The Unicorn Agenda

The Unicorn Agenda

by William L. Culbertson

The Unicorn Agenda

by William L. Culbertson
http://wculbertson.com/

Cover Art: Randi Schumaker

Other Books by William L. Culbertson

Chronicles of the Dragon-Bound
King's Exile: Book 1
King's Dragon: Book 2
King's Crown: Book 3
Dragon-Bound Bard
Scarlet Jewel
Dragon-Bound Thief

Science Fiction
The Starships Saga

One

Walking down the street one morning, I saw a unicorn. Its unsullied white coat stood out in the shadowed gray concrete canyon of Third Street. Ordinarily I wouldn't have paid much attention. All my life I've seen strange things that others don't notice, and I've seen lots of odd creatures in our city. Early on I'd learned to keep my mouth shut about what I saw—or at least imagined I'd seen. My dad would smack me every time he thought I made something up.

But this unicorn noticed me watching, and that was unusual. He stopped and swung his head to stare at me. After a brief inspection, his lips curled into a contemptuous sneer, and he trotted on his way. Staying in the bike lane, he ignored the rest of the pedestrians plodding blindly by on the sidewalk. A speeding courier cycled around the corner. The unicorn deftly stepped out of his way without slowing. The courier himself showed no sign of noticing anything out of the ordinary.

Curious because of our moment of interaction, I watched the supposedly mythical creature as he continued on his way. At the corner of the next block he took a right at the bagel shop and headed east on Talbot. Halfway down the block, he turned a corner and I lost sight of him

I almost started to follow, but I remembered my appointment. Even so, I lingered at the corner, watching and wondering what a unicorn was doing downtown. The towering buildings of the business district surrounded me. I'd never seen a unicorn in the central city. They were rare enough in the suburbs.

But my meeting. Alexander Stuyvesant, plenipotentiary administrator of Sterling Fund Investments, wanted to see me, and it was a meeting I couldn't afford to miss. Why had a man who controlled billions of dollars of other people's money selected an unremarkable private investigator like me? I'd asked myself that question several times since Stuyvesant's secretary made the appointment last Thursday. As a private eye, my usual clients' definition of high finance involved renegotiating the payment schedule on their car loan.

However, I wasn't going to look a gift horse in the mouth—even a horse with a horn on its head. I straightened up, adjusted my tie, and started walking again.

Stuyvesant's office was so far up in the DAMA tower it would have been a three-day hike up the stairs. My appointment was for midmorning, so I missed the morning crowd on my trek in from a parking garage up the street. Although the DAMA tower had its own garage, Stuyvesant's office hadn't included a parking pass for a visiting tradesman like me.

Dark polished granite framed the outside entrance to the building. The entryway transitioned to a lighter marble that continued into a vaulted, three-story interior. The main lobby featured several high-end retail establishments. Since I didn't need to be reminded of my humble station in life, I ignored them and headed directly to the bank of express elevators.

There were only two other passengers with me on the run up to the sky lobby. The car glided in swift silent contempt past the first fifty floors before it deposited us at the two-story marble concourse dotted with more small shops. Gold-trimmed escalators led up to a second level of shopping. The elevated location of these boutiques made it obvious they were not interested in casual, walk-in trade. I suspected they'd charge somebody like me admission to come in and browse, but I didn't check.

Local elevators to the upper floors stood waiting down the way. I thought I would continue my journey all alone, but just as the doors started to close, a woman in a business suit carrying a briefcase slipped through the door.

"Floor?" I asked politely, hand poised over the buttons. She ignored me and impatiently reached in front of me to punch in her destination. Just for that, I didn't offer her a comment about the weather.

I was all by myself when I got off at the seventy-first floor. Outside the elevator there was an acre of dark-patterned Persian carpet. The elevator vanished behind me, and I realized I was already inside the Sterling Fund's main office. The reception area alone was as big as my whole apartment. Paneled in wood with lots of brass accents, large green plants lined an aisle that led to the welcome desk.

Out of curiosity I brushed against a shrub—real vegetation. Through strategic clearings in the underbrush I glimpsed three other people working at desks.

A young woman sat on alert behind the substantial wooden desk facing the elevators. A name plate labeled her as J. Tavers. A scruffy-looking gnome sat on a corner of the bare, polished desktop, doing his nails with a tiny pen knife. He'd glanced at me when I'd gotten off the elevator, but at the moment he was trimming a hangnail.

I approached the desk. Oblivious of the gnome, J. Tavers smiled politely. "May I help you?"

I too ignored the ugly little fellow who shared her desk and gave her a smile of my own—level two, pleasant enough but neutral.

"Hi. My name is Mickey Holmes. I'm a private detective, and I have an appointment with Mr. Stuyvesant."

Even though I was in my good suit, she blinked twice at Stuyvesant's name. Although she arched an eyebrow skeptically, she was smooth. Her smile never wavered. "Just one moment, please." She looked down to a screen partially recessed into the top of her desk.

Maybe I should have used a level three smile.

One point in her favor was that she had said nothing about Mickey Holmes being a private detective. A detective named Holmes? I've taken a fair amount of ribbing about my name over the years. My clients seem to find the temptation to be witty irresistible—and repetitive. And no, I don't look anything like those illustrations of the fictional London detective. Like the legendary literary detective, I'm trim and taller than average, but I have a winning disposition and a cute smile—at least according to a former girlfriend.

What I don't tell people these days is that Mickey is a nickname I chose for myself long ago. When my parents named me, they must have wanted me grow up tough. Or maybe they just decided to inflict their weird sense of humor on me in perpetuity. As of this moment, none of my friends—or enemies for that matter—have discovered my true given name.

The receptionist looked up. This time she beamed a welcoming smile that radiated on at least a level six.

"Yes, Mr. Holmes," she gushed, obviously overjoyed to see me. "Marcus will be down in a moment to take you up. Won't you have a seat?" She gestured to a rank of leather armchairs nearby.

Sterling Investments was an international operation. That much I'd found out with the quick internet check I always do to make sure a prospective client can pay. And yes, if Sterling paid Stuyvesant in line with their ostentatious headquarters, Stuyvesant could pay. Could he ever! The elegant atmosphere of their reception area hinted at the full meaning of all those extra zeros in their financial statement.

I was out of my element. Even the soft, cushioning armchair intimidated me. This one piece of furniture outclassed anything in my apartment. I was sitting in a masculine version of my great-aunt's tea parlor. Maybe if I scuffed the chair some, slopped coffee on it, and otherwise used and abused it for a couple of years, I could make it fit in with my apartment's bachelor-casual decor.

Uncomfortable in unknown territory, I stayed alert. Who knew what else besides a gnome might be lurking in all the surrounding foliage? Fortunately, I didn't have much time to vegetate amongst the vegetation.

A young man in a well-tailored suit strode out to greet me. I stood to greet him as he extended his hand. "Mr. Holmes? I'm Marcus. Welcome to the headquarters of Sterling Investments." After he shook my hand, he took my elbow and guided me toward a carved wooden door that slid aside to reveal another elevator.

Marcus—was that a first or last name?—kept a controlling hand on my arm, something I detest. I stumbled to one side and excused myself for clumsiness. My wobble gave me the chance to casually slip out of his grasp. Once inside the elevator, I kept my distance lest Marcus grab me again. It also meant he didn't have to worry about accidentally brushing against me and soiling his clothes.

The ride up one floor was short and almost imperceptible in its smoothness. The door opened onto what looked like a classic Victorian library. Dark wooden cases full of books lined the walls. An oil painting of an older gentleman hung above a marble fireplace.

Marcus made no further moves to guide me. He stretched out his hand to the archway on the right. "Through here, if you will. Mr. Stuyvesant is waiting."

Alexander Stuyvesant was a couple of inches taller than my six feet. He looked to be in his late forties. A couple of character lines in his face along with hint of gray at his temples gave his good looks a distinguished cast, a clear reassurance that this was a man who could be trusted with money.

Leaning against a large carved walnut desk, Stuyvesant straightened up as I approached and took my hand. His dark gray bespoke suit had a conservative faint chalk stripe and fit his trim physique like a glove.

"Mr. Holmes. So good of you to come."

I braced for a domineering businessman's grip, but he applied a very civilized pressure. "Nice of you to invite me," I replied. Really nice since he was one client I shouldn't have to hound for a payment.

"Why don't we have a seat over here?" He gestured toward a furnished nook on one side of his expansive office.

More greenery set off two leather love seats that met at right angles. On the end table between, there was a leather folder beneath a lamp with a porcelain base. He took one seat. I took the other. Quiet, cozy, and we didn't have to face each other.

"What can I do for you?" I asked as soon as we were seated.

He smiled. "Right to it, then." He picked up the leather folder, opened it, and took out a picture of a good-looking woman also in her mid to late forties. "My wife," he announced. He put the picture back and slid the folder to my side of the end table. "I suspect she has a lover. Maybe more than one. I would like you to find details of any"—the corner of his mouth curled down—"trysts on her part. If she has betrayed me, I will divorce her."

The rich may be different, but they still have good old everyday human problems. "What's her name?"

"Samantha," he said and anticipated my next question by adding, "We got married in college twenty-seven years ago."

He paused and looked at me with a frown. "Don't you want to write any of this down?"

"Yes, sir. I'll take copious notes after our interview."

His offer of advice might have been well-intended, but it felt patronizing. During a first interview, I gather information about my clients by watching them while we talk. In this business I depend on my instincts as well as my detective skills. Details are easy enough to find, and his folder probably had most of them. What I needed was a sense of the man I was going to work for. At the moment, Alexander Stuyvesant, the cool, collected business man, wasn't giving me much.

I gestured to the folder. "Is all your wife's information in there?"

He nodded curtly. "Of course."

"Do you and your wife have children?"

"Two, Shane and Jeffrey, but they're not at home anymore. They have their own lives."

And how close or far away they'd chosen to live those lives might tell me something, as well.

When I'd come into the office, I'd noticed a gnome with a blue hat sitting on a lower shelf of the book case. After Stuyvesant and I had started to talk, he strolled over to a corner of our nook and pulled himself up into the pot of an indoor tree. He sat down on the mossy ground cover and crossed a leg over his knee while he watched. I might not know a fichus from an ornamental fig, but I could tell the gnome was interested in our conversation. So far at Sterling Investments, I'd seen two gnomes in ten minutes. Why so many, and why were they hanging around Sterling? And in particular, why was a gnome watching the conversation I was having with Alexander Stuyvesant?

"Mr. Holmes?"

I blinked and turned my attention back to my client, embarrassed he'd noticed my distraction. "Sorry." Attempting to recover my professionalism, I frowned thoughtfully. "What makes you think your wife is having an affair?"

He glanced away for a moment, then leaned closer. Instead of responding in turn, I stayed where I was. If I'd moved closer as well, I would have signaled recognition that he was sharing an intimate confidence. If he hired me, his secrets would be private, but we would not be friends. I'd already sensed his disdain at having to deal with the likes of me. He worked to conceal it, and that made me wary.

He looked at me directly, eyes flat and emotionless. "I know for a fact she regularly visits various hotels around the city—hotels that are not in the best parts of town."

Yes, that could be a sign. I raised my eyebrows and gave a slight nod to indicate I understood. "When did you discover this?"

He looked away and gestured dismissively. "A couple weeks ago. Margo, the secretary who does my bills, showed me copies of her credit card charges at the hotels." He tapped the folder. "It's all in there."

I could have given Samantha a few pointers in the arts of deception, but I nodded my understanding. "Do you see any particular pattern? A schedule?"

He leaned back and shook his head. "None that I can see, but I won't pretend to know everything she does."

His mouth turned down, and he waved negligently. "She's very social. On the boards of lots of organizations, non-profits mostly—I guess. Women's groups. Fundraising. That sort of thing"

High-powered business man—neglected wife. I'd seen it before. Married as long as the Stuyvesants had been, in the settlement he could be on the hook to lose a fair share of the assets he'd accumulated since they were married. The fact he wanted to hire me to investigate told me they probably didn't have a no-fault clause in their pre-nup agreement—if they had one at all. If I found evidence of his wife's infidelity, singular or plural as the case might be, I could save him a bundle of money.

"Do you have specifics on her friends, memberships, and that sort of thing?"

He tattooed his index finger on the folder.

I ignored the patronizing signal and nodded. "Sounds pretty straightforward, Mr. Stuyvesant. Just so you know right up front, I charge a hundred dollars an hour for surveillance work, plus any related expenses. There's a minimum of five hours in advance to cover my basic costs to set up the investigation. Those charges cover a final written report with documentation."

Rather than yield to temptation to up the ante, I'd quoted him my standard rates. Proud of my restraint, I handed him the contract I'd prepared. "I'll send you regular updates every ten hours of work."

I crossed my arms and leaned back in my seat. "In a case like this, if there's something to find, I can't see it would take much beyond three or four weeks. Maybe fifty hours total."

He sniffed. "You charge like a lawyer, for Christ's sake."

I shrugged. "If you decide to divorce her, you'll need one of those too."

The corner of my mouth twitched a bit, but I suppressed the smile. No need to gloat. "Remember, I provide in-person, eyes-on surveillance. Computer-based checks are quicker and cheaper, but they don't tell the whole story." I'd practiced that line.

His glare was frigid—and arrogant. "When can you start?"

"It's Thursday morning." I paused and thought about my calendar. "Tomorrow, I have to give testimony in court."

I showed him a level-one smile of ironic amusement. "I also charge for my time in court if it comes to that, but only at half rate."

He glowered, and I sobered.

Stop being snotty and focus, Holmes, I told myself.

"Once I'm done tomorrow, my schedule's clear. Sign the contract, and I'll be ready to go. You know your wife's habits. When would you suggest I start?"

He tapped the point of his chin with his index finger thoughtfully. "We'll be busy all weekend. The governor's reception is Friday night. We leave from there to our place in the mountains, where we'll stay through Sunday afternoon."

His chilly blue eyes locked on mine. "Monday would be good. She'll be off on her usual social rounds." He pressed his finger on the folder. "Our home address, a description of her car, and her phone number are all in there. If you need anything else, check with my secretary."

So far he'd been pretty frosty toward me, but unexpectedly he smiled warmly. "You know, Holmes, I like your unconventional attitude. I don't see that much, especially among independent operators like yourself."

He looked at me appraisingly and nodded. "I handle retirement fund investments for several of the largest law firms in the city. Their clients often need the services of a good private investigator who knows how to be discreet. You were recommended to me." He held up his hand. "I'm not going to tell you by whom. Don't ask."

I was flattered, and I wouldn't ask—especially since he'd said not to.

So, if you can impress me, I would be happy to offer others your name."

I felt a big old off-the-charts grin starting, and I stifled it. Reputation. That's what it took to move to the top of the snoop business. If I could deliver for Stuyvesant, I could move on to more challenging—and more lucrative—work. No more long, slogging hours of tracking down people who had delinquent debts, overdue child support, and other irresponsible behaviors.

Not wanting to appear too eager, I frowned and pretended to mull it over.

Be professional, I reminded myself before I looked up to meet his eyes again. "A good recommendation would be appreciated, sir. I will do my best to earn it." Including standing on my head if needed.

He stood up, signaling the meeting was over. "I'll send the signed contract and your advance over by messenger," he said. "Will cash be satisfactory?"

I picked up the folder and stood as well. "Of course," I said as he led the way back to the elevator.

On the way down, I took a deep breath and sighed. Stuyvesant in his element had been cool and competent. I'd felt some contempt in his attitude toward me at first, but condescending or not, he was a client who could pay. If he referred me to his friends, this assignment could make my career. And about time, too.

Two

Back on the street again, I finally released the big, goofy grin that would have betrayed my unprofessional elation. I'd been hoping for a chance to prove myself again to a wealthy client. Two years ago, my investigation of a real estate deal for Atwater Bank and Trust revealed not only that the deal was shady, but also that Teddy Sticker, one of the bank's own officers, had led the fraud as well as masterminding several similar deals.

While Sticker's involvement wasn't good news for the bank, uncovering it should have at least earned me a gold star. Unfortunately, my work also turned up solid evidence that Teddy-boy was a serial sexual harasser. The bank had insisted I keep my lip zipped about his lecherous behaviors for fear that knowing proof existed would encourage anyone who had been harassed to sue. Since they were paying the bill, I handed over everything I had found to the bank.

Somehow, unfortunately, word about the existence of the evidence got out anyway. Suddenly Teddy—along with the bank—was the subject of seventeen harassment lawsuits. Rather than accept that they'd overlooked Teddy's bad behavior for years, the bank turned on me. Although they never took me to court for breach of contract, they'd bad-mouthed me—unofficially, of course—to the point where big, reputable clients avoided me these days.

If I made Stuyvesant happy, I might be able to redeem myself. His recommendation could give me entree to an elite class of customers who could pay well—a refreshing change. Perhaps I could even afford to move my office out of my apartment's second bedroom.

However, before I got too far ahead of myself, I had to deliver for Stuyvesant. My favorite bistro, the Coffee Berry Ferry, was close and a good place to jot down notes while the meeting was fresh in my mind.

"Hey, it's Mick the Dick." Jessica Jones greeted me with a smile as I pushed through the door. "How they hangin,' big guy?"

There were only a few regulars in the place, so I gave it right back to her. "Well, hello to you, JJ, the lewd, crude, and rude." I bowed ostentatiously low. "Yep, I keep comin' back because you know me here."

"The usual?"

"Please. And a spiced donut if they're fresh."

I took a seat at a table looking out the window toward the river. Fishing my notebook out of my jacket pocket, I started jotting down impressions. The job Stuyvesant had hired me to do was pretty ordinary. Not for him of course, but I'd worked for plenty of suspicious husbands—most with good reason to be. The rich may be different, but they screw up their lives in pretty standard ways. The amount of money at stake if the Stuyvesants divorced might be poles apart from that of my usual clients, but the tawdry details of the case would be distressingly familiar.

"Got something going?" Jessica asked. She set down a large cup of black coffee and a donut. "And you're in luck. They're fresh out of the oven. That'll be six seventy-five."

I fished a ten out of my pocket. "Here you go. Keep the change."

"A tip? Now I know you've got something going."

She slid into the chair beside me. "Give! Is it juicy? You've got Stuyvesant at the top of that page. Is that Stuyvesant as in the Sterling Fund? Holy shit!"

I closed the cover of my notebook and looked at her. Jessica was easy on the eyes in an unconventional kind of way. Unlike most women, she wore her hair cut close to her scalp in a tight brown nap. Her dark complexion emphasized her bright, pretty smile.

And Jessica was quick. Too quick most of the time. I smiled and rolled my eyes. I turned the closed notebook facedown for added emphasis. "For business reasons, my client's name is confidential."

She smirked. "Gotcha. Mum's the word."

After a brief pause, she said, "But since it's Stuyvesant, you're going to need help with the research."

I sighed. "At the moment, it's mainly a surveillance job."

Jessica had access to the LexisNexis database as well as assorted corporate and municipal resources. She was a formidable researcher and enjoyed doing it. I enjoyed letting her, especially since I could charge her time to my clients.

I took a bite out of the donut and opened the folder Stuyvesant had given me. I flipped the pages. There was information about his wife's car, her memberships, and other activities. I closed the folder, pushed it away, and frowned.

"But who is she?" I muttered.

"Who?" Jessica's dark eyes flamed with curiosity.

"Samantha Stuyvesant." I took out her picture and showed it to her. "His wife. He gave me information about where she goes and what she does, but there's nothing about who she is."

"You're the detective. Isn't that what you're supposed to figure out?"

"Eventually, but a little background would have helped me get started."

Since I had it in my hand, I checked the back of the picture. It was blank. "I don't even think he listed her maiden name. He said she does volunteer work, but does she have a paying job? Does she come from a wealthy family or is she a street kid who's punching above her weight? Does she have any assets in her own name, or is she totally dependent upon him?"

I frowned. "For that matter, it might help to know Stuyvesant's own financial situation. Has he been transferring assets lately or doing anything else affecting their joint ownership property that might fall under a pre-nup?"

"See, you need me."

"Don't you have any classes this summer?"

"Just a seminar on domestic violence."

The corner of my mouth curled up, and I raised my eyebrows. "Is it a 'how to' guide? Is there a boxing tutorial with it?"

"No, smartass." She frowned. "But if somebody gets clobbered, I can coach the punch-ee on how to sue the ass off the punch-er."

There was a snip in her tone that hadn't been there before. When it came to wise cracks, she could give as good as she got. However, I could tell she'd taken my remark the wrong way.

I held up my hands defensively. "Sorry. I shouldn't kid about domestic violence—or your education." Jessica was putting herself through law school one course at a time by working at the coffee shop and other jobs. Earning a law degree piecemeal was no picnic. In spite of my smart mouth, I had a world of respect for her accomplishments.

I nodded briskly. "You want to help, you're in. Right now all I need is a quick background check."

"You still pay twenty an hour?"

"Along with my undying gratitude," I said. "Don't forget that."

"Yeah, that and five bucks will get me a cup of coffee just about anywhere."

Jessica could make me smile. That's why we were friends. "Twenty an hour," I agreed. Given my uncertain feelings about my client, I wanted to make sure what was in the folder was accurate. If she found additional relevant information about Samantha, so much the better. Besides, I'd charge her time to Stuyvesant at twenty-five an hour.

From across the coffee shop came a call. "Hey, hot stuff!" A regular held up his empty cup.

"Comin', Safi," Jessica chirped.

She leaned closer to me. "Gotta go. Send me the details."

Social minute over, I turned my attention back to my notes. How should I put my estimation of Alexander Stuyvesant into words?

I stared thoughtfully down at the cross-river ferry dock. Every time I took on a new investigation, I recorded my reaction to the client after our first meeting. When a client wasn't completely upfront with me, the evasion was usually obvious. I was pretty good at reading people, and I trusted first impressions. My notes would make sure I recalled any nuances supporting my feelings. It's particularly important when I take personal dislike to the person who hired me.

As I watched the eleven o'clock ferry approach the dock, I considered my new client. Stuyvesant's demeanor had been entirely cool, calm, and unruffled. A high achiever in his profession, the man had received unsettling information that his wife was visiting hotels around the city. I would have expected him to have been more worried and anxious. Then again, if he had suspected such behavior for a time, he might not have been as visibly upset.

I jotted a note to that effect.

And what was the deal with the gnomes? I'd seen two of them inside the Sterling Fund's headquarters. The one with a blue hat had even listened to our conversation. I didn't like to document my delusions where others might see, so I just jotted the question, "blue hat?" to remind me of his interest.

I watched the ferry. A crewman tossed a line at one of the pilings on the dock. He missed his first throw.

I looked down at the notebook again and added the note: Not quite right.

I put my elbow on the table and propped up my chin. The crewman's second try at the piling went astray as well. His lips moved, and I imagined a swear word.

My apartment was too small, and the neighborhood was ratty. New, well-paying clients would be a refreshing change. They could change my life in fact.

I looked at the words I'd written and sighed. Not quite right was not quite right. I put a question mark after the words. Maybe when I knew more about the Stuyvesants, I would be able to clarify my feelings.

On the way out, I went over to the end of the counter where Jessica was busy making a latte. "Hey, JJ. You think you'll have anything by Sunday?"

She looked up and smiled. "You bet, Mick. You want it by phone, or do you need a hard copy?"

I waved dismissively. "Just call or text me. I'm starting surveillance Monday, so all I need is some general info—you know, memberships, interests, and stuff like that—so I can be prepared." I waggled the folder. "It'll probably confirm a lot of what's here, but I'd like an unfiltered survey just to make sure."

"Gonna get your disguise ready?" She smiled. "Maybe if she does the gym scene, you could get a little treadmill time in while you're keeping watch." She poked a finger in the direction of my gut. "You know, belly management?"

"Is it starting to show?" I'm actually in good shape, and my toned gut is as flat as a board. In response to her teasing, I pushed my stomach out over my belt and patted the bulge. "It must be you and the damned donuts in this place."

As I left, I smiled and pointed a finger gun at her. "Thanks for your help, kid."

Bart Stewart was hunched over his keyboard when I looked through the window in the door to his home. He lived in his office, a converted garage behind his parents' modest home. Its separate alley entrance made it private. Sort of.

He didn't look up when I knocked. I was used to this, and I let myself in. "Hey, Bart," I said, "you interested in some work?"

He waved a hand for me to wait, and I did. I was also used to this. He had a ratty old chair just inside the door, and I took a seat. Bart was deeply immersed in whatever he was doing on his computer. We'd talk when he came up for air.

Bart was a computer geek, and he looked the part. He weighed half again as much as he should have, and his nether parts sagged over the rim of the stool on which he'd perched. Although his hair might have started the day combed, by now his shortish, blondish locks resembled a well-churned field of hay. Much to his embarrassment, last year I had stumbled on the fact that Bart's real name was Bartimus. Far be it from me to kid someone about a hated first name. His secret was safe with me.

The clatter of keys stopped with a measured series of taps followed by an authoritative poke of the enter key. His stool squeaked as he swung around to face me.

"Hey, Mickey. You got something for me?"

"Ever heard of Sterling Fund Investments?"

He nodded. "Yeah. I've got some money in Euro-based merger arbitrage hedge funds with them. What's up?"

I blinked. I didn't understand what he'd said, but the implication was clear. When it came to finance, Bart operated in a world I knew nothing about.

But maybe this was a good thing.

I looked thoughtful and said, "What about Alexander Stuyvesant?"

"Oh, yeah. He's one of their major muck-a-mucks." He smiled. "Only the biggest investors work with him."

His eyes widened. "Ooo! Is that who you're working for? You want me to investigate something for him?"

"I'm investigating his wife, actually."

"Uh-oh." His smile turned sly. "She cattin' around?"

I sighed. "That's the question I'm supposed to answer."

I pulled out my notebook and handed him two pages that I'd copied. "Her name's Samantha Stuyvesant. For a start, her husband gave me her email and social media accounts—at least the ones he knows about."

Bart took the list and glanced at it before he dropped it on the pile beside his keyboard. "Right. You want anything on her financials or other stuff?"

"Yeah, but only if it looks like there might be something off the books. Jessica's going to do her thing in that area, but she's only going to see the official records."

I scratched my head. "I'd like you to focus her social media activities since that's probably where something will turn up. So, you know, look at the usual places, but keep an eye out for anything hinky."

"Hinky?" His smile was back, and it was naughty. "What about kinky?"

I made a finger gun and pointed it at him. "That too."

Back at my office, I created a new folder for my latest investigation. Once I had the hanging file labeled, I put all the information Stuyvesant had given me, along with my notes, and dropped it into place in the drawer. I rolled the file drawer closed and leaned back in my office chair. The setting was familiar. My view out the narrow window was much the same as my bedroom's, since my office was right beside my bedroom. The space is small, so I have to be diligent about keeping things neat and organized—at least in my office.

My classy new client had me thinking ambitious thoughts of moving up in the world. What would it be like to have my own store-front office? I'd likely have to start with a location in some small strip mall, but if I cultivated a list of clients with offices downtown, maybe . . .

Before I drifted too far into fantasy land, I leaned forward and opened my laptop. This was no time for self-absorption—although I'm good at it. Stuyvesant expected results, so I put my dreaming on hold.

Wanting to get a broader sense of the man, I went to his corporate website. Although there would be no personal information here, it would give me an idea of how Stuyvesant portrayed himself to his clients. The company's webpages made more of a hard sell than I'd expected. Stuyvesant's management profile emphasized all the exciting ways he could put his clients' money to work to maximize their gains. The direct appeal to greed was not as subtle as I expected.

I browsed around checking some other related links and sites, but I preferred to let others do my serious research for me—even when it costs me money. My main problem comes from the fact that on the computer, I'm easily distracted. Is it an attention disorder, or does the surplus of instant information fan the flames of my out of control curiosity? Whatever it is, when I prowl the internet, my brain generates too many new thoughts, questions, and diverting ideas, all only a click away. An hour into a search, I find myself mired in a disorganized jumble of information only tangentially related to my original query.

By now it was late in the afternoon, and I was hungry. For supper I snagged one of my gourmet-guts frozen entrees. While I waited for the microwave to finish, I conjured pleasant thoughts about being able to go out to eat more often. Unfortunately, while I stood there, my eyes landed on the dining debris on top of my stove. While I wouldn't call myself slovenly, some visitors have suggested my standards of cleanliness rate somewhere below relaxed. I don't entertain much, but it does happen. Therefore, I try to clean whenever I notice a patina of dust on my kitchen counter's stationary items—or any other blatant signs of creeping crud.

The signal was clear tonight, so after I ate, I decided to swab the decks. Once I'd cleaned the kitchen, I kept the momentum going and tackled the rest of my apartment. I saved my bedroom for last. When I ran the duster over the items on top of my dresser, I saw the ceramic beer mug Heather had given me.

I sighed. Heather Kaymeyer. It had been two years since we had broken up.

Broken up? No, she'd dumped me, and even after two years the memory hurt. Her final speech had included an accusatory recital of all my faults. Although she'd enjoyed the time we spent in the bedroom, her main complaint centered around her conclusion that I wasn't ambitious enough. According to her, I'd been coasting, using my wits and charm in place of hard work. She had great expectations of a house in the suburbs someday and didn't see that in her future if she stayed with me.

On the other hand, Heather herself had plenty of drive and determination—especially drive. That last night she told me she was driving to Wisconsin where she was going to meet up with a guy she'd met online.

Since Heather had given me the mug, I probably should have chucked it. However, it had an elaborate image of a dragon sculpted in sinuous relief around the outside. I liked the art. Plus, I'd started calling the snarling, reptilian beast "Heather."

Once I'd rearranged the dust, I went over everything with the vacuum cleaner. I even pulled out my bed so I could get behind it— an extra effort that always made me feel particularly virtuous. On the second swipe under the bed, the sweeper bumped something out of sight.

I dragged the bed out another two feet and found a woman's shoe. It looked nice, a kind of white-on-white plaid with brown trim and a high heel. The only name on it was Fendi, but that meant nothing to me. Could it have be one of Brittany's? How long had it been there? What had Brittany been wearing that night?

I half smiled at the memory—or rather the lack of it. I'd known her casually for a while, and we'd started flirting one night at a party. She'd come home with me, but I'd gotten carried away with the bourbon that night. I remembered that nakedness had been involved, but I couldn't recall the whole event. The next morning, she was gone when I woke up.

I looked at the shoe. I looked back under the bed and found the mate to the first shoe. Had she left barefoot?

I checked back under the bed to see if there was anything else but saw nothing but a dust bunny I'd missed. Had she brought other shoes, changed, then forgot? Then again, she'd been drinking too, so maybe she didn't notice she'd forgotten her shoes.

I looked at them again. Surely I'd cleaned under the bed since our one-night tryst . . . hadn't I?

However long it had been, Brittany hadn't spoken to me since. She didn't even my acknowledge my texts.

I tossed the shoes into the trash and finished the job.

While housework isn't in the same class as a gym workout, it lasted longer. By the end, I was sweating and took a shower. Satisfied with a full day's work and the promise of a new source of income, I watched a movie and had a beer.

Okay, I felt so righteous after my cleaning, I had two beers.

Three

"Hi ya, Mick. How was the call with your mom?"

It was Sunday evening. I'd warned Jessica that my mom always phoned at six o'clock to check up on me, so she had waited until seven.

"Hey, JJ," I said. "Well, Mom was pleased to hear I'm working for a better class of client these days."

"She still thrilled with the whole private eye thing?"

I ignored her sarcasm. "So what've you got for me?"

"You don't want to talk more about your mom?"

She was teasing, so I said nothing.

After I'd waited her out, she said, "Okay, some news. Her maiden name is Astor, Samantha Astor Stuyvesant."

They way she'd said it, I knew she thought it was interesting. Being coy, she waited for me this time. Finally I prompted, "Yeah, so it's Astor?"

"Astor. Doesn't that name mean anything to you?"

"You don't mean the rich ones?"

"Got it first try, Holmes. The mega-bucks, family-fortune Astors."

I blinked. "Okay, that I didn't know."

"Astor, as in ancient, old-type money from the west-coast fur trade; summers in Newport, Rhode Island; college at the Sorbonne—"

A little awe-struck as she rattled off the list, I interrupted. "The Sorbonne? In France?"

"You bet, Mickey baby. Know the school?"

"Sure, JJ. Their basketball team's the Wildcats."

Jessica's information had turned my initial impressions upside down. I'd been thinking of Alexander as the consummate business man with his wife an ignored, bored spouse. How much of Alexander's success had come from money his wife had brought to their marriage?

"Made ya think, didn't I?"

I blinked and came back to the conversation at hand. "Yeah, that kind of puts a new perspective on things."

"She may be rich, but she's also big into social causes and charity work. I'll send you the list."

I nodded thoughtfully even though she couldn't see. "Got anything else, kid?"

There was a long pause.

"I've told you before, I'm not a kid."

Yes, she had, and in no uncertain terms. "You're right." I sighed. "You're twenty-nine, and only two years younger than me. I know all that, but you seem so . . . ." My thoughts trickled to a stop.

"Immature?" There was sarcasm in her tone. "And I'm thirty."

I sighed again and rolled my eyes. "Yeah? Well, happy birthday. No, I was going to say that you're young . . . and vital."

I took a deep breath before I continued. "I guess part of it is knowing you're still going to school."

"For a post-graduate law degree." Her voice held an accusation.

"I told you I dropped out because I was bored."

"So process serving and skip tracing really gets your heart rate up?"

"The bane of my existence." After a pause, I added, "But it pays the bills."

I waited, but she didn't say anything else. After a few more seconds, I figured the fight was over. "And I'm sorry. You're not a kid."

"Except when I act like a snot-nosed infant."

"Except that."

I had to smile at her implied apology for over-reacting. "You do good work . . ." I fumbled a moment because I almost called her kid again. "Nice job, Jessica," I finished. "With this new information, I'm going to have to take another look at things. Thanks for your help."

"You'll get my bill," she said, but she chuckled as she said it. "See ya later, Mick."

By Monday, my calendar was clear to start surveillance of Samantha Stuyvesant. Warned of her family's wealth and connections, I'd decided to keep my distance on day one. Someone as rich as she was might have a personal security detail. There was nothing about it in the information I'd received from her husband, but I didn't want to trip over anybody until I had the lay of the land.

The Stuyvesants' condo occupied the top two floors of Carrack Center's south tower. That morning I sat across the street from that prestigious address under the awning of a café, nursing a cooling cup of coffee and pretending to read a newspaper. About half the tables were occupied. At one table a couple was conversing. All the other customers were by themselves. Two of them had newspapers. The rest were on their phones.

One patron I hadn't expected was a gnome, this one a bit chubbier than most. He wore a conical red hat and sat on the broad arm of a concrete bench idly swinging his short legs back and forth. I'd never seen too many gnomes in the city—maybe one a month if that. In the last few days, I'd seen three. Why?

While I looked idly at the gnome, I let my mind wander. Sometimes free association will bestow meaning to an observation.

Nothing came.

Then again, since I knew nothing about gnomes, I didn't have much to associate with.

The gnome glanced up and saw my attention. He made a rude gesture and turned his attention back to the table in front of him. The customer sitting there stuck his phone in his pocket and got up, leaving half a sweet roll behind.

As soon as the customer turned away, a gull swooped in. The bird cocked its head and inspected the sweet roll. The bird hesitated, but the gnome didn't. He hopped across the space to the table and booted the bird in the butt. The gull squawked with indignation and flapped away.

Several customers looked up to follow the gull's noisy exit, but nobody noticed the gnome as he carried the remains of the sweet roll back to his perch.

That's how it always worked. I saw the gnome, but the rest of the people didn't. Everyone else was busy reading newspapers, scrolling on their phones, talking to their companions, or picking bugs out of their lattes.

I'd always wondered about myself. When I was really young, I learned to keep my mouth shut about seeing gnomes or unicorns—or any other odd faerie creatures. I could see them, but they ignored me. No one else was interested in hearing about strange beings they couldn't see. I remember my mom sitting me down one day and telling me in no uncertain words to stop making things up about what I saw.

I wasn't making things up, but nobody believed me. They didn't even want to hear about it. So I kept my mouth shut about what I saw. That secret had always made me feel weirdly different. I noticed the faerie fauna, but no one else did.

The other customers at the coffee shop paid no attention to the gnome's actions—they couldn't see him. When the little fellow saw me obviously watching him, he stuffed the last large crumbly bite into his mouth and flipped me off.

I sighed and turned a page of the newspaper I wasn't reading. I glanced at the entrance to the underground parking garage. Although there was another exit on the north side of the complex, I figured Samantha would use this closer one.

I'd come early today, planning to go into the parking garage to find her car. That strategy had ended as soon as I arrived. I found a place to park on the street and approached the entrance to the parking garage on foot. There was plenty of security on display, both uniformed and video. Instead of going down the ramp, I walked on and found the cafe. I had a tracking beacon in my pocket I'd intended for her car, but the garage obviously wasn't the place to plant it.

At 9:33, Samantha's silver BMW emerged from the ramp and headed north on Beach Street. Today I wasn't going to follow her. I just wanted to know if she travelled alone. Although the car's side and back windows were tinted, I had a moment to look at the front of her car. She was at the wheel herself with no one beside her. After she left, the ramp remained empty for several minutes. The next car up, a Mercedes SUV, turned in the opposite direction.

Satisfied that at least some days Samantha traveled without security, I folded up the newspaper and tossed it and the remains of my deceased coffee into the trash. A quick glance showed me that the gnome had left as well.

It was time to call Bart to see what he had found.

". . . and six local non-profits." Bart paused. "You want a printed list of her board memberships, or should I just send the file to you?"

"Geez, save a tree. Send it." I leaned back and sighed. Bart had confirmed what Jessica had found out about Samantha Stuyvesant's involvement with the community. Starting at the top, she was on the boards of nine different prestigious universities, five on the west coast, three on the east, and one in the middle of the country. She was also a trustee at twelve major international charitable foundations, and on the governing boards of innumerable non-profit agencies. "How would one person find the time?" I wondered aloud.

"Some of these are probably ceremonial positions given in recognition of contributions. You know, donor mining?"

"Yeah, probably." I scratched my head. "Any way to tell? I mean, can you find out which boards she's actively involved with?"

"That'll take some time. Do you want to know only the ones she attends in person, or should I include telepresence as well?"

"For now, just get me the ones she shows up for. Personal contacts are more likely to lead to the type of personal contacts her husband hired me to look for."

Bart chuckled at my implication. "Hey, you want me to check her credit card for local activity?" He charged me extra to get a person's specific credit card transaction records. Accessing confidential credit records was illegal, and he took his risk into account when he billed me.

"Not necessary. I've got the last three months of statements right here." I glanced at the folder Stuyvesant had prepared. "Her husband even underlined charges at local hotels that made him suspicions."

However, as I said it, I remembered my reservations about Stuyvesant himself. I reconsidered. "Tell you what. To make sure he's dealing off the top of the deck, why don't you run a check on what he's highlighted to make sure they're real?"

I frowned at another idea. "While you're at it, go back another three months on these accounts to see what else pops up. And check to see if she has any credit cards he doesn't know about."

Technically, when it was time to figure the bill, I probably shouldn't charge Stuyvesant for double-checking records he'd already given me. Although I'd keep that in mind, I've been known to vary my billing practices.

"So what are you doing tomorrow, Mick? Are you actually going to follow her?"

"Yeah, I've got to get a feel for her activity. Where does she go? What does she do? She and her husband have a joint social calendar. That's the one I have, but he says she does lots of stuff on her own. She probably keeps another calendar that her husband doesn't have access to."

"If she keeps it on her phone, I might be able to give you a look at it."

Something in Bart's voice sounded sneaky. "Oh? I thought you specialized in confidential business information. Are you branching out? I thought you didn't like phone hacking and other illicit stuff."

"Uh, it's . . . not me." He fumbled a bit then added, "I know a particularly talented, uh, person who does that sorta shit. Guy's kind of weird, but I can ask if you think it'll help."

"Couldn't hurt to ask. It would certainly save me a lot of time."

After I'd said it, I had second thoughts. Anti-social behavior permeated Bart's world. I'd seen it in Bart as well as some of the other people he hangs out with. "Weird" in that world covered a lot of ground. "So how far out of touch is this guy? He won't get me in any trouble if I hire him, will he?"

Bart smiled faintly. "I wouldn't worry about that. My guy is really good about getting what you need and not being noticed."

The extra information about Samantha's activities would certainly make my life easier, and my extra efficiency might raise the chances of a recommendation from Stuyvesant to some of his big money pals—maybe. "Okay, see what he can turn up." A moment later I added, "But find out what he'll charge first. Just out of curiosity, who is this guy? Do I know him?"

Bart cleared his throat and didn't meet my eyes. "Name's Kurse—with a K. I met Kurse last year at a hacker get together in Des Moines."

He paused a moment before he continued. "Kurse likes to operate real private like, but we, uh, did a project together."

"Your hacker group met in Des Moines? Des Moines, Iowa?"

He chuckled. "Yeah. That Des Moines."

I frowned thoughtfully. "Not exactly a tech-heavy location . . ." I scratched my head. "Or am I missing something?"

"There were other considerations. The hotel had good internet and an outstanding bar. That's all we needed. Why go someplace where people might actually recognize what we were doing and get suspicious?"

Why indeed? "So, can you give me Kurse's contact information?"

"Nope. Kurse won't work with anybody unknown. You'll have to go through me." He paused. "It won't be cheap, but if all you want is a peek at Samantha's calendar, that shouldn't be too bad."

And I could bill it to Stuyvesant as part of Bart's research.

I nodded. "Okay. See what your Kurse friend can find."

Four

The Stuyvesants' joint social calendar for Tuesday showed they had a political fundraiser together that evening. I hadn't been invited, but it didn't bother me. In the first place, I didn't like the candidate and wasn't interested in what he had to say. Besides, if they were both attending, her husband could watch her.

The information Stuyvesant had given me, however, listed nothing for Samantha that day—the type of gap he had hired me to fill. In order to follow her through her daily routine, I needed to be on the street ready to go at eight o'clock. However, yesterday had showed me that if I wanted to park where I could see her leave, I had to get there early to find a space. No way would I screw up this job the very first day I tailed her.

I'd set my alarm for three a.m. At four o'clock, I found plenty of open spaces. Once parked, I had extra time and a need for coffee. A city that never sleeps? Maybe in some places, but at four in the morning, this part of town was decidedly somnolent. I walked three blocks before I found a place to buy a cup.

Back in my car, I put the coffee in the cup holder and started to review the material Bart had sent me.

A sudden banging on the car window jolted me awake. Early morning sun silhouetted a cop staring in at me. After a couple of blinks, I checked my watch—quarter to seven. Shit. I sighed and got out of the car. "Morning, officer." I rubbed my eyes. "I'm waiting to meet a client."

Sort of true.

I took a deep breath and stifled a yawn. "I must have dozed off."

She stepped closer and held out her hand. "Can I see some ID?" I knew she was also checking for the smell of alcohol and looking for other signs of intoxication.

I fished out my wallet and showed her my driver's license and PI identification. While I waited for her to check, I saw an open cafeteria nearby. I hadn't finished my earlier coffee, and it had died long ago.

I nodded toward the cafeteria. "They have decent coffee in there?"

She handed back my documents and looked over her shoulder. "Their food's not bad, but the coffee'll kill you."

She jerked her thumb down the street. "I'd go to the cafe around the corner on Fourth." She nodded briskly. "Have a good day, sir."

Yes, around the corner they did have good coffee. While there, I took advantage of their restroom. I don't know what part of me dislikes the dull humdrum of surveillance work the worst—my brain, my butt, or my bladder.

This time I stayed awake. Samantha's shiny car poked its nose up the ramp a little after nine o'clock. I tailed dutifully along behind her on the busy streets. If Bart's friend Kurse could get me a copy of her personal calendar, I could bypass most of the waiting and watching.

One thing I'd learned over the years is that I can discover things about people's personality by watching their driving. Samantha had been raised a privileged child in a wealthy family. I was curious. Did she show an entitled sense of immunity to the rules of the road when dealing with lesser mortals?

Within minutes I saw quite the opposite. Samantha of the Astor family was a conscientious driver who used her turn signals consistently. From several cars back, I couldn't see her eyes in the mirrors, but she swiveled her head appropriately to keep track of traffic in the other lanes. At one corner she gestured at another car to go ahead even though she probably had the right of way.

Samantha might have been socially and monetarily advantaged, but she showed no indications of having that sense of divine-right-of-way I'd seen in other rich people who drove expensive cars. In other words, I liked the way she drove. I would have ridden with her.

She turned and headed uptown. The traffic was heavier, so I closed up a bit.

She was a careful driver, but driving in the city rewards one for being opportunistic. We were both in the right hand lane when she darted into an open parking spot along the street.

I couldn't do anything except drive on past. At the corner, I flipped on my blinker and turned right. By the time I could get around the block, she would probably have disappeared, but I'd give it a go.

At the next corner, I caught a red light. I waited impatiently for it to change, drumming my fingers on the wheel and watched the review mirror. As a reward for clean living, Samantha came walking around the corner and turned into the first door along the block.

I smiled. Now that I knew where she was, I took my time and found a good parking spot with a view of where she had gone.

With her car parked on the street, I could finally plant the GPS tracker. The battery on the little bugger would last only a couple of days, but once I knew where she was, it would be easy to swap out the unit with a spare. Bart had found the trackers for me last year, but this was my first time using one. It also meant I could legitimately bill the cost of the trackers to Stuyvesant. I would, of course, be happy to give the units to him when we settled up—if he asked.

I knelt by her BMW and retied my shoe. A glance around showed no one obviously watching. I reached under the car and planted the tracker on a support bracket behind the front bumper.

Back on my feet, I strolled confidently to the corner of the block, following the same path Samantha had taken. At the door she had entered, a small brass plate said, "Floraison." Whatever might be behind the door, I wasn't about to barge in to find out.

Back in my car, a quick search showed me that Floraison was a French word for bloom. In this case Floraison was the name of the exclusive, high-end spa listed at this address. So exclusive, there were no business hours given nor any specific services named. Their slogan promised *premier elegance* but no details. Their customers must know because the internet didn't.

Now came the fun part of surveillance.

Waiting.

And more waiting.

I used the time to run some simple data searches on my tablet for other clients. I also worked my email and composed a draft of my final report on another case. After several hours, my stomach told me it was lunchtime.

I checked, and it wasn't.

My stomach isn't a good judge of time—especially since today's breakfast had been premature and hasty. I tried to focus on work, but my stomach kept growling.

By eleven-thirty, I gave in and decided two hours of diligence justified a break to eat. After double-checking the motion alert setting on the tracker app on my phone, I got out of my car and stretched out the kinks.

Earlier, when I'd walked past Floraison, I'd noticed the next retail bay's frontage had been painted and trimmed to match its neighbor, probably indicating a related business. The sign over this door said, *Raffiné*. The letters were in a different style, but had the same size and brass sheen as the first shop. Best of all, *Raffiné* had a menu posted.

Now that I was hungry, I stopped to inspect the menu. There were no prices, but in fine print at the bottom, I read *"In Partnership with Floraison."*

The connection of the two businesses told me I might be able to get information about the spa. The classy connection also warned me that the information could cost me. I considered the humble available balance on my credit card.

My rich client wanted information about his wife's activities. Samantha was right next door to a restaurant connected to the exclusive spa. I'd never get in the spa, but . . .

The restaurant had food, and my stomach grumbled the deciding vote.

I pushed the door open. Inside, the lighting was subdued. Tables sat in little nooks created by planters and wooden dividers. Sleek contemporary lines finished in subdued tones suggested quiet intimacy rather than aggressive modernism.

"Welcome to Raffiné." A young man wearing an embroidered vest over a tailored, open-collar shirt gave me a small bow of recognition. He had also demonstrated how to pronounce Raffiné.

He smiled. "I'm Leonard." He gestured to the nearly empty room. "It's early, so you can sit where you like. Do you have a preference?"

A quick scan showed me a table where I could keep an eye on the street through the heavily tinted windows. "How about over there?"

"Very good, sir. Are you dining alone, or will someone be joining you?"

I returned a level two smile, preoccupied but with pleasant intentions.

"It's just me today, Leonard. I had an early morning, and I need to catch a quick bite."

"Do you need a menu, or do you know what you want?"

"I've never been here before, so I guess I'd better see a menu."

He smiled, and his smile had dimples. "Yes, we're rather hidden. Antoine opened this as a little side venture to go along with his husband's business next door."

"Floraison? I saw the name plate, but I no idea what it was." I paused as if considering possibilities. "Is it an investment company or something?"

He chuckled. "Not hardly. It's an exclusive spa. They don't even advertise. You have to know somebody."

I looked around. "And Raffiné too?"

"We do take walk-in trade." He showed his dimples again. "And I'm glad you came in. Are you ready to order?"

No, I was not ready. I had glanced at the menu on the door. Now with it in my hands I realized it was in French—I think. Whatever it was, my two years of high school Spanish wouldn't cut it.

And there were still no prices.

I handed the menu back. "I just want a light lunch. Is there something you would recommend?"

"Do you like fish? Antoine fries sea bass in a really light batter. I could give you a luncheon portion. On a bed of light baby kale, it's just scrumptious."

With no price tag, I was a little reluctant to commit. However, since the two businesses were connected, Leonard could probably tell me about Samantha's spa.

Rationalization complete, I nodded. "Sounds good."

"Maybe a nice white wine with that?"

Wine in a cafe like this was certain to be a budget buster. I shook my head. "Thank you, but no. I was up early, and I'm afraid a glass of wine would put me to sleep. How about some coffee?"

He frowned looking concerned. "If you need a wake-up, how about an espresso? That always perks me up."

"Eh," I sniffed. "I've tried it, but I don't really care for it."

"Starbucks?" He sounded suspicious. When I nodded, he touched my arm confidentially. "Listen, Antoine roasts his own beans. That mass-produced stuff isn't even in the same league."

He looked around as if afraid someone would overhear. "Tell you what. I'll bring you a little half-demi to try. If you don't like it, I'll bring you coffee. We usually do a French press. Would that be okay?"

When I agreed, Leonard bustled away.

Bemused, I watched him go. *Was this how the rich were always treated, or was Leonard particularly taken with me?*

I returned my attention to the window. While I didn't expect Samantha to come strolling by, I wanted to watch the foot traffic.

When Leonard reappeared, he had a little glass cup half full of a dark, nutty brown liquid topped by a layer of lighter brown foam.

"Try this," he ordered and set the cup in front of me.

As I brought it to my mouth, the first thing I noticed was the rich, smoky scent. The texture of the liquid was almost like cream. The espresso had a rich hint of caramel and a bitter bite at the end.

"Oh, my goodness!" was all I could say. I swirled the little that was left and finished it.

He nodded knowingly. "Would you like a double?"

I savored the lingering aftertaste. "Do you do triples?"

"For you, anything's possible." His dimples were back.

When Leonard brought the espresso, I quizzed him about the business next door. Yes, it was a high-end spa that offered services, treatments, and therapies to hair, skin, and nails—remedies I'd never even heard of, let alone experienced. Then again I'm pretty much a shower, shave, and comb kind of guy.

When my fish came, it was truly outstanding. When I was younger, my family would visit my aunt and uncle at their lake place up north. I'd always thought that nobody could fry bass better than Uncle Jim. I was wrong.

When Leonard brought the bill, I passed my compliments along before I checked the damage. It was under three figures—but not much. Still, I'd gotten information about Samantha's day as well as having had a chance to absorb a little ambiance from the world in which the Stuyvesants lived.

Leonard brought back my freshly dented credit card. When he laid it on the table, I saw a slip of paper underneath.

"Listen," he said. "I don't usually do this, but you seem like a really great guy. Here's my number. Would you give me a call—maybe?"

Yes, Leonard was nice, but I don't bat from that side of the plate.

"Gee, I'm sorry," I said with as much concern as I could manage. "I'm already in a relationship."

It was a lie.

Then again, hope springs eternal.

Five

After a much better lunch than I'd planned, I went back to my post in the car. I did more emails and other bookkeeping, all chores that made the time just fly by. The BMW gleamed right where Samantha had left it.

I checked in with Bart. He said he'd made contact with Kurse and would have something in a day or two.

Since the Floraison spa offered its customers fine dining while in the throes of the beautification process, the length of her stay didn't surprise me. By two-thirty, I decided there was no longer time for her to have an illicit assignation and still make the fund raising dinner the couple had scheduled for five o'clock.

I laid my tablet aside and reached for the keys. Before I could start the car, a belch from the back seat startled me. I snapped a look back over my shoulder.

A gnome sat in my backseat.

"'Scuse me," he said.

"What the hell . . ."

"I said I was sorry."

He covered his mouth for an additional small burp then frowned. "You anthros aren't supposed to notice us anyway."

"Why not?"

He shrugged. "Sort of like trying to see your backside in a mirror." He smiled and added, "I guess that means they're the lucky ones."

"But why do I see you, and they don't?"

"You're unlucky?"

That was less than informative, so I tried another tack. "What are you doing in my car?"

"Watchin'."

"What are you watching?"

"You." He yawned broadly. "Got to say, you sure don't do much. I'm Gary, by the way."

"Gary?"

"It's short for Garhezeigenbusch. It's an old family name."

"Why?"

He shrugged. "Garhezeigenibusch is too long to say?"

"No." I made a face and waved away his answer. "Why are you watching me?"

"Mel told me to."

I'd sort of adjusted to actually talking with one of the beings I'd been half afraid were figments of my imagination, but we'd just rounded a sudden conversational curve. "Who's Mel, and why is he interested in me?"

"His real name is Melocartazenilis. You wouldn't know him, seeing as how he's a unicorn."

He stood up and frowned, putting his hands on his hips. "Mel says that Alexander Stuyvesant hired you. He wants to know why."

"Why would a unicorn care what Alexander Stuyvesant does?"

"Long story," he said. "It has to do with some property out west that Stuyvesant's wife owns. It's the only unicorn breeding ground on this continent, and Alexander wants to drill for oil or somethin' there." He shrugged. "You might say the details are above my pay grade. You really don't want to ask a unicorn too many questions. Especially not when the questions concern personal business like their . . ." He chuckled. ". . . breeding."

Maybe unicorns didn't like to be questioned, but since I had the gnome talking, I circled back to a question that had been on my mind for a long time. "So why is it that I can see you and nobody else can?"

"Not nobody, but there aren't too many of you sensitives around. I guess you're just born that way." He crooked a wry smile. "I imagine those of you who can see us learn pretty early to keep their mouths shut."

I certainly agreed with that, but I pressed on. "Are there any others, you know, other sensitives like me in the city?"

He shrugged. "Beats me. We gnomes don't keep track of things like that."

"So what do gnomes do?"

"Scouting and snooping. We're are good at that."

"For Mel?"

"And others." He smiled. "You anthros really are pretty entertaining."

Gary looked out the window then back at me. He frowned. "So, you want to tell me if you're going to do something that matters today? I've been bored to sizlets back here."

I took a deep breath and tried to collect my thoughts enough to remember what I was doing. "Actually I was about to head back to my office. It doesn't look like Samantha is going to do anything today."

"So you really are following his wife, huh?"

He walked across the seat to the door. "Well, if you're heading back, I'm checking out. See you later."

He lifted the door latch and opened the car door just enough to slip out. When he closed the door, there was scarcely a sound.

The third day, the BMW and the tracker never moved from the parking garage. The fundraiser the night before had lasted well into the early hours—at least it had on their joint appointment calendar. There was nothing on that calendar for today, but I was ready in case Samantha had something on hers.

At least by now I'd figured out how to set up for my morning watch. The city allowed overnight parking on the street. Last evening, I'd located a good spot for the car across from the Carrack Center. My apartment was only two miles away, walkable in a half hour or so if I humped it. The distance was several lightyears in rental prices, but there and back again made for good exercise, especially since I would be sitting most of the day.

As usual, I'd brought my tablet to do work, but today I also brought one of my old law books. Yes, I'd dropped out of law school. The demanding and detailed coursework had bored me. Composing comprehensive legal briefs was tiresome beyond belief. I found splitting legal hairs down into their component molecules just for the sake of argument to be pointless.

So why had I gone to law school in the first place? A crime.

I went to college with the idea of being a high school chemistry or physics teacher—a nice, safe job for an insecure kid. My mother's father sponsored my education at his alma mater, a small private college in Ohio. Having led a sheltered life, my expectations of college were similarly limited.

The biggest revelation at college was the large number of gorgeous babes who were my fellow students—not to mention the effect that those girls had on my youthful libido. If you'd charted my study time over the four years, you would have concluded my major was women's studies. Considering the amount of independent research I did on the subject, my grades in my actual academic classes were pretty good.

The seminal event of my college education occurred my senior year. Over spring break that year, Myron Toff, the college's vice president of finance and chief financial officer, absconded with the majority of the school's money. When he didn't come back after break, the school found that glib, smiling Myron had cleaned out his office as well as most of their assets. He'd even taken the award he'd been given by the alumni group the year before in honor of his fundraising efforts—funds he'd been raising for himself as it turned out.

It took another week or so for the college's accountants to discover that somehow, over those three years, Myron had pilfered, diverted, embezzled, and outright stolen not only operating funds but also a goodly portion of the institution's endowment.

The college canceled commencement that year. Three months later, I received a printed piece of paper vouching for my degree.

In the end, the school did not close. For several years it limped along, teetering on the brink of insolvency. The last I'd heard, my alma mater had found two wealthy brothers who had agreed to fund the school. It's no longer a liberal arts college. They kept the name the same, but it's become a business institute devoted to propagating the ideology of its benefactors.

The details of the embezzlement case fascinated me—on a strictly intellectual level of course. How had smooth-talking Myron hidden his actions for the time it had taken to loot the funds? What devious tricks had he used? That spurred my interest in the legal system, and I enrolled in law school.

That first year, I took courses like Contract Law. The course spotlighted the delightfully subtle interpretations of such concepts as offer and acceptance, invitation and acceptance, intention to be legally bound, both consideration and capacity, not to mention the rigors of regulatory requirements.

While the instructor's voice echoed in the large hall, I found myself contemplating such enigmas as the Mona Lisa's smile, the difference between degrees of mathematical infinity, the ethereal structure of the asteroid belt . . .

Don't get me wrong. Isolated aspects of the course work fascinated me. What was the history and reasoning behind the Supreme Court's dreadful Dred Scott decision? How was *Brown v. Board of Education* still influencing education today?

The required material in Contract Law? Not so much.

I stuck it out through the first year because I couldn't admit to myself that I'd made a mistake. That summer, most of my fellow students eagerly sought out positions as legal interns. I had gotten acquainted with Phillip Woodland, a local private investigator, and he offered to pay me to shadow a client's daughter through her course work at a nearby university's summer remedial program.

I loved the job. With my natural nosiness about everything and everybody, the work was effortless. While I'm not particularly a people person, I found I had a talent for pretending to be someone I was not for the purpose of chatting up people to gather information. Not particularly comfortable in my own skin, I could ooze confidence in someone else's.

At the end of the summer, Woodland offered me a permanent position with his agency. Since it was way more fun than law school—not to mention easier—I became a full-time private investigator. Illicit behaviors were a lot more fun to work with before they became court cases.

So why did I bring my dusty law book along today? Alexander Stuyvesant might have been a high-powered international financier, but I didn't trust him. I wanted to review subjects like torts, negligence, and liability—just in case the subject came up during the discussion of my bill. And maybe I wanted to check to see if there might be a defensible rationale for billing Stuyvesant for the cost of yesterday's lunch at Raffiné.

Turned out I had plenty of time to do research. I never saw Samantha that day. I saw no torts either, but I did develop a craving for the sweet tarts they sell at the Berry Ferry.

On day four, my stakeout yielded results that turned my view of the case around.

Samantha spent the morning at a fitness center. It didn't have the exclusive look of the Floraison beauty spa, but they'd displayed enough high-end exercise equipment in the front window to advertise their service while making a clear statement that this was not a place to come expecting to find a pickup basketball game. Stuyvesant's surveillance job had preempted my normal morning fitness regimen. I sat in my car envying Samantha the opportunity to sweat productively.

I had to tail her visually today because the signal from the GPS tracker I'd planted on her car had disappeared yesterday evening. My first thought was a weak battery. While she was in the gym, I checked under the car. The unit itself was gone. Something had probably kicked up off the street and dislodged it—an accident.

Probably.

I stared at the car and debated with myself about planting a second tracker. What if someone had found the unit? If they recognized it as a tracker, they would have told Samantha and be alert for a replacement. If they found a second tracker, they'd start investigating.

For that matter, they might be watching right now.

I glanced around hurriedly but saw no one obviously keeping watch on the BMW. Pretending to be just another car ogler, I ran my hand admiringly along the car's fender line and walked away with the second GPS unit in my pocket. Her husband had been adamant that his wife not know anything about my surveillance, and I didn't want to jeopardize my payday.

Samantha was dressed for the gym in jeans and a sweatshirt with her hair in a ponytail, and that's how she came out. Even with her more casual look, I saw the same focused, no-nonsense woman. From the gym she walked around the corner to a fast food restaurant. No Floraison today. There she met another similarly dressed woman of about Samantha's age. I watched from a bistro across the street while they ate lunch. I had to scramble when they left because they took the other woman's car, a nondescript Toyota parked on the other side of the street and going in the opposite direction.

They drove into a rough neighborhood of decaying brownstone apartment buildings. I kept my distance and slid into the space beside a hydrant when they stopped. They got out of the car and went into one of the buildings. A few minutes later, they hustled out with a third woman. This woman clutched a bundle to her chest. A child? Samantha carried a bag. The two women helped the third into the back seat, and a moment, they later were on their way.

What had I just seen? I followed them reflexively, but my mind wandered about uncertainly in a bemused neutral gear. They headed to the outskirts of the city. Just past the outer belt, they pulled into the parking lot of the MotoGo Motel.

I cruised on down the street until I found a spot to turn around. The type of motel fit with information Stuyvesant had given me, but the context was completely wrong. This was no clandestine sexual assignation. It looked for all the world like a rescue mission.

That idea was confirmed when I pulled into motel's lot and parked the car. Samantha and the others were out of the car. The bundle now had arms and legs. The woman beamed as she held up her baby. After an affectionate little jostle, she pulled her baby close for a kiss. I couldn't hear their conversations, but there were smiles and fist-bumps all around as the two women escorted the woman and her child into the hotel.

I sat in the car and looked at nothing.

Ever have one of those moments when your entire frame of reference comes tumbling down? Maybe Samantha was stepping out. But maybe her activities meant something completely different from what her husband thought. Maybe Stuyvesant had been misled by idle gossip.

Maybe so, but my not-quite-right feeling edged closer to something's-fishy territory.

Six

Patricia Wentz? So who's that?" Jessica looked up from the note I'd given her. We sat in the living room of her apartment that evening.

"She's the woman who helped Samantha."

"How'd you get her name?"

I'd already given her an abbreviated version of what I'd seen Samantha and her friend do that day. I'd skimped on details, but Jessica had shifted into cross examination mode.

"They took Wentz's car."

I shrugged, trying to be casual, but her stare demanded more. "I took a picture of it, and Bart got her name from the plate number."

"I didn't know Bart had a pipeline into the DMV."

She frowned and her eyes narrowed. "He doesn't, does he? He got this illegally, right?"

Bart was a friend of hers. Once before she'd given me a hard time when she'd found out his help for me had taken him into outlaw territory.

"Bart didn't do anything this time. He told me about a guy he knows who can get into just about anything." I winked. "I think Bart's taking a peek at the dark side."

"What? He's apprenticed to a Sith Lord?"

When I stared at her blankly, she sighed. "You know, *Star Wars*? The Sith?"

Sort of. I knew the movies, but only casually. Still, I'd used the reference first. Jessica had raised my ante—and called. Not the first time she'd been a step ahead of me.

She looked at me skeptically. "I went to school with Bart. I don't see him as a real hacker type guy."

"They're not all bad guys who'd bring down the power grid or rig an election, you know. Some see it as a challenge—like climbing mountains." I shrugged. "They'll break into a system but report how they did it so the weakness can be fixed. Maybe Bart'll be one of them."

"Yeah, I know," she said with a sigh. "Maybe I'm overprotective of people I know."

She looked at my note again. "Okay, I'll see what I can do with the name."

Just then her phone went off. She glanced at it and took the call. "Hi, Dad. I've got something going right now. Can I call you back?"

When she hung up, I raised my eyebrows. "Your dad? You've never mentioned him."

She smiled slyly. "He's a cop."

"Oh? Where?"

"Right here in the city." She sighed as if anticipating my next questions. "My mom's dead. I have one brother who lives down in North Carolina. I moved out on my own when I got out of college." She dusted her hands. "There. Any other questions?"

Jessica had never shared her background with me before. It felt . . . good. It also explained a few things I'd seen.

"So that time last year at the Berry Ferry when you broke that guy's wrist when he tried to get fresh with you?"

She nodded. "My dad's showed me stuff. It was supposed to be a standard wrist twist so I could dig my thumb into his ulnar nerve, but the guy tried to turn it over. The ulnar, uh, funny bone's my standard move when a guy tries something cute, but that time he had me off balance."

"Yeah, remind me not to get out of line with you."

"Maybe it depends on which line you want to cross."

Was that a challenge in her eyes? I didn't know what to say. It almost sounded as if she was . . . flirting?

I realized I was staring blankly. "Yeah, uh, okay."

Change the subject, idiot! I thought madly.

"So, do you think Samantha and her friend today were really out to rescue that woman and her kid?"

She frowned. "It sure sounds like it. You said it went slick with no resistance, so they probably timed it for when the guy was at work or something."

She gnawed at a knuckle thoughtfully. "Maybe if I find out who Patricia Wentz is, we'll have a better idea."

"Exactly why I came tonight." I stood up to go but remembered another tidbit I wanted her to check. "I had a reference to a property that Samantha Stuyvesant owns out west. I'm curious about it, but since I don't have details, it can wait. You said you've got a paper to finish, and you still have to call your dad. I'm glad you let me drop by."

She stood up too and looked at the spread of books on her table. "Yeah, gotta love those responsibilities."

She smiled at me. "And thanks for coming by, Mick. You're a good study break."

The next day, Samantha Stuyvesant left for England to attend a board meeting for a non-profit charity based in London. Although I followed her to the airport, her husband wasn't interested enough to send me across the Atlantic to continue following her. To me, a couple of nights alone in London would have seemed a perfect time for her to indulge in an affair. Too bad Stuyvesant didn't agree. I'd never been to London.

Since I had other irons hanging in the fire, I used the rest of the morning to take care of my business. That afternoon, I went to the Coffee Berry Ferry to see if Jessica had found anything. The cafe was busy. Once I had my coffee, I waved at her from across the room and found a table.

A few minutes later, she plopped a folder of papers on the table and slid into the seat across from me. "Oh, you're going to like this one."

She glanced back at the line of customers at the order counter and sighed. "Busy afternoon." She dug into one of her shoes. Coming up with a little piece of grit, she looked at it disdainfully and flicked it away. "Didn't even have time to get that out of my shoe. I was waiting for you before I took a break."

I opened the folder and glanced at it. "So what's the scoop? Who is Patricia Wentz?"

"She's a lawyer who runs a rescue mission for victims of domestic violence."

"Mission? A church thing?"

She shook her head. "Nope. They're independent. They get a little state money, but most of it comes from donors in the city." She shrugged. "I couldn't get into their records that far, but I wouldn't be surprised—"

"Yeah. You're thinking Samantha's a donor, right?"

"You do catch on."

She dug out one of the sheets of paper and plopped it on top. "Time To Go is the name of the operation. Wentz founded it twelve years ago. Their website says they help women in abusive relationships—counseling, restraining orders, direct help, that kind of thing."

I looked at the paper and nodded. "Even picking them up when it's time to go." After I heard what I'd just said, I added, "Ah, clever."

I shuffled around in the papers. Later, I'd read them in detail, but I scanned them for anything that jumped out. "She's thirty-seven."

"Right. Married with a ten-year-old daughter."

"Married? And her husband?"

She shook her head. "Her status was listed as married but no name. I haven't checked the official state records yet."

Glancing back at her notes, she continued. "Wentz was born in Arkansas. Left home after high school for the University of Oregon. Then Harvard Law. No record she ever went back to Arkansas."

"And made abused women her life's work."

I put the papers back in the folder and looked at Jessica. "Any bets about the family she grew up in?"

"Sadly, no." She nodded to the folder. "Time To Go has filed a number of court cases over the years. Wentz handled every case in the beginning. For the last six years, they've filed a lot more suits, and several other lawyers' names are on them. Also six years ago, they moved their office to where it is now."

"Six years, huh?" I rubbed the end of my nose thoughtfully. "Suppose that's when Samantha . . . ?"

She shrugged. "I can't tell you for sure, but expanding their operations would take money."

She tapped the folder again. "Different subject: you said heard something about a property Samantha owns out west? I took a quick look. She owns a lot of stuff here and there, but there's one that caught my eye. It's a property south of Bozeman, Montana, just north of Yellowstone Park. Turns out it's one of the largest privately-owned parcels of land in the country."

I raised my eyebrows. North of Yellowstone? "So I'm thinking wild animals and undeveloped land? Forests? Mountains?"

Jessica nodded.

With that in mind, I couldn't help but wonder. Would that be the type of scenery that would make unicorns randy?

Rather than think raunchy thoughts about a supposedly mythical beast, I turned my speculations back to Samantha. With assets like the landed gentry, she could have lived a life of leisure, yet she actively protected ill-used women.

"I can't help wondering about her and what she does," I mused out loud. "Is Samantha this active with other charities she supports, or does helping abused women tell us something about her husband?"

I focused back on Jessica and smiled. "You do good work, uh . . . JJ, Thank you."

Dammit. I'd almost called her kid again.

Her eyes squinted just a bit as if she had read my mind, but then she smiled. "And thank you, Mick, for the work. I appreciate a little something to do that doesn't involve either coffee or looking up case law references."

The window on the door read "Time To Go." Below, the words "Welcome - Come In" had friendly smiley faces inside each "O."

Inside, a small woman sat at a desk.

I smiled at her. "Miss Wentz? Hi. I'm Bob Parker, from the *Tri-County Gazette*. We had an appointment?"

She got up and came toward me with her hand outstretched. "Yes, I'm Patricia Wentz." She gave me a quick, firm handshake. "Let's go into my office where we can talk."

As soon as we were seated, she fixed me with a cool gaze. "Mr. Martin called and offered me a contribution if I'd talk to one of his reporters. I wasn't aware that the *Tri-County Gazette* did feature articles. I thought they mainly sold real estate ads and ran topical domestic pieces taken from the wire services."

I adjusted my enthusiastic level three smile down to a sincere and earnest level one.

"Sean is trying . . . uh, that's Sean Martin, the owner. The guy who called you? Anyway he's trying to include more local content— something you can't get online."

Better yet, Sean Martin owed me big time after I'd tracked down a guy who had scammed him out of twenty grand. The *Tri-County Gazette* was one of his projects, and he was more than happy to vouch for Bob Parker's fake credentials.

"So what do you want to know?"

"You offer help to abused women. Exactly what types of services do you offer?"

"These aren't *abused* women. Not even battered. Call it what it is. They're victims of domestic violence. Vi-o-lence, get it? Punched in the face. Arms broken. Skulls fractured."

She locked her hands behind her head and leaned back in her chair. "Or doesn't your little suburban sales paper like to deal in graphic violence?"

I blinked. My friendly bumpkin approach wasn't working. I recalibrated to something more professional.

"Sorry, you're right. I want to deal with this realistically so the readers will understand your work." I added sheepishly, "You have the expertise, and I guess I need some education."

Hoping to defuse the tension I'd roused, I tacked toward getting her to talk about the organization's history. "You founded Time To Go twelve years ago?"

"Yes." She sat and looked at me.

Oh, good, I thought, *a talker*.

I leaned forward a little, trying to project earnest interest. "So what was your motivation? Did you have any help getting started?"

It took a few minutes, but I managed to extract confirmation of most of what I already knew from Jessica's research. Wondering if I could puzzle out to what degree Samantha supported the group, I asked Wentz about the source of her group's funding.

"That's confidential," she snapped.

Once again I'd clumsily stepped on a tender area. I figured she'd never give me Samantha Stuyvesant's name directly, but I'd hoped to get a feel for the accuracy of my hunch that Samantha had contributed money as well as time.

I nodded earnestly. "I understand completely, but can you speak in general terms? Do you get any state or federal funding?" I already knew from what Jessica had found, but I wanted to hear how she said it.

"A little. At least from the state." And she clearly resented the amount of that support.

"Are your individual contributors mostly local or is your fund raising more widespread? Can you talk about general numbers of donors?"

"No comment," she snarled.

Obviously the group's finances were a sensitive area. That suggested to me that one of those contributors supplied the majority of her group's funds.

Since I'd hit a wall with this line of questions, I took a new tack. "Do you offer your services to anyone who has been the victim of domestic violence or just women?"

Given the tenor of the interview so far, I was pretty certain of her answer, but I was surprised by the vehemence of her response.

"We rescue only women. Children have their own agency. Members of the male patriarchy have ways of taking care of their own. Show me an abused husband, and I'll show you a sneaky son of a bitch who's good at provoking confrontation."

Land mines all around. I didn't react to her absolutist statement, but I remembered one case two years ago where the wife, an obese alcoholic woman, had regularly beaten her smaller husband. Wentz's chilly glare warned of danger if I pressed her on the issue. From her answers as well as the general tone of the interview, Wentz had a clear grudge against men in general.

I nodded brusquely and changed course again. "Would you care to share any information about a recent case?"

Even as anger flashed in her eyes, I held up my hands defensively. "I don't want any details that might compromise anonymity. You said you rescue women. That sounds dramatic. If you could help me convey some of the tension of the situation, the drama of the rescue, the publicity might help your fund raising."

She frowned, but after she'd thought it over she nodded. As I'd hoped, she described in general terms the episode I'd witnessed.

What I'd seen had indeed been a rescue.

With a few more softball questions, I brought the interview to a close.

Once safely back in my car, I called Jessica. I got her voice mail, and asked her to call me back.

A few minutes later, she did. "Hey, Mick. How'd the interview go? A little rough?"

"Yeah, thanks for the heads-up on that one," I said with more than a little sarcasm.

"Sorry about that. I had suspicions she might be difficult, but I didn't know for sure until Melanie got back to me an hour ago. Melanie does social work. She's counseled several of Wentz's clients and knows her. She told me Patricia doesn't suffer fools gladly."

She chuckled slightly. "She even said that once her client's safe, little Patricia isn't above going back for a physical confrontation with the abuser."

"What, is Wentz a ninja or something?" How close had I come to getting physically kicked out of the interview?

"More like a black belt. She's into those martial arts things." She chuckled softly. "Yeah, when she's not woman-handling a man-handler, she gives classes at a local dojo."

I nodded as I thought about the larger situation. Wentz had not reacted well when I'd probed her agency's finances. While I still had no confirmation of Samantha's support of Time to Go, I suspected Wentz's concern might be protecting the confidentiality of her major donor.

As challenging as it had been, Wentz's interview had confirmed my interpretation of what I had seen Samantha doing that day. It also deepened my problem with my client. Stuyvesant had clearly implied that I would find evidence his wife was catting around. Yes, he might have been suspicious, but he might also have been trying to motivate me to dig up something that would make his divorce easier. If he was looking for a way to cash in on a divorce, he wouldn't be happy if I handed him documentation that his wife deserved nomination for humanitarian of the year.

Thank goodness Stuyvesant had signed a contract to pay me, one way or the other.

"Mick? You still there?"

"Yeah . . . Yeah, sorry. Just wondering—"

"If you still have questions, why don't you go back and ask your new friend Patricia?"

She was taunting me, and I laughed good-naturedly. "Thank goodness I won't have to go into that lion's den again."

Seven

I still had one last task before I called it a day. My phone had been acting funky lately, and it ate its charge like a dog eats its breakfast. Bart had fixed a problem with it before, so I headed over to see him.

When I saw he wasn't at his desk, I knocked.

After a time with no answer, I knocked again. When he still didn't show, I tried the knob. Locked? Bart never locked his door.

Worried now, I knocked more insistently.

"Yeah, yeah. I'm comin'." His call was muffled by the door. A moment later he shuffled into the room from the direction of his bedroom, barefoot and tucking in his shirt tail.

He looked out, saw me, and opened the door. "Hey, Mick. What you need?"

I stepped inside and held up my phone. "I'm having some problems and wondered if you could take a look."

"Yeah, sure," he said and took the phone from me. "You try restarting it?" He went through a couple of other standard questions as he flipped through screens.

"Whoa," he said and looked at me strangely. "You're on Textickle?"

"What's that?"

He looked at me and chuckled. "Come on. You know, the sexting app?"

"Never heard of it."

I grabbed my phone back. On the screen there was a list of apps and down in the Ts was Textickle.

I looked at him. "What is it?"

58

His smile was sly. He gave me an exaggerated wink and took back the phone. "Well, let's see what you've been up to." He gave the phone a few more flicks.

"Ah, here you go." He pointed the screen to me so I could see. "You don't remember this?" He winked again. "She sounds like a good time."

I took the phone. On the screen there was a running back and forth text chat. I skimmed the first posts then went back and read them in disbelief. It was sex talk—an explicit, unrestrained, libido-driven flirtation between two people discussing the extravagantly nasty things they wanted to do to each other. "Where did this come from?"

Bart laughed out loud. "Oh, you're good," he said slyly.

He took back the phone and scrolled through the texts. "Did you send her a picture of your dick?"

A moment later, he said, "Whoa!" and backed up his scroll.

He showed me the screen and asked, "Remember now?"

Samantha Stuyvesant was nude, a look of coquettish flirtation on her face.

After a bit, I realized my mouth was open. Before I closed it, I took a deep breath. "That . . . that . . ." And that was all I could think to say.

Over the last few days, I'd enjoyed tailing the beautiful woman. I'm a guy, okay? Maybe I'd even conjured up a speculative image of what she looked like undressed while envying her husband and/or lover.

Just the once, you understand.

When my brain began to operate again, my thoughts turned ugly. "Is this some kind of a joke?"

"What joke? You gave me your phone five minutes ago. It's not like I've had time to do anything." Bart grinned. "You're just embarrassed I found your little secret."

"Secret? Yeah, secret from me! This is the client's wife I've been tailing. I've never even spoken to her, let alone . . ." I gestured wordlessly at the phone.

"All right. Stand down, you two."

Startled by the interruption, I looked up. While I'd been arguing with Bart, another person had emerged from the bedroom. In jeans and a rumpled, shapeless sweat shirt, I couldn't tell if the individual was male or female. Unkempt short brown hair offered no clues, nor did the intermediately pitched voice.

The person walked over to Bart and glanced at the phone.

"Sorry, Kurse," he said. "I was just going to get rid of him, but . . ."

Kurse? This was the hacker genius Bart had told me about? At first glance I had taken the slight figure for a youth, but a closer look showed mature lines and angles in his or her face.

Face? I scanned for traces of a beard and found none—so female? It was a deduction, and I added a small mental question mark of uncertainty.

"You're Kurse?" I asked. The question had already been answered, but I wanted in the conversation.

She eyed me coolly. "And you're Mickey Holmes, the private detective who's working for Alexander Stuyvesant."

I nodded but didn't have the courage to risk saying "yes, ma'am" if my gender check had been faulty. "He hired me to investigate his wife." I gestured at my phone that Bart still held. "I've never seen that, uh, information before."

Kurse looked at me unenthusiastically for a bit. Finally she turned to Bart and held out her hand. "Gimme."

She flipped through the file a bit, then favored me with an ironic smile "Pretty in-depth investigation."

I glanced at the ceiling for a moment and sighed. "That's what I was trying to tell Bart. I have no idea how that got on my phone."

Kurse looked at Bart, and they shared a smile.

My aggravation boiled over. "It wasn't me!"

She offered me the phone back. "Okay, if it wasn't you, then who? If somebody put it there, it wasn't some random hacker. Whoever did it knew who you were investigating." She smirked. "And where to get the file."

Mentally I kicked myself for not thinking through the implications. Who knew, and who would also have access to nude photos of Samantha?

The only answer I came up with made no sense. "Her husband?" I breathed. "But why?"

"Good question," Kurse said. "Perhaps you've been investigating the wrong spouse."

She pointed at my phone. "You can always delete it if you don't want it on your phone, but remember, there's probably a duplicate on the other end. It won't go away unless she deletes it. Even then, Textickle will have a copy."

I took another look at Samantha's nude form and shut down the app. After a deep breath, I said, "I guess I need to do some thinking."

"I would think so, hot stuff." She chuckled, then looked crafty. "Do you want me to check who else has the file?"

"You can do that?"

Kurse smirked. "Sure, unless the owner has taken precautions. Of course it would require considerable expertise to do it. So, say four benjamins worth of expertise to make sure this is the only copy?"

"Four hundred?" I hadn't paid that much for the phone in the first place.

She raised her eyebrows speculatively. "And if you want, I can even dig down into Textickle's archives. Of course that would take time and effort to get past their security . . . and would take even more money."

I stared at her uncertain, what to say.

With a shrug she added, "Then again, the company's policy is to not give up their files without a court subpoena. Maybe not even then. Still, if you want to make sure there's no record . . ."

Kurse was definitely a for-hire mercenary looking for new business. Wherever the app and its bawdy conversation had come from, it could cause me no end of trouble if Stuyvesant—or his wife—were to find out about it. Four hundred bucks seemed steep, but it would be cheap compared to what I'd lose if I botched this job for Stuyvesant.

I nodded, "Make it go away, at least the regular stuff. I'll have to think about what you said about Textickle's archives."

She held out her hand for my phone. "I can't do it from here. I'll bag and tag a copy of your file with its tracing data and send it to myself. As part of the service, I'll even delete the app, its files, and any activity record of it from your phone."

I got the gist of what she'd said, so I unlocked my phone and handed it to her.

Kurse flicked and tapped at the screen, fingers moving too quickly to follow. I had started to have thoughts about other parts of my business that were open to her inspection when she looked up. "You want to keep a copy of the file itself?"

My first thought was to have the whole thing just disappear, but a niggle of caution made me hesitate. "Maybe you should. There might be a clue to who made it."

"Maybe. I'll check the tracing data and let you know." She gave me a crafty smile. "I could send you just the pictures if that's all you want to look at."

I waved away the thought. "Get rid of the app, but send me a copy of the, uh, conversation. Can you do it—I don't know—as another type of file so I can access it from different app if I want to check something?"

"No problem."

She looked up and waggled my phone at me. "So, four hundred bucks: I make all traces of the app go away and see if there's anything that tells me where it came from. Then I check for other copies of the file and send you a copy in a different format. Right?"

She was pricey, but that file could cause me a world of trouble. I nodded. "Do it."

She spent a couple minutes tapping on my phone then handed it back. "There. Your end's clean. I sent myself a copy of everything. I'll find and scrub any other files tomorrow when I'm back at the shop. I'll convert the conversation to a plain text file and send it to you."

I started to put my phone back in my pocket, but she added, "Remember, I can't promise there won't be another copy at Textickle unless you pay me to look."

I nodded agreement and slid my phone back into my pocket.

"Hey, did you check his cell usage?" Bart asked Kurse. "It seemed awfully high, but I got distracted by the other stuff."

I handed the phone back to Kurse. She started tapping and flicking again then stopped. She frowned intently at the screen. A moment later, she went back to work. After a several minutes, she pulled out a stool and perched on it while she continued her efforts.

"What?" I asked.

Intent on the screen, she didn't look up. "There's some serious shit down under here I didn't see at first." She held the screen toward me, showing a chart full of meaningless numbers. "Something's sharing your activity and location data. Probably all of your cellular communications too."

She tapped the screen with her finger nail. "It's spy stuff, so there's some heavyweight fuckers behind this. I'd guess the feds." She looked at me and smiled. "Jeez, who'd you piss off?"

Dumbfounded, I just looked at her. Finally I said, "Well, the IRS did dispute a deduction on my taxes last year."

"Smart ass. You know the IRS would just haul your butt into court."

I took a deep breath and tried to steady myself. I don't always do my clearest thinking when I'm in trouble. "I'm sorry. You're right. This is serious."

She shrugged away my apology. "So, you want me to clean up this other shit for you?"

She paused and pursed her lips thoughtfully. "At least I think I can. But if I was you, I'd just get a new phone. It'd be cheaper. If you get a new one, get a burner and let Bart know before you use it the first time. I'll set things up so it won't happen again."

She frowned. "At least not without you knowing about it."

She handed the phone back to me. "I'll send you the Textickle file as a pdf. Can you handle that?"

"I'm not a complete illiterate," I protested. I was sure I had followed what she'd been talking about. Pretty sure, anyway. "And you'll send the picture too?"

"You bet, hot stuff." She grinned. "And remember, you owe me four hundred for wiping your ass. Give Bart the cash, and he'll get it to me."

Pointing at my phone, she added, "I'd turn that off if I were you. Even off, it might still be tattling on you, so you might want to take the battery out. Best thing to do would be to bury it with a stake in its heart."

I looked at my phone, an essential tool of the investigation business. "So how'd these things get on my phone in the first place? I'm pretty careful about the links I click and other stuff."

She shrugged. "Only takes one. For that matter, how's the security on your home wireless network?"

"I use . . ." I started, then stopped as I thought about my internet access. I used the ACE Properties' communal network that served my own apartment building as well as three others. "I guess maybe I need to look into something a little more secure."

After I left Bart's place, my contaminated phone hung heavy in my pocket. I'd turned it off, but Kurse's warning echoed in my ears.

What was going on?

Where had that file come from?

Why was I being tracked?

What did it mean?

Who was behind it?

What had Stuyvesant, my potential meal ticket, gotten me into?

All the way back to my apartment I peppered myself with questions that had no answers.

Safely home, I plopped down on my sofa and took out my lifeless phone. The smooth glass and metal rectangle no longer felt like a familiar extension of my job. Something alien lurked inside. I tried to remember which of my conversations with Jessica about the case had been by phone and which were in person. I wanted to call her right now, but the thought of using a phone that was broadcasting everything to an unknown somebody repelled me.

I got up and went to my desk, where I keep a couple of contract phones stashed for emergency use. It was later than I usually call, and Jessica didn't know this number. I shot her a text to warn her before I made the call.

"Hi, JJ. Sorry it's so late."

"Mick? Where are you calling from?"

I explained the circumstances and described what Bart had found on my phone. I recited a few excerpts from memory, but I sort of forgot to mention the provocative picture of Samantha. Fortunately she couldn't see me blushing.

We speculated a little bit, but collectively we came up with no new thoughts.

Finally she asked, "Should I take a look at your client—Samantha's husband? Maybe there's something that will suggest a connection."

Since I had been having some second thoughts, I said, "Sure."

"Now tell me about this Kurse," she said. "You said she was with Bart? What were they doing?"

I had mentioned the circumstances I'd found at Bart's when I arrived. "It looked as if they were in the bedroom when I got there." I thought for a minute then added, "Uh, it looked as if they might have been . . ."

"Doin' it?" she finished for me. "Huh. Bart never had a girlfriend when he was in school. So he's finally found one. A hacker to boot."

I told Jessica about my marginal identification of her gender. "Given the evident connection of their minds," I said, "I'm not going to speculate about the connection of their genitals."

That finally got a laugh. "Mick, you are a character. I wouldn't worry about their genitals. They're big kids."

She chuckled again and sighed. "Good thing you didn't say anything snide to them." She paused. "You didn't, did you?"

"Jessica, you know me. I'm the soul of tact."

"Yeah, and that's why I asked. If they're working that closely together, they might put all kinds of incriminating evidence on your phone if you make them mad."

Yeah, incriminating evidence. After I ended the call with Jessica, worries about Stuyvesant and incriminating evidence kept me awake for a long time.

Eight

With Samantha Stuyvesant in England for several days, I had more time to reflect on what I'd found on my phone. I didn't like the thoughts I'd already had. Lying awake in bed last night, I'd thought of a really good reason why her husband might have been involved in putting the pornographic file on my phone. I'd been following Samantha around. If I didn't find any evidence of Samantha's infidelity, my actions—and that file—would make me the designated perpetrator of cuckoldry in his divorce filing.

Stuyvesant was an investment counselor, no doubt a field with its own dirty tricks, but did he do digital tricks? Could an investment counselor make and plant a file like that? Then again, he had plenty of money to hire the expertise.

In the end, I decided to go ahead and continue my surveillance of Samantha when she returned. I'd already planned a half-dozen ways to use Stuyvesant's money, not to mention the possible new business it might bring.

And just in case, I would keep an eye on my back.

A break from the Stuyvesant case gave me time to follow a lead on a job I was doing for First Capital Bank. The bank was trying to repossess a car, but they couldn't locate it. Four months ago, Harmon Thomas had taken out a sizable bank loan to buy a used, late-model sports car. Although he had put a little money down when he took out the loan, he'd had no chance to make a regular payment before the car went missing. Thomas maintained that the car had been stolen. He'd filed an insurance claim, so the bank would get their money—eventually.

The bank called me because, while the car might really have been stolen, Thomas had lost two previous cars in a similar fashion—cars the bank had also financed for him. Thomas might have been really unlucky, but the bank officer figured it was much more likely that Thomas was just really stupid.

Jessica had researched Thomas's background for me and found a tidbit that piqued my interest. Thomas's older brother, Eddie, owned Speed-E Repairs, a body shop on the other side of the river.

Today, I drove out to Speed-E Repairs to play a hunch. When I went by the shop on the street, I saw a large, well-kept garage with five bays and an attached office. I turned down the side street and went down the back alley behind the shop. From the rear I saw several cars parked together at the side of Speed-E's back lot, including one that was the same make and model as the missing car. This car, however, was a sleek and shiny blue instead of cherry red.

Back on the main street, I parked my car and went inside. A guy with the name Daryl stitched into his denim shirt was at the desk.

"Excuse me," I said, giving him a level four smile with a goofy, over-enthusiastic eyebrow rise. "I was admirin' that blue car out back. Do you know if it might be for sale?"

Daryl looked up. "Could be if the price is right." He studied me coolly. "We just detailed it for a guy who's thinking of selling it. You interested?"

"Well, whatcha gotta have?" I licked my lips with excitement. "I've always admired them babies. They're hot, if you know what I mean." I gave him a big wink in case he didn't get it.

Daryl quoted me an exorbitant price, and we dickered a bit. I persuaded him to take me out back so I could get a closer look.

I made a point to drool a bit as I ran my hand over the fender. "Real clean interior too," I said while ogling the VIN number at the edge of the window.

Back inside, we dickered some more. Finally, with the price still too high, I told him I'd have to think about it and walked out.

I retrieved my car and headed back into the city. On the way I called the bank and told them where to find Thomas's car.

Once in my office at my apartment, I prepared my bill for the bank. *Another day, another dollar*, I thought, looking at the invoice. The cliché applied a little too literally to pieces of work like this. I still hoped Stuyvesant's job would start me on the path to more lucrative cases, even if I'd stumbled into more problems than expected.

I was feeling quite pleased with myself once I finished up the paperwork on the misplaced car.

Then Jessica called.

"Mick, he was in the military—Special Forces."

"Who? Stuyvesant?" I couldn't think of anything else to say. "Oh, shit," I finally managed.

"I couldn't find the details," she said, "but it looks as if he left high school early with some kind of agreement to join the army. From basic training, he went on to Special Forces school. After six years, he left the service and enrolled at UCLA. That's where he met Samantha."

Stuyvesant was older than I'd thought and older than his wife as well. The fact that he'd been a Green Beret meant there was a whole episode of his past I had to factor into my thinking.

Many of my reservations vanished. While it was improbable that investment-banker Stuyvesant could have planted evidence of a liaison with his wife on my phone, special-forces-veteran Stuyvesant might have the expertise. And even if he didn't know how himself, it was for sure he would have connections to people who would know—in spades.

"Mick?"

"Sorry. Lost in thought," I apologized, then sighed. "You keep throwing these bombshells of information at me."

"Do you think you've got a problem?"

I'd already shared some of my thoughts and speculations with Jessica, and now she had zeroed in on my as yet ill-formed misgivings. "I . . . I don't know," I answered truthfully. "But you can bet I'm going to find out."

After offering her a few more heartening words I didn't feel, I said goodbye.

I sat at my desk and let my mind wander a bit. Special forces? My thoughts drifted into territory full of dangerous hidden pitfalls and booby traps.

I opened my bottom desk drawer to check my gun. I don't like to carry it because I don't want to give myself the option of using it— in most circumstances. There are times, however, when I need the comfort of something more than my glib mouth to protect me. I flipped back the lid of the storage box.

Empty.

When had I checked it last? Two weeks? More?

I blinked and looked at the ceiling.

Had I taken it out to clean it? Practice? Stupidly left it somewhere?

I pulled the drawer out all the way and emptied it. I even checked the next drawer up.

No gun.

I looked around my office. Where had I seen it last?

Then I had a new thought. A burglar? That sent a chill down my back. I looked at the array of files, equipment, and other paraphernalia in my office—all familiar tokens of my life. I was so accustomed to their presence, I hardly saw them anymore.

Had anything been moved?

Was anything else missing?

I took a deep breath and checked the drawer one last time. Alexander Stuyvesant had been in the special forces. They trained in unconventional tactics—ways to unsettle an enemy's life. Did those tactics include bugging my phone, planting a fake sexting file—and stealing my gun?

On the other hand, what resources did Samantha Stuyvesant bring to the table herself? Could she have gotten wind that her husband had hired me and called on her deep-pocketed Astor assets to create mischief for me? Because the sex text would be personally embarrassing for her, that seemed unlikely, but was there something I didn't know about? How devious was she? How deep might her conflict with her husband be?

I took another deep breath and asked a more reasonable question. Had I bitten off more than I could chew?

Rampant, unbridled speculation proved nothing. At the moment, all I had were unsettling pieces of information. Why not go to the source?

I checked the time. Stuyvesant should still be at work. I picked up my infested phone and turned it on to check his office number. With it in my hand, I realized that if Stuyvesant really was monitoring my phone, there was no reason not to use this phone to make the call.

Not only was Stuyvesant in, he would see me at five o'clock. If I didn't like his answers, I might be better off staying with my current client list.

The suspicion my apartment had been invaded made me restless. My home no longer felt like a safe refuge. Since I had time before my appointment with Stuyvesant, I decided to take a walk in the park to think.

Just outside the door, I stopped. A gnome sat on the baluster at the end of the stair down to the sidewalk. He looked around at me when I closed the door. "Gary?" I asked, uncertain if this was the same gnome I'd met before.

"Right the first time, bub." He smiled broadly. "Even though we gnomes all look alike."

He jerked a thumb toward the street. "Let's walk to the park. He wants to talk to you."

"He?"

"Mel. He says you're getting into things that concern him."

We started off up the street. We hadn't gone far when it occurred to me to ask, "How does he know what I'm doing?"

Gary looked up at me with a sly smile. "Since we found out you can see faerie folk, Mel's had pixies watching you." He chuckled. "They're not the brightest things, but nobody, and I mean nobody, can see 'em unless they want you to."

Another type of faerie folk? At least he'd given me a name for the new category of fauna. Now I knew in addition to unicorns and gnomes, there were pixies.

Gary didn't have much to say as we walked. He led the way, setting a brisk pace despite his short legs. I had no experience making idle chitchat with a gnome, so I kept my mouth shut.

Across the street from the park, I saw a unicorn waiting by one of the trees that lined the shaded path. Was this the same unicorn I'd seen before? His body, obviously male, was that of a small, delicate horse. His long, silky mane hung down the left side of his neck. Mel's coat was pure white with a bone-colored spiral horn. He could have been an illustration out of a book of fairy tales except there were no sparkles or rainbows.

One other familiar feature of unicorns as they are popularized was missing—a happy look of benign naiveté. This unicorn stared across the street at me with the same challenging glare I'd seen before.

"Hey, Gary, how do I talk to a unicorn?"

"Carefully."

The gnome chuckled as we crossed to the park. "We'll go someplace a little more private. Mel can't talk, of course, but when he touches you with his horn, you'll hear his thoughts."

He chuckled again but this time it was more of a grim snicker. "And be sure to let *him* put the horn on *you*. Unicorns don't like to be touched—especially there."

The unicorn turned as we approached and led the way. Self conscious about passersby, I followed him into the park on the path. Other people strolled blissfully by, never glancing at the unicorn or the gnome. I feigned casualness as well while keeping pace with the fairytale creatures.

As we walked, I studied the unicorn. The horn in the middle of his forehead was about two feet long. Several dark, narrow lines twisted along its length and emphasized its corkscrew pattern.

The unicorn led us well into the park to an out-of-the-way bench with a clutch of bushes nearby. The bench wasn't private, but then again, no one but me could see my companions. Anyone who glanced our way would think I was some poor lonely guy sitting on a bench talking to himself.

And what was the proper way to address a unicorn? I had no idea, but Gary had made Mel sound touchy.

The gnome invited me to sit. Before I did, I made a respectful half bow toward the unicorn. "I am honored to meet you, sir," I said then held up my hands helplessly. "Gary has told me your proper name, but I don't remember it. I hesitate to address you informally."

The unicorn took a step forward and nodded to the bench. I took that as my cue to sit. Once I was down, he stepped closer and delicately touched his horn to my shoulder.

"Greetings, Mr. Holmes. My name is Melocartazenilis, but you may call me Mel."

I heard the words clearly in my mind. Unsure if I could make myself understood the same way, I said aloud, "Thank you, Mel. Gary said you wanted to talk to me."

"What is your connection to the Stuyvesants?"

Right to it then. "I'm a private detective, and Mr. Stuyvesant has employed my services. Beyond revealing that, I am bound by rules of client confidentiality to say no more."

How much of that would a unicorn understand?

How much did I understand? I wasn't even sure I was going to continue the investigation.

He pulled his head back out of contact and glared his unicorn glare. A moment later, he put his horn back on my shoulder.

"You are following Samantha Stuyvesant. Why?"

I shook my head slightly, all too aware of how close the sharp point of his horn was to my face. "Again, because of my contract with Mr. Stuyvesant, I am required by law not to answer."

I almost shrugged my shoulders under his horn but caught myself.

Mel took his horn off my shoulder for a time, then touched me again. Even if I had not been able to feel the tenor of his thoughts, the unicorn's eyes were expressive. *"Garhezeigenibusch has already told you that a particular property Madam Astor owns in the western part of your country is important to us."*

"You mean the unicorn breeding—"

His angry snort right next to my ear interrupted me. *"A fact that anthropoids are forbidden to know."*

His thought came through with stunning volume. With his horn touching my shoulder and head close to mine, the unicorn's disgust felt very personal.

"I have information that Alexander Stuyvesant is maneuvering to put his wife's property under his control. Please understand that I, and all those of our world, will use any means necessary to prevent this from happening."

"So you don't want them to do anything like drilling for oil."

"Willing to broil what?"

The new voice startled me. I glanced away from the unicorn and toward the path. A grandmotherly woman with a shopping cart in tow stood looking at me. I hadn't been paying attention to passersby.

"Sorry, just rehearsing a part I'm going to try out for." I gave her a level two smile of embarrassed contrition. "You know, a community theater thing."

"You're an actor?" She smiled broadly. "I've done some theater work myself. What play is your group doing?"

I really wanted to get back to my conversation with the unicorn, but I didn't want to be rude—at least, not too rude. "It's called 'Naked As Amanda.' It's an experimental work by one of our members." I shrugged. "I managed to get a speaking part, but it's not one of those where I have to take off my clothes."

"Oh," she said blinking uncertainly. After a bit of hesitation, she said, "I'd better leave you to it then. Good luck." She smiled pleasantly as she walked quickly away.

On the other side of the path, Gary the gnome rolled on the ground, laughing hysterically.

I looked back at the unicorn. His scowl hadn't changed. At least it looked like a scowl to me. "Sorry about that," I said. "You were saying you wanted to make sure the property out west was undisturbed?"

Once more the unicorn approached me and laid his horn on my shoulder. *"We will not tolerate extraction of any natural resource from that property. Nor will we allow anyone to develop the land in any way."*

I had a natural conversational urge to shake my head, but I was all too conscious of the long, pointed horn resting against my shoulder. "I can tell you my involvement with Alexander Stuyvesant has nothing to do with that property."

As I said it, I realized that if the information I gathered led to a divorce, those legal proceedings might well involve property ownership issues. Before Mel could reply, I added, "However, I have to concede that my investigation might result in an event that might . . . let me emphasize, *might* affect ownership of the property."

I hesitated. How far would the ethics of confidentiality stretch? "At the moment, I have found no information that makes that event seem likely." Thinking about Samantha's rescue work, I added, "In fact, from what I have seen so far, I think that such a . . . a situation would be very unlikely."

The unicorn stepped back. Was he thinking? A moment later, he lowered his horn and made contact again. *"We would like to have information about any threats to this property now and in the future. Will your anthropoid laws and ethics allow you to provide relevant particulars to us?"*

I couldn't answer right away. The unicorn breeding ground was not a direct part of my investigation of Samantha's activities. Technically, any details I might find related to finagling with the property would not be relevant to her extra-marital flings. Unless they were. Then again, if Mel was interested in a continuing monitoring—

Perhaps we can offer you a professional incentive.

Lost in my thoughts, I almost jumped. Fortunately, I caught myself before I pushed Mel's horn. Was that horn on my shoulder a two-way street? Could he hear my thoughts?

"What kind of incentive?" I asked.

Garhezeigenibusch and the other gnomes are good at gathering information, especially about anthropoids. Would their services be of value to you?

Unseeable snoops? I started salivating, but swallowed instead of licking my lips. "Yes," I said coolly. "Yes, they could be a great help." Especially if the Stuyvesant case gave me access to a better class of employers.

Old Philip Woodland had emphasized ethics when I worked with him. I had suspicions about Stuyvesant's ethics, but with Mel's tempting offer, I now had doubts about my own standards.

I sucked it up and made a self-righteous declaration. "Yes, that would be very helpful to me. But, remember, I still can't reveal anything I find that relates to what my client has hired me to do."

Yes, you have mentioned your moral code several times. I will be interested to see exactly what standards you display.

With a snort of disgust that echoed the obvious distaste I felt in his thoughts, the unicorn stalked away.

I sat on the bench, a little dazed by the implications of the confrontation. As if the idea of having a conversation with a unicorn was not surreal enough, it turned out the unicorn had an agenda.

Gary leaned against the tree that shadowed the bench, picking at his teeth with a twig. He'd obviously enjoyed watching the conversation. I took a deep breath and started to get up but stopped when I thought of one more really important question. I looked at the gnome. "How worried should I be about Mel?"

Gary huffed in amusement and shook his head. "Old Mel's a pussycat. He talks tough, but he don't do dick himself."

He tossed the twig away and hiked his trousers up around his pudgy middle. "No, when Mel gets upset, he sends a troll." With a jaunty wave, he strolled off in the same direction as the unicorn.

A troll? None of the strange, fairy-tale creatures I'd seen over the years had seemed troll-like, at least not to me. I've always ignored internet trolls, but I had a hunch they were of a different species than the one Gary had mentioned. No, the sum total of my knowledge of trolls came from stories about gruff billy goats and movie fantasy adventures.

I looked around the park. Off in the distance I heard the shrieks and squeals of a kids' game of tag. A breeze rustled leaves on the trees.

I had just spent ten minutes talking to Mel-something-or-other the unicorn and Gary the gnome. And there were trolls as well? This was something new to think about, especially since the gnome had implied the creature was dangerous.

I shook my head. If I was having hallucinations, the figments of my imagination were getting increasingly complex—and realistic.

And yet the unicorn's offer was too good to pass up. I sighed. My ambitions had betrayed me. I really wanted to be able to accept it even if it meant having to once and for all admit that my world contained creatures that everyone else thought existed only in myths and legends. One of the reasons I got into the private eye business was because I wanted to go my own way. So was I being independent . . . or delusional?

But my time for idle contemplation had passed. I had an appointment with Stuyvesant at his DAMA tower office, and now I had to hustle. Even though I had plenty of concerns to think about, including sex-texting phone files, my missing gun, and other worrisome tidbits, I couldn't help thinking about unicorns and gnomes.

And trolls.

Nine

"Mr. Stuyvesant." I nodded respectfully and reached for his offered hand, a hand that with Special Forces training was no doubt a lethal weapon.

We sat down in the same conversation nook in his office as before. Safe enough—for the moment. The window across the way showed a sky that held a dark, hazy-gray threat of rain. A gnome, the same one I'd seen before in this office, sat on the wooden side table between us. He leaned back against the wall, eyes flicking back and forth as he followed our conversation.

"So what's on your mind, Mr. Holmes?" Stuyvesant smiled graciously. "Or may I call you Mickey?"

"When you're writing the check, you can call me whatever you like." I gave him a pleasant but not over-friendly number two smile. When a client doesn't play straight with me, we're not pals.

"I had a couple of questions about things that have come up. Things that make me wonder if I should continue investigating."

"Fire away."

Unfortunately, since my gun had been stolen, I couldn't take him up on his invitation.

"I've followed your wife for several days now. Recently, she and another woman staged a rescue of an abused woman and her child from a residence. They took them to a hotel on the outskirts of the city."

I paused to purse my lips and look thoughtful. "Could activities like this be the source of the reports of her frequenting hotels?"

He looked solemn. "Would that be the Time To Go group?"

When I nodded, he sighed and flipped a hand in casual dismissal. "Yes, I know she does things like that with them from time to time. I suppose it's possible, but the information I have led me to believe there were additional . . . incidents."

The side of his mouth turned down. "*Unexplained* incidents. Not rescues at all."

His emphasis made clear my information had not answered his questions about his wife's behavior. I nodded again and took out my phone. "And there's another problem. My tech guy found a file on my phone that appears to be an intimate text conversation between me and your wife."

I wasn't going to play show and tell, but I tapped the phone for emphasis. "I have never had any direct contact with her, yet the file made it appear that we have had . . . rather extensive communications."

He looked at me, down at my phone, then back at me. He sighed deeply. "I don't know what to tell you, Mr. Holmes, except I evidently didn't give you enough information." He appeared concerned and sincere, but investment counselors make their living looking concerned and sincere.

"Well, now would be a good time."

"I think I know the file you are referring to. It was from an incident several years ago when I discovered Samantha had developed an online flirtatious relationship with a man. When I confronted her, she admitted it and broke it off." He scowled. "However, her 'friend' evidently was one of those hacker people, a cyber stalker, or something. The application and that file kept reappearing on her phone. I finally hired an electronic security firm, and the attacks stopped. I thought the problem had been resolved."

"So you're saying he's back? But that doesn't explain how he was able to put that file on *my* phone."

Stuyvesant nodded. Worry lines appeared on his forehead. "That's what particularly troubles me. First, it tells me that the problem has not gone away. The man is still an active harassment threat. But worse than that, the fact he was able to put it on your phone indicates that he, or someone working with him, must be one of my household's domestic employees." He spread his hands helplessly. "A spy."

I looked at him for a time before I responded. I saw guileless earnestness. Heart-felt integrity. Then again, he made a living convincing people he had their bests interest at heart. "I can see how that would worry you," I said. That sounded a little more sarcastic than I'd intended, so I added, "Would you like me to have my guy look into the origins of that file to see if I can find any connection to your staff?"

He settled back in his chair and stared at the ceiling for a time. When he lowered his gaze to look me in the eye, his intensity was obvious. "Tell you what. I've recently brought on a new chief of security. If you forward the file to me, I will have him see if it's the one from before. My security chief and his team have access to all our employees' personnel files and records. Whether it's the same file or not, they will check it out. I would prefer to keep this in house if I can."

He leaned forward. Palms together, he poked his finger tips toward me with pointed candor. "I will let you know when they have it resolved. If you're not satisfied at that point, you may notify the police or whatever you wish."

Evidently satisfied he'd addressed the issue, he nodded decisively and straightened. "Now, is there anything else is on your mind?"

The intensity of his sincerity convinced me he was lying. "What's your head of security's name?"

He hesitated and frowned. "Matthew Holt. He comes well recommended. I'll give him your contact information so he can get with you if he needs to."

Was I satisfied? No, but it seemed our conversation was over. While I didn't think he'd put all of his cards on the table, he'd answered my concerns with an explanation that, while reasonable, would require more checking out. I wasn't free from doubt, but it would be nice to be free from debt. Stuyvesant held the ticket for that, and I wasn't ready to give that up just on the basis of my instincts alone.

I stood up. "Then we've covered everything I have, Mr. Stuyvesant."

We hadn't, but I wasn't about to tell him I knew about his effort to acquire the unicorn breeding grounds. I also hadn't brought up my worries about the other spy software Kurse had found on my phone. So far there was nothing to indicate it was related to this case, but there was nothing that said it wasn't. If he had planted it on my phone, I wouldn't tip him off that I'd discovered it.

"I'll get back to work then. Thank you for your time," I said as I stood up. He had been as cordial as the first time we'd met, but this time he didn't offer to shake hands as we said goodbye. As I headed for the elevator, I had lots to think about. At the least, I wanted to know more about his new security advisor.

With Samantha Stuyvesant out of the country, I took care of other, more mundane, tasks. I sent the bill for the car recovery job plus three dunning notices reminding previous clients that their payments were overdue. From time to time I've toyed with other methods of collecting from clients who were disinclined to pay. So far, I've yet to find a method that is effective—and legal.

Two nights after my meeting with Stuyvesant, I got a call from Jessica. I thought she was calling with information I'd asked her to find about Matthew Holt, Stuyvesant's new head of security.

"Mick?" Instead of her usual breezy self, Jessica's voice trembled.

"What's going on?"

"It's Bart." I was about to say something when she squeaked, "He's been shot."

I couldn't think of anything to say. Finally I asked, "How bad's he hurt?"

"He . . ." Her voice caught. "He's dead."

Dead?

The concept that someone I knew and worked with had been killed confounded my world.

Neither of us said anything for the longest time. Bart had been my tech guy since soon after I set up shop five years ago. Sure, he was kind of a funny duck, but that's the way some tech guys are. But dead?

"What happened?" I finally asked.

"They don't know yet. Dad phoned a while ago to tell me. He didn't get the call when they found him, but he heard it at the station. He knew Bart from when Bart and I were in school together. He knew Bart's parents too."

"Where was he shot? At home?"

"No. Dad said it was down in the south end near the international docks."

"Why would Bart be down there?" I wondered out loud.

"Yeah, it doesn't make sense."

My heightened suspicions gave me a bad thought, a thought that turned my hands cold. "You don't suppose it was anything he was doing for me, do you?" Bart snooped into confidential records for me, but nothing he'd found would have made someone want him dead—at least nothing I knew about.

A wave of guilt rose up to eclipse my shock and grief.

"I don't know," she answered, "But if it is, it's my fault too. I sent him to you, remember? It's been a few years."

She paused. "But let's not jump to conclusions. Remember he met this Kurse person recently. Maybe it's got something to do with her."

I knew she was trying to make me feel better. While I appreciated her effort, I'd already lined up a dreary list of regrets.

Jessica wanted to talk, and I let her distract me from my pangs of conscience. Since we had few facts to go on, she started reminiscing about when she and Bart were in school. "He asked me to a dance once upon a time."

"Did you go?"

"Huh? Of course I went. It was our eighth grade dance—a tradition at our school at the end of the year."

She sighed wistfully. "All the kids dressed up. They had refreshments for us. There was even dancing. Slow dancing, I mean." She chuckled a little. "You know, the kind where you hold on to each other? The parents were there too, and everybody was super self-conscious."

She sighed again. "I don't remember too much about that night except the gym was hot."

A moment later she added, "I don't know if Bart ever had another date while he was in school."

I snorted. "Yeah, I know how that goes. I had more than one, but I definitely wasn't part of the social scene."

We shared stories back and forth until I realized it was almost midnight. "Hey, JJ, I think I'm going to have to wind it up for tonight. I've got to work tomorrow."

"Yeah, me too." After a moment, she said, "Thanks for letting me talk your ear off, Mick. I guess I needed someone to listen."

"No trouble at all," I said. "Keep me informed if you hear anything more."

After I'd hung up the phone, I returned to the thought that had disturbed me. Bart had been gathering information for me about Alexander Stuyvesant. He hadn't told me that he'd found anything corrupt about the man.

But then again, maybe he hadn't gotten the chance.

That one thought kept me awake a long time. Although this investigation could really help my bank account, I continued to be uneasy.

I filled the next day with routine tasks and tried to avoid thinking about Bart. Especially my worry that he'd been killed because of something I'd asked him to do.

I don't do guilt well.

That evening Jessica called again. "You wanted to know about Matthew Holt?" Her voice sounded weary.

"Hey, how are you doing?" I asked before she could give me her report. "You sound beat."

She sighed. "I slept about two minutes last night."

A moment later she said, "The funeral's going to be Saturday. Could you . . . take me?"

"His death really bothers you, doesn't it? Of course I'll take you."

"Thanks, Mick," she said. "Yeah, it really got to me. I mean, it's not like we were an item, but he was a long-time friend."

I could tell she had more to say, so I waited for her to go on. "I guess I'm having one of those moments when I confront my own mortality. You know, when you finally realize that the life you've been so blithely living could come to an end . . ."

We ended up talking for another two hours without ever getting to what she had found on Matthew Holt.

Just before she hung up, Jessica said, "Oh, and that Holt guy? He doesn't exist. At least there's no record of anyone with that name in any of the places I check."

Mathew Holt was still on my mind the next morning when I went out for a run. Gary the gnome sat waiting for me on the front stoop just outside the building. Since there was no one around, I addressed him directly. "Good morning, Gary. Still keeping watch on me?"

"It's exciting." He sighed and looked away. "Especially when I get to sit here and watch a dog poop."

"I'm going for a run, but I've got a question for you." Just then a dog walker came around the corner headed our way. "Can you meet me up in my apartment when I get back?"

"You're not ducking out on me, are you?"

"No, I'm serious. I need information."

I shut up and did some extra stretching on the stoop until the dog walker passed.

"You guys are keeping track of Stuyvesant, and I've got a question about his operation. My apartment's locked, but I'll be back in about a half hour."

He waved me on my way. "Lock's not a problem. I'll make myself some coffee."

My apartment was still locked when I got back, but as promised, the gnome was waiting for me inside. Not only had my locks not been a problem, he evidently knew his way around a coffee brewer as well.

However, my questions about Stuyvesant took precedence over more gnome knowledge. I grabbed a towel to wipe the sweat off my face and sat on one of the hard kitchen chairs.

"Yesterday Stuyvesant told me his head of security was Matthew Holt, only there doesn't seem to be any such person."

I felt a drip forming on my forehead and swiped at it with the towel. "I know there's been a gnome watching Stuyvesant, at least at his office. Do you guys talk?"

Gary took a sip of coffee. He'd found an old espresso mug in my pantry, but the small cup looked like a flagon in his diminutive hands. "That would be Teddy," he said and paused for another sip. "So you want to know who this Matthew Holt is?"

I thought for a moment. "If he exists, then yeah. But I've got a feeling Stuyvesant lied about the whole thing. What I really want to know is if Stuyvesant has somebody who does illegal stuff for him."

"Hoo, hoo!" he leered. "You mean like maybe the guy who put that sexy file on your phone?"

"I . . . Wait. You know about that?"

He made a throw away gesture. "Just 'cause folktales about us gnomes go back to the Middle Ages, that doesn't mean we don't get out and about these days."

"Even with a password—"

"Be sheer luck to find it, huh?" He wiggled his eyebrows and chuckled smugly.

I made an immediate resolution to change my password, but I refused to be diverted from my basic question.

"Can you tell me if Stuyvesant has a guy like that or not?"

He nodded. "Yeah, I think he's got somebody that does that kinda stuff. Teddy mentioned a guy named Lou once."

"Lou? Is that all? I need more information."

"It'll take a little time." He smiled and looked me up and down. "I'd say, keep your shirt on, but you really should change that one."

Ten

Friday Samantha was back in town. While things had gotten more complicated for me the last few days, her husband was still paying me to keep track of her movements. So despite my doubts, I waited in my car, watching the parking garage for her car to appear.

"Louis Sherman."

I jumped. The voice from the back seat was unexpected, but it was Gary. I took a deep breath and turned to look at him. "So, what did you find out?"

"Louis Sherman's the security guy's name," the gnome said. "And he's not new. Teddy says he's seen him come and go a few times at the office, but from what he and Stuyvesant say when they're together, they meet other places too. Teddy's never paid too much attention to him because he hasn't done anything related to Mel's property."

"Who is he? Does Teddy know anything about him?"

"He said they act like old friends. Stuyvesant calls him 'his operator.' They use a lot of military jargon."

I pursed my lips and thought, *Maybe old friends from their special forces days?*

Now that I had another name, Jessica might be able to find something. I sat there and considered the new information. When I went to ask Gary another question, he'd gone.

As for Samantha, I followed her through another exciting day. She worked out at her gym in the morning. From there she went to Floraison, where she spent the rest of the day. Fortunately, it all paid me the same.

The next morning, low clouds darkened the sky and dampened the pavement with drizzle. Bart's funeral made the already gloomy Saturday especially bleak.

That morning, I did paperwork and paid bills, but I kept thinking of Bart—Bart and why he'd been killed. Had his association with Kurse led him to get cross-wise with dangerous people? Not that I knew much about what else he might have been doing, but a more troubling question haunted me.

Did I ask him to do something that triggered his murder?

After an early lunch, I got dressed for Bart's funeral. I have only one suit, but it's a good one. My old boss Phillip Woodland had taught me the private investigation business. One of his tenets was to spend the money to have one good suit custom-tailored. Woody used to say, "A good suit makes a good impression."

I wore my suit when I had to testify in court or meet an important client. Bart wouldn't care what I wore today, but I would.

I picked up Jessica at her apartment at 12:30.

"Hey, Mick." Her tone was subdued when she answered the door. "Let me get my purse, and I'm ready."

She had on a dark dress, and her purse matched. I'd never seen Jessica in a dress before. She even wore a hint of makeup.

"What?" She'd noticed me noticing. "Is there lint?" She twisted around trying to see the back of her dress. "I tried to brush it off."

She looked perfect, but to make her feel better, I went through the motions of checking.

"You are faultless," I finally said. And it was the truth.

"You clean up pretty good too." She smiled. "I like your suit."

Neither of us said much on the way to the church. The weathered stone edifice sat at the corner of Park and Third. At the center of its neighborhood, twin spires towered over a working class community of mainly two and three-story row houses.

We walked in through the great carved wooden doors of the main sanctuary on our way to the chapel where the service was held. At least two hundred people were there. We were early enough to be able to express our personal condolences to Bart's parents.

I've never liked funerals. A funeral for someone I'd known and liked pushed my usual hopeful cynicism over the line to a discouraged world-weariness. I sat in the pew beside Jessica and tried not to stare at the casket. A lead weight of guilt rested in the pit of my stomach.

Jessica dabbed at her eyes with a tissue. She blew her nose in it, and I gave her a fresh one. She sighed and laid her head on my shoulder. I felt the hitch in her breathing as she wept silently. I reached back and put my arm around her shoulders. She leaned gratefully against me, the dark nap of her hair brushing against my neck. I hoped my presence made her feel better because having her close helped me.

At the end of the service, the clergywoman spoke to the mourners in terms of living life to the fullest and looking forward to what each new day would bring.

New days that Bart would never see.

When I shifted in the pew, Jessica leaned away and sat up. She looked at me with red eyes. "Thank you," she mouthed.

As we made our way out of the church, Jessica tugged me over to the side where an older Black man with a touch of gray in his hair stood with his arms folded. "Somebody I want you to meet."

As we approached she said, "Hi, Dad."

The man smiled and embraced her warmly. When they finally separated, he patted her shoulder affectionately. "Hey, how's my little girl doing?"

He looked up at me over the top of her head, his eyes considerably cooler. "And who's this?"

"Dad, this is Mickey Holmes. He's the private detective I sometimes do research for." She looked at me. "Mick, this is my father, Devon."

He stuck out his hand. "Pleased," he said without sounding pleased at all. He wasn't in uniform, but his eyes had that hard, skeptical cop look.

"Glad to meet you, Mr. Jones," I said as I shook his hand. A church after a funeral was not the place for a toothy, level-four grin of false delight. I nudged out a restrained but pleasant level-one smile, hoping it looked sincere enough.

Devon turned his attention back to his daughter. "I got here as soon as I could after my shift."

He looked at me. "Thank you for bringing her, Mr. Holmes."

He held out his arm to his daughter. "Come on. I'll take you home."

Jessica's eyes were mournful when she looked up at me, but she took her father's arm. "Thanks, Mick," she said. As they started to step away together, she turned her head back. "Thanks for everything. I'll call you later."

My feelings were mixed as they walked away. I wasn't feeling at all sociable. I wouldn't be good company for anyone. And yet . . .

I watched Devon escort his daughter to a car.

And yet, I had enjoyed sharing the pew—and my sorrow—with Jessica.

Later that evening, Jessica called. "Hi, Mick. Sorry about this afternoon. Leaving like that, I mean."

"What? He's your dad." I shrugged even though she couldn't see me. "He's family. You do what you gotta do."

"He kind of gave me the third degree on the way home." After a pause, she added, "About you."

"I would have too. Disreputable line of work, private investigating."

She didn't say anything for a time. "No, he was worried about . . . the racial thing."

"What racial thing?"

"I know what you're doing, Mick." I could hear the smile in her voice. "You're trying to pretend you're oblivious."

"I'm not oblivious, I just didn't think it mattered."

She sighed. "This is the United States, after all."

"Yeah, where some people like to make racial and ethnic mountains out of mole hills just because they can."

I scratched my head while I thought about how to say it. "You know, until I met your dad, I hadn't really thought about your . . . family. I mean not in that way."

"What? You think I was from Tonga or something?" She chuckled. A moment later, she added, "The law school thing dazzled you, huh? Or was it me being a cute barista?"

She sounded cheeky, so we were playing games again. I felt more confident.

"Oh, I'd figured out you were a girl and all that a long time ago."

"Was it that time when I wasn't wearing a bra and ran into you at the MetroMart? I saw you look down my top."

"A most delightful confirmation of what I had already surmised. I am a trained investigator after all."

I felt much easier having this kind of exchange with Jessica. Yet, there was still an unresolved piece of business hanging out there. "Jessica, I like you for who you are. You're a good researcher, but you're also a good friend."

And now the dangerous part. I was getting signals from Jessica that she was fond of me. She deserved a word to the wise. "And because you're a friend, I've got to warn you that I'm kinda gun-shy about the whole man-woman thing."

At that point, the conversation turned in exactly the direction I'd feared. Jessica's curiosity was boundless, and I'd just given her a topic to research.

"Gun shy? Does that mean you've been shot down before, or that you aren't attracted by my gender?"

It didn't take long until she had pried the sordid, painful story out of me. I sort of left out the parts where Heather had accused me of just sliding by in life. Jessica had already called me on that side of my personality.

"So you're saying that all you and Heather had together was sex? That was the whole basis of your relationship?"

"That's pretty much what she said. Pretty crass, huh?"

"Were you married?"

"No, thank goodness." That had made things easier—but not less painful. I'd learned that when you give your heart to someone, she won't give it back when she leaves.

"And she just dumped you for this other guy?"

"Last I'd heard they'd moved to British Columbia and had a kid."

After a long pause, Jessica finally said, "Thanks for telling me this, Mick. It kind of explains some things."

After another moment, she added, "You still have defensive feelings, don't you? You don't like to show your real emotions. I'll bet that's why you give people those goofy smiles of yours."

"I don't . . ."

But I did.

And I was about to get defensive about it.

I took a some time to get my thoughts in order. "You're probably right," I finally admitted.

"It obviously still bothers you," she said. "Have you thought about counseling?"

I knew her suggestion was well intentioned, but I brushed it off. "I don't think so. I'm doing okay."

"So okay that you call yourself gun shy and try to mask your feelings?" She snorted. "Typical guy thing. Be a manly man. Tough it out." She sighed. "And how's that working for you, Mick?"

Although I'd never thought of myself as a typical guy, much less a particularly manly one, I didn't correct her. Worst of all, I had no answer to her question.

Eleven

Monday morning I was back on the street watching the parking garage. I was halfway through my first cup of coffee when a policeman tapped on the window. He motioned me to get out of the car.

I started to set the coffee down, and he jerked his gun up.

I froze for a second, then lifted my hands.

He pulled open the car door. "Step out of the car, sir."

His gun never wavered.

"Sure," I replied. My heart thumped in my chest. "I'm going to set my coffee down to unbuckle my seat belt. Okay?"

I glimpsed another cop on the passenger side with his gun drawn, but I focused on the officer at my door.

He stared at me, then glanced at my seatbelt and nodded. "All right, but slow and easy." He backed away from the door.

Once out of the car, they laid me over the hood to frisk me before putting me in handcuffs.

The unreality of it had derailed my thoughts, but now I had an important question. "What's this all about, officers?"

The first policeman took me by the arm and steered me to a police car. He ignored my question. Instead, he informed me of my rights. It was good to know I had rights, but I still didn't know why I needed them.

I tried again. "So what's this all about?"

The officer opened the back door of the police car and motioned for me to get inside. Once I was in the seat, he told me. "Samantha Stuyvesant. She's been murdered."

The words were so out of place, it took time for them to penetrate.

"Murdered? What do you mean murdered?"

Suddenly my lights clicked on. "Wait! You think that I . . . What? Are you arresting *me* for her murder?"

Panic? Oh, yes. I gasped for air. Sweat broke out on my forehead. A surge of adrenaline burned through me.

Fight or flight?

At the moment, I sat handcuffed in the back of a police car. I had neither option. Therefore, I stayed where I was, mouth hanging open. Wild, nonsensical ideas buzzed around in my head. I scarcely noticed when they closed the door.

When we pulled into the parking lot at the police station, my brain's hysterical yapping finally slowed. I started having a few rational thoughts. By this time, I was pretty sure I wouldn't be able to sweet talk my way out of this situation. I had a right to a lawyer, and I definitely needed one.

Inside the station, the booking process and all the other checks and procedures kept me occupied. The officers even gave me a chance to call Eli Dushinsky, my lawyer.

Once the door clanged shut on my holding cell, I had time to think. In fact, I had nothing but time to think—at least until Eli got here.

Or until the cops took me into a little room and started asking questions while they looked at me with greedy eyes and slapped their palms with rubber hoses . . .

I blinked, took a deep breath, and tried to force that image out of my head.

Focus on the situation.

Except I hardly knew anything about my situation. Samantha Stuyvesant was dead—the cops had told me that fact. But how? Where? Why? With no answers to these rather basic questions, I could only speculate about what was going on.

One major question ate at me. I'd already had suspicions about Alexander Stuyvesant, a former special forces soldier who was trying to broker an oil deal on his wife's property. He'd also lied about the name of his security man. What else had he lied about?

My current circumstances gave me time—and motivation—to rethink the case. I played around with a whole raft of possible scenarios in my head.

I didn't like any of them.

"Holmes, you've got a visitor."

I'd dozed off. Worry and anxiety are exhausting. When the guard called me, I sat up and rubbed my eyes. The bars on the cell hadn't changed. I looked at my watch. I'd slept two hours.

Being locked up was a piece of cake.

My visitor was my lawyer, Eli Dushinsky. He was a small wrinkled and rumpled man in his early sixties. His bushy, graying eyebrows curled into pearl-colored caterpillars above his intense brown eyes. He dropped his briefcase to the concrete floor and eased himself onto the chair outside my barred holding cell.

"Oh, my goodness, Mickey." He sighed. "What have you gotten yourself into? A murder?"

"Murder's what they said, Eli." I took a deep breath. Saying the word aloud gave it a fresh new reality. Fortunately I was already sitting down because my right knee started to tremble.

I took another deep breath to steady myself and told him the story of how I'd been hired by Alexander Stuyvesant to investigate his wife's activities.

"So you can see, there must be some mistake," I concluded. "Sure, I've been following her, but I was being paid to do it."

"Did you get paid? What about a contract?"

Ah, the contract! "Stuyvesant gave me a cash retainer in advance, but yeah, he signed a standard contract." I smiled. "That will verify my story, right?"

He nodded. "So, now that I know what's going on, I'm going to go see about getting you out."

He left, and I heaved a big sigh of relief. It was all a misunderstanding. It would be cleared up in short order—at least short in the bureaucratic sense of the term.

But it wasn't short, and it wasn't cleared up.

It was a good three hours before Eli came back to see me in my cell. He frowned as he sat down with a sigh that sounded too world-weary for good news.

A moment later he looked over at me. "Alexander Stuyvesant is making an accusation against you. He said he never hired you. His security people have been tracking you as you followed his wife, but they thought you were harmless."

"What?" I was on my feet, holding on to the bars.

Eli raised his hands and motioned for me to sit back down on the bunk.

"That's what he says, Mickey." He sighed again. "I told them your side of it. Based on the conflict between your statements, the police are getting a search warrant for your apartment to go find the contract. The warrant and the search will take time. With a murder charge pending, they can't let you go. You'll have to go through a full arraignment process. If they decide to charge you, there'll be a bail hearing."

He paused and looked at me. "The arraignment will be tomorrow."

I blinked a couple of times. "So you're saying I'm going to spend a night in jail?"

"Maybe more if they decide to charge you."

Nothing but good news.

I leaned back against the wall. "Okay, then . . . I guess you'll do what you've got to do." I couldn't think of anything else to say.

"They gave me a list of things you're permitted to have someone purchase for you while you wait."

"Huh?" My imagination had wandered off into a bleak landscape. Distracted by my dark thoughts, I'd lost track of what he was saying. "What do you mean?"

"Do you need anything for the next day or two? Do you have any prescription medications or other medical devices you require on a daily basis?"

"Oh." I blinked again at the reminder that it could be a day or two, but I focused on the question. "No, I'm good on medications and stuff."

My mouth felt gummy. "But I guess I'll need a toothbrush . . . deodorant . . . other stuff."

"Is there somebody who could do this for you?" He smiled. "You probably don't want to pay my rates to have me shop for a tooth brush."

"Oh, yeah. Right."

I thought of Jessica, and I gave him her name. "She'll help."

And never let me forget it, but that was the least of my worries right now.

Once Eli had delivered his bad news, they got serious about the jail thing. From the holding cell, they processed me through as a prisoner and took me to a different cell in the detention wing. My new quarters were just as bleak but bigger. This new cell measured one more restless pace in width.

Seven-thirty that evening, they took me out and led me to the visitor's room. It wasn't Eli this time. It was Jessica. I sat down in my fluorescent-orange striped jumpsuit on the other side of the glass from her.

I saw her familiar face, and suddenly my vision blurred. Embarrassed by my tears, I turned away.

"Mick?"

I took a deep breath and wiped my cheeks. Turning back to face her, I smiled. Or, rather, I tried to. Out of habit I tried to force out one of my calibrated smiles, but this was Jessica.

I couldn't pretend.

Finally I just let my face do its thing.

"Good to see you, kid." As soon as I'd said it, I wanted the word kid back.

Jessica didn't even blink. She leaned closer to the glass. "Are you okay, Mick?"

Was I okay? I huffed an unfunny laugh and summoned up what little bit of assurance I could. "Never better," I said and swung my eyes over to look at the guard, up at the barred windows, over to the locked doors . . .

She half smiled. "You never quit, do you?" She sighed. "One of these days, I'd like to understand you."

"Maybe then you can fill me in."

That slipped out. Rather than wallow in my insecurities, I tried to summon a bit of confidence. "So, here I am. There they are. And *illigitimi non carborundum*."

"Yeah, well these bastards are pretty darn good at wearing you down, you know. Make sure Eli's with you when they ask their questions."

She looked into my eyes for a time before she asked, "So what happened?"

I looked away and shrugged. "They arrested me this morning while I was sitting in my car watching the Carrack Center's parking lot. I was going to follow Samantha again. I had no idea somebody'd killed her."

After an afternoon spent thinking paranoid thoughts, I had plenty of suspicions, but few facts. And this was not a good time to share my speculations. I didn't think the police or anyone else would be monitoring our conversation, but I wasn't sure. With only a hunch about Stuyvesant and his capabilities, I didn't want to take any chance that he might somehow be listening either.

Still, I had one piece of new information that Jessica might clarify for me. I faced her and rested my elbows on the wooden shelf on my side of the window. "I've got a name. I wanted to give it to you the other night, but I got distracted."

I glanced around. No one appeared to be interested in our conversation. I leaned closer to the glass.

"Louis Sherman. Stuyvesant lied to me when he gave me the name of his head of security. I think Louis Sherman is the right name."

She nodded thoughtfully. "Where'd you get it?"

For a single moment, I had a foolish temptation to tell her the truth—a gnome told me. However amusing her reaction might be, it would distract her. My goal was to get out of jail.

"I asked around, and one of the guys gave me a name."

"Good enough then. I'll check it out."

I didn't have much more to say, and neither did she. However, I was loath to see her leave. We sat for a time just staring at each other.

Finally she said, "I'd better be going." She looked down a moment before she took a deep breath and met my eyes again. "Take care of yourself, Mick."

As a prisoner, my fate was not exactly in my own hands, but I heard the sentiment behind the admonition.

"Thanks for coming, Jessica." I don't think I'd ever meant something more sincerely in my life.

Back in my cell, I tried to settle myself for sleep.

Easier said then done. The same old thoughts wanted to chase around in my brain some more, but a new one popped up. Gary had told me that they had pixies watching me. I looked around my cell but saw nothing. Were they there but invisible? Had the pixies lost track of me after I was arrested?

I took a deep breath and sighed. The idea that someone, even a supernatural someone, was watching reassured me. I decided to go with that option.

Twelve

"Get yer stuff, Holmes," the guard said. "Yer leavin'."

I rolled over on the thinly padded bed in the cell where I'd spent the night and sat up. I checked my watch—three o'clock in the afternoon. They'd taken me down to an arraignment hearing early in the morning. Nothing was said there I didn't already know, but process is process. I did have a speaking part. When the judge asked if I understood the charges against me, I said, "Yes."

Ever since, I'd been waiting restlessly for a decision. What was the hold up? Were they going to charge me or not?

Last night had not been the worst night of my life, at least that's what I tried to tell myself. I yawned and ran my hand through my hair as I regarded the sterile concrete walls around me. No, there'd been that night of inflamed itching back in elementary school, the result of a dare I'd taken to run through a poison ivy patch. Then in high school—

"Move it, Holmes."

The guard had a lower tolerance for boredom than I did. Then again, in the last thirty-some hours I'd built up quite a bit of sedentary inertia.

I sighed and got to my feet. Exchanging a prison jumpsuit for my own clothes went a long way toward restoring my sense of self. After that, it took all of two seconds to gather the small sack of things that Jessica had brought me.

The guard gave me another sack of items they'd taken from me when I'd been arrested, then led me to an office where I signed papers. I waited some more while clerks shuffled more documents to properly check, recheck, and categorize what I'd signed. It all took too long, but my impatience didn't count. Eventually I walked out through a heavy door into a brightly lit but spartan waiting room.

Eli rose to greet me. "Mickey." He smiled happily and patted me on the back. "Good to see you on this side."

He gestured to the outside door. "Let's go get some coffee. We have things to discuss."

I shuffled along out the door and to Eli's car. After Jessica had left last night, I'd numbed myself to my surroundings by not thinking—as much as possible, anyway. Outside now, my brain circuits were slow to restart.

Even if I wasn't thinking at full speed, I knew one thing. "Uh, okay, but not at the Coffee Berry Ferry." Eli liked the place, but we had business to talk about. I didn't want to be distracted if we ran into Jessica.

Eli found a nearby coffee shop. Once we were settled into a quiet corner, I asked him for the news about my case.

"The good news is you're out. However, I'm afraid most of the rest is bad, Mick." He sighed. "I passed along to the police where you said the copy of your contract with Stuyvesant would be." He shook his head sadly. "They found nothing. No folder. No notes. There was nothing anywhere in your apartment to indicate you had a professional relationship with Alexander Stuyvesant."

He paused to take a sip of coffee. "On the other hand, even with Stuyvesant's accusation, they don't feel they have enough real evidence to charge you with murder." He paused again. No coffee this time, but he continued to stare at me before he said, "Yet."

The coffee was doing its work on me. I had functioning brain cells, and this news spelled trouble—spelled it out in all capital letters. I'd told Eli exactly where in my files the police would find the contract, along with my other papers about Stuyvesant. I may not get my laundry folded each week, but I keep my business meticulously organized—another thing Phillip Woodland had drummed into me.

Both Jessica and Bart knew about the contract. Bart was dead. I'd never actually shown the contract to Jessica, so her testimony would be dismissed as hearsay. Although she'd been doing research for me on Stuyvesant, she had only my word that he'd employed me.

I nodded to show I'd heard. What was worse, I finally understood what was happening. I was being framed.

Memories flooded back.

In my second year of high school, I had worked two study hall periods each week delivering messages for the school office. One of those periods happened to be the period when senior star athlete Blake Forrester snuck into the girls locker room and stole head cheerleader Lisa Sammons's panties for a souvenir.

I'd seen Blake in the hallway that morning, and, as required, dutifully reported his name to the office. When Blake had been called into the assistant principal's office and confronted with his crime, he instead had pointed the finger at me. Someone had tipped Blake off that I had ratted him out to the office. Blake had turned the tables on me.

Eli's report gave me that same moment of sick horror I'd experienced when the high school assistant principal had searched my locker and found Lisa's panties, red with cute little white hearts, stuffed in the back.

In high school, I'd had massive insecurities and zero self-confidence. As a dweeb, the miserable humiliation of that moment had overwhelmed me. The panties incident had stunted my social life from then on.

Although some of those insecurities lingered, these days I have more belief in myself. This time, instead of abject embarrassment, a thrill of anger-fueled adrenaline focused my attention.

Stuyvesant wasn't there, so venting my temper to Eli was useless. Even if Stuyvesant had been here, nothing I said or did in a hot-headed tantrum would change a thing. For the moment, the only thing I could do was circle the wagons and play defense. Spending the night in jail had convinced me my glib tongue would only take me so far. I may not have applied myself as diligently as I might have over the years, but if I let Stuyvesant win, I would go to jail. Time to pull out all the stops and focus my brain for a change.

"Okay, Eli," I said, "Then I guess you need to know some other things. Somebody stole that contract out of my office. I know they did because they took my gun at the same time." I couldn't help making a sour face as I said, "The police reported Samantha had been shot?"

Eli nodded. "Once in the chest. Once in the head."

"And when they get the ballistics report back, I'll bet anything that it was a 9mm slug that was fired from my gun."

He looked at me for a time before he said anything. He was not about to let me charge on unchallenged. Since I don't check my gun often, he pointed out I couldn't be sure that it had been taken at the same time as the contract. While that might be true, with both of them missing and me accused of murder, this was no coincidence. They had been snitched at the same time.

I was also certain I knew who did it, but I had to build a case to my lawyer. I moved on to describe the sexy text I'd found on my phone. The police still held my phone and my work tablet as evidence. They hadn't seen the copy of the file Kurse had given me because I hadn't told them the passwords. They'd asked.

"I don't know how good the police's electronics forensic people are," I said, "but I'll bet they won't have to take me to court to get the password. Whoever killed Samantha will make sure they see a copy of the file regardless

Eli sighed and leaned back. He blinked owlishly at me a couple of times. "So you were set up," he observed. "And next you're going to tell me it was Alexander Stuyvesant who did it."

I nodded. "It hangs together, but there's more." The next part of what I wanted to say would be tricky because I had to dance up to—but not across—the borders of fairy land. "I've run across information that shows Alexander Stuyvesant could profit from his wife's death."

I told him what Jessica had found out about Samantha's wealth, but then I fuzzed things a bit. "I think one of the parcels of land out west that Samantha owned might be connected to an oil deal her husband is interested in."

Oh, how I hoped he didn't ask me how I knew that. I didn't want to dodge a murder rap only to end up in the looney bin.

Eli nodded, but he held up his hands helplessly. "I understand what you are saying. So far, the police have Mr. Stuyvesant's sworn statement that you are involved. But . . ." He paused dramatically and held up his finger. "They must have no other evidence in hand besides that sworn statement. That's why you were not officially charged."

"Yet," I finished for him.

He nodded and pursed his lips thoughtfully for a time before he leaned forward. "I know you're going to investigate this on your own now that you're out, but you must be careful to keep your nose clean. I know you're not stupid enough to contact Stuyvesant in any way, shape, or form."

His hard stare told me he actually had doubts.

After I nodded my understanding, he shook a warning finger at me. "Because if you do, you'll end up right back there." He jerked a thumb back over his shoulder the way we had come—the jail. "And don't count on me for your bail money if they even offer that option."

He settled back in his chair and wiped his hand across his face. "So, okay. I'll ask a few questions on my end, but I have other cases."

When I got up to go, he smiled and winked. "So be sure to let me know if you happen to find anything interesting."

Judging by the tornadic scramble the police had left behind in my apartment, their search had been thorough.

Eli had explained that if they'd found the contract right off, they would have called off the full search. Since the contract had not been where I'd told them it was, the police had looked at everything. High and low, inside and outside. It couldn't have been much worse if they'd turned it upside down and shook it. I estimated I would have at least a full day's work to put all of my things back in order.

At the moment, I had other, more immediate priorities. I found my spare phone and called Jessica.

"Hey, Mick," she answered. "Eli must have sprung you like he said he was going to. Good to hear from you."

I spent a few minutes bringing her up to date on what the police had found, or rather, not found. "So I'm kind of grasping at straws where to go with this," I said. "Did you get a chance to look at Louis Sherman?"

"Oh, yeah, but I didn't want to worry you until you were home and had your feet up."

"Worry me?"

"Mick, Louis Sherman was special forces too. When he got out of the service, he started a company called BlackOut, Inc. They do business security work here in the city and elsewhere. They also handle personal protection for celebrities and other rich folks."

She was right. That was not a piece of news I would have easily digested inside the jail. After I'd thought about it a minute, however, the news gave me confidence I was on the right track. Maybe instead of Stuyvesant getting his well-manicured fingers dirty, it had been Sherman or someone at his BlackOut company who had put the tawdry sex file on my phone and burgled my apartment.

It also warned me I was playing out of my league. And by asking Jessica for help, I might have I involved her more deeply in something that had become dangerous. Stuyvesant's friend Sherman and his company were pros at the business of security and clandestine operations. In comparison, I was strictly a beginner. Could I compete with the pros?

But then again, I did know someone who was a pro, at least in the computer end of things. I smiled.

"Jessica, did you do any checking on Kurse?"

"Bart's girl friend? No, why?"

I heard her denial, but there was something in her voice. "So what did you find?"

She didn't answer right away.

Finally she said, "Well, I wanted to make sure, you know, that Bart wasn't going to have—"

"What did you find?"

She sighed. "Karen Hernandez. I think that's Kurse's name. She's twenty-eight and originally from Portland, Oregon. She did three years at Cal Tech but never finished her degree."

"Atta girl."

"I don't know for sure she's Kurse, Mick, but I think so. Do you want me to send you her contact information?"

"Absolutely."

If I was going to go up against people with a background in military security and intelligence operations, I needed someone who might be able to find the key to their back door. Kurse's connection with Bart had been personal, so she would be even more motivated to help.

I hoped.

"There's one more thing." Jessica's voice sounded tired.

I braced for another piece of bad news.

"My dad talked to one of the detectives on the case. Stuyvesant has an iron-clad alibi. He was in Brussels when Samantha was shot."

I huffed an unfunny laugh. "Of course he was."

Everything I'd seen so far in the effort to frame me for Samantha's murder showed careful planning. Stuyvesant wouldn't have ignored the obvious element of giving himself a cover story.

The mountain I had to climb kept getting higher.

After I'd gathered my thoughts, I said, "I guess I'll need as much help as I can get. Do you think you could find anybody who knew Samantha personally? Maybe by going through lists of women who were together with her on a couple of boards of directors or something? I really would like to find someone who may have heard her comment on her marital situation."

"I'll see if I can find some possible names."

After a pause, she asked, "What about someone that her husband might have screwed?"

"For business or pleasure?"

"You never stop, do you?"

She hesitated a moment before she went on. "I was thinking in the business sense, but, yeah, it wouldn't hurt to see if I if can find any sign that he's been stepping out."

"And don't forget that land deal."

I saw a vision of the research bill for the questions I had asked her to look into. "I guess we should talk about a payment plan sometime."

"Mick, you ain't gonna pay anybody if your butt's in a prison cell." She sighed. "Let me worry about that part later, okay? You need help, and you're going to get it."

After we said our goodbyes, my eyes were a little misty.

After a roller-coaster day, I was exhausted. Even so, I was far too keyed up to fall asleep easily. It was time for Beethoven therapy.

Growing up, my mother had insisted I take piano lessons. That skill never blossomed, but my attraction to the classical music I'd encountered stayed with me. Although I like popular music well enough, when I'm under stress, I turn to the heavy-weight themes from the masters.

I chose his Third Symphony and sat in the dark staring out the window at my limited view of the city. The music danced through gay frolics and swelled into minor-key battles.

The themes came and went. My urge for an immediate bloody confrontation ebbed.

Instead, I felt a growing sense of purpose.

People with money, power, and the skills to use them menaced my life and my friends' lives.

All I had was my brain.

That and tenacity—a highly motivated and concentrated tenacity.

The thunderous conclusion of Beethoven's symphony focused me on using all the skills and resources I could muster to defeat Stuyvesant and his allies.

No doubts.

No reservations.
I would do what it took.

Thirteen

"What?" Kurse met me in the hallway outside the door to her apartment. Arms folded, she glared at me.

I hadn't even knocked. It was the morning of the day after they let me out of jail. I hadn't warned her I was coming because I'd wanted to catch her unprepared. However, I was the one taken by surprise. I blinked at the unexpected confrontation.

"I want to ask you about Bart." And other things.

"You got him killed."

A conclusion I feared was all too true. I spread my hands helplessly. "You may be right." I took a deep breath before I continued. "If that's the case, I'm truly sorry. Bart did work for me, but I liked to think of him as a friend too."

I waited a moment for the thought sink in, but her angry stare never changed. "I want to talk to you about how I can find out who killed him. Can I come in?"

Her steady scowl showed me the depth of her feelings. She and Bart had definitely had a romance.

Finally she sniffed dismissively and swung open the door for me. Once inside, she pushed the door shut behind me. She stood facing me, hands on hips, without inviting me to sit. "You know who did it?"

"First of all, I want to tell you how bad I feel about Bart. While I don't feel like I knew him well, I've always thought he was a nice guy."

Kurse stared, eyes still hard.

Hoping to make things more personal, I asked, "Look, would you mind if I called you Karen?"

She bristled. "Only if you want all of your digital devices to stop working," she snapped. Her eyes narrowed, and her scowl deepened. "You're not supposed to know my name," she hissed. "It's a hacker culture thing. When you're female, you gotta scare the shit out of the guys before you get any respect."

I nodded. While the culture among private investigators might be different, I'd noticed that women investigators often had way more attitude than the men.

I backed up and tried again. "You're right. I'll call you Kurse, because I certainly want you to know I respect you."

Her smile crooked up slightly, and her glare eased. "And because I scare the shit out of you."

I didn't dispute her.

To introduce my needs, I told her my story about working for Alexander Stuyvesant. Her eyes gave away nothing, but she listened to the end.

"So it was Stuyvesant who shot Bart?"

I shook my head slowly. "I think he was behind it, but at this point I don't think he pulled the trigger. He was in Brussels when his wife was killed, so I'll bet he's got a cover story for Bart's murder as well."

By now there was fire in her eyes. "So who did it?"

I thought about Gary the gnome's information.

"Stuyvesant's head of security is a guy named Louis Sherman. Both he and Stuyvesant were special forces. From what I hear, Stuyvesant treats him more like a good buddy than an employee."

I handed her a hard copy of the information Jessica had given me about Sherman.

She scanned the material and looked up. "BlackOut?"

When I nodded, she pulled out a straight back chair and sat down. She pointed to another chair for me.

She studied the material intently.

When she finally looked up, she asked, "What kind of gun did they steal from you?"

"A Glock 26."

"Nine millimeter, right?" She looked thoughtful. "Registered in your name?"

I nodded. "Yes, to both." I sighed. "However, I haven't been able to find out what caliber gun was used on Bart." A moment later, I added, "Or Samantha."

"But you're thinking they used your gun for both of them, right?"

I nodded again. "I expect the murder weapon to turn up pretty soon. It's been four days and not a trace." I huffed an unfunny laugh. "That's why I'm still out walking around."

"Maybe they're not done killing."

That was a new thought and one that brought me up short. "I'm going to have to think about that."

"Don't think too long. You might be next."

I definitely hadn't considered that aspect. I took a minute to roll the thought around. "You mean maybe a fake suicide?"

"That would let the cops close the case pretty quickly."

"I agree."

It felt funny talking about my own fate this way. I thought some more. If the money from Samantha's property was the primary motive for Stuyvesant, the price he'd be willing to pay to keep his plan on track would be high. High enough that he could buy all kinds of help.

That gave me a new thought. "A lot would depend on how well they thought they had me framed. Maybe Stuyvesant even has an information pipeline to someone on the police force."

After I heard the words come out of my mouth, I held up my hand in caution. "I don't know that, but when movers and shakers are involved . . ." I let my voice trail off and shrugged.

"Yeah, it's not the movers who get shaken."

I sensed this was the time to ask directly for my favor. "Would you be willing to help me find out who's behind this?"

She narrowed her eyes and raised her eyebrows. "You think you can bring this guy down if he's the one that killed Bart?"

"Not by myself."

I wasn't about to bring up the faerie folk because so far they hadn't given me very much real help. Besides, while they might be a lot better at clandestine observation, I doubted they had access to anything Stuyvesant and Sherman were doing in the digital realm.

I had one specific task in mind for her. "You told me before there was stuff on my phone that was watching what I was doing. Can you tell me who's watching?"

She nodded. "That would be a place to start. I haven't had the time to dig into it yet, but what I saw of it looked like military stuff. Since your guys are special forces, that's just about guaranteed."

Frowning, she said, "Look, get the phone to me. I'll look to see if there's anything else that might point in that direction."

"You know how you said it was sending location information and other stuff all the time?"

"You stupid shit. You didn't bring it with you, did you?"

I shook my head and motioned for her to sit back down. "No, it's lying in a police evidence drawer."

"You going to get it back?"

I shrugged. "Probably, but not until after the police close the case."

Her smile was grim. "So after you're dead?"

She obviously was more amused by the thought than I was.

Gnawing on her knuckle, her eyes looked off into the distance. Finally she frowned. "If I don't have the phone, there's no way I can backtrack who's responsible for that spyware shit."

But I was no longer hunting in the dark. "Is there some way you could monitor Sherman and maybe Stuyvesant for signs of other shady behavior?"

She nodded. "But if Sherman's any good, it will be difficult to do it directly without him knowing somebody's looking at him and maybe even who's looking."

"So you can't do it?"

"No, but it means I'll have to be extra cautious." She smiled sourly. "Boy, you'd pay me through the ass for this—if this weren't for Bart."

"For Bart," I agreed.

Before I left, I had one last question. "I'm curious. You were waiting for me. How did you know I was coming?"

She smiled smugly. "I'd called out for a pizza, but you got here first."

Since we'd already talked way longer than any reasonable delivery would have taken to get here, I ignored her. "Are you watching me or what?"

"Don't flatter yourself." She sniffed and looked away. "I've got security cameras the landlord doesn't know about watching all the doors to this building. It sends me an alert whenever anyone enters the building who it knows."

"Knows? How would it know me?"

"Facial recognition." She pointed at her vest. "I run a body camera all the time. Anybody I meet, I extract their picture for my facial recognition system. Cops too. I make a point to get as many of them on my cam as I can."

She paused then shrugged. "I met you at the door so at the very least I could chew your ass about Bart."

She smiled grimly at me. "And what if you'd been the one who did Bart? You could've been trouble, but if I don't safe my system after you leave, it sends an alert to the local precinct with a video of our interaction. Dead or not, I'd have your ass anyway."

I swallowed hard. Kurse was paranoid to a degree I'd never encountered before.

"And you are going to cancel the alert after I leave, right?"

"Don't worry," she said disdainfully. "I already said I'd help."

Fourteen

My next goal was to contact the faerie folk, but I hadn't seen Gary or any other gnomes since I'd gotten out of jail. You can never find a gnome when you want one. Rather than trust to luck that sooner or later I'd stumble across one, I walked to the park and sat on the bench where I'd had the conversation with Mel. Maybe it was a faerie hotspot.

While I watched to see if anyone from the faerie world strolled by, I got on my burner phone. First on my list was Jessica. I knew she was at work so I sent a message asking her to dig up more information on the large land parcel that Samantha Stuyvesant had owned near Yellowstone—short and to the point.

I also needed to call Eli Dushinsky—his firm anyway. I'd had a vague idea that maybe if the gnomes pilfered the original deed, it would prevent, or at least delay, the sale. But where would Samantha have kept the deed, and what did it look like?

As I expected, the law firm had several lawyers who specialized in real estate. One of them was willing to answer my quick question with the information that standard deeds varied from state to state, and formats had changed over the years—something I should have realized myself. In order to tell the gnomes what to look for, I would have to know the location and the date the land was first acquired by the Astor family before I could get an idea what the deed might look like.

That meant a lot more research. It also meant I had to let Jessica know that I also needed dates including the year of the land's original survey. The more I'd thought about the emotional upset I'd felt after her visit at the jail, the more awkward I felt about talking to her.

I sent her another text.

Unfortunately, this time, she was on her break. She not only got the message, she called me back. My requests had triggered her suspicions.

"You're thinking about going snooping in Stuyvesant's office, aren't you?"

Yes, but not the way she imagined.

"Uh, I was hoping to have a description of what the deed looked like, so I could check, you know, for filings at the clerk of courts office and such."

"You're not a good liar, Mick."

Actually I'm a pretty good liar, but my impromptu dissembling is weak.

"You're right," I admitted. "I'm hoping to find a way to get a look at the deed, and I want to be ready."

"So you are going to do something stupid."

I sighed. She was good. "No, I'm not dumb enough to think I could get into either Stuyvesant's home or his office."

That was perfectly accurate. However, I'd seen the gnomes come and go as they pleased. If I told them what to look for, they might get lucky.

"I admit it's a long shot, but if the deed does surface, I want to be ready."

"What if there's more than one or two properties involved? Back in the day, the Astors did a lot of business, especially out west. There could be a whole portfolio of relevant deeds. Not just the one."

"I hadn't thought about that," I admitted. "I guess you won't know unless you look."

She let me go on that one, but tossed me another hot potato. "My dad says he'd like to talk to you."

"Your dad? Uh . . . what about?"

I had visions of confronting her stern-faced father asking questions about how cozy we must have looked at Bart's funeral.

"Well, I've told him a few of the things you've told me, and he wants to hear the details for himself."

My vision switched to an interrogation room with hot lights and one-way mirrors. "Uh . . ." was all I managed.

"Look, he said to tell you to come over to my apartment this evening to talk about the case with him. He may have some ideas for you."

While I weighed the pros against the cons—con as in conviction—she added, "Do you want me to be there to supervise?"

Yes, I would be more comfortable if Jessica were there to ensure things stayed civil, but then the resulting conference might resemble a meet-the-parent night, a context that made me uncomfortable in a whole different way.

Still, if a member of the police force wanted to give me ideas . . .

"Yeah," I finally agreed. "I'm free tonight."

"Good. We'll see you at seven here at my apartment."

Still waiting in the park on the bench, I continued down my list of calls. Since I had to concentrate on the Stuyvesant case, I had to let my other active clients know I couldn't work their jobs. My income would take a serious hit, but it was the ethical thing to do. If I had to spend time in court—or in the big house—I wanted to make sure I didn't leave any of my current clients hanging over the fire.

I'd finished two of the three calls, when I glanced up and saw Gary leaning against a tree watching me. Relieved, I put away my phone and waved him over. He hopped up on the bench beside me.

I turned to talk. For the benefit of anyone who might stroll by, I pretended like I was engaged in the solitary contemplation of nature.

"How was your time in the slammer, big guy?"

That was not the first topic I wanted to deal with, but it told me that Gary—or somebody—was keeping an eye on me. The way my luck had been breaking lately, the snooping was actually reassuring.

I ignored his question and got right to my business. "I know you guys are watching Stuyvesant. Can you tell me if he had his wife sign any papers lately—maybe the last couple of months?"

The gnome nodded. "Yeah, probably. What Teddy didn't see, Ethel will have." He thought for a moment. "Anything special you're looking for?"

"One thing Stuyvesant might have done is trick Samantha into signing off on a transfer of the deed to the property that Mel . . . you know, is interested in. I need to know if she signed any papers for him. I've also asked a friend to find out what the deed looks like so if needs be you or somebody could take it . . . or something." I waved a hand uncertainly. "Maybe if the deed disappears, so does Mel's problem." There was undoubtedly an official record of the property, but a missing deed might complicate or delay the land grab.

"Sounds easy enough."

Unfortunately talking about the deed gave me an additional complicating thought. "Another way he could have played it would be to have her change her will—assuming she has one."

I thought how that might be done. "If she did have a will, did she have it registered?"

"You're talking lawyer stuff, and that's over my head."

"Do you guys have lawyers?"

He smiled broadly. "Sure. We got lawyers, or at least what passes for lawyers. You think maybe they could play a part in this on our end?"

It was a new thought—one that might be worth exploring.

"Could be. I'm fishing for information, so anything you can tell me would help. Meanwhile, I'll have somebody check to see if Samantha has a registered will, and if so, when it was registered."

"Is Jessica the one who's doing all this for you?" He grinned. "You're going to work that poor girl to death."

Was I surprised the gnome knew about Jessica and the work she did for me? Not really, and the more I thought about what Stuyvesant was trying to do to me, the better I liked the idea that the gnomes were keeping an eye on her as well as me. Not that a gnome could ever have testified in a court of law, but their eyes and ears could provide me with useful information.

I nodded. "Yes, Jessica does good research."

"You gonna get in her pants?"

I took a deep breath and frowned. "That's not on the table," I said with some heat.

"Table'd be uncomfortable. You should do it someplace soft like the couch or in a bed."

"We don't have that kind of a relationship. This is strictly professional."

The gnome smirked and rolled his eyes. "And pigs fly."

Sensing a chance, I opened my eyes wide with innocence. "Pigs? Really?" I gasped. "Your world is so much more exciting than mine."

Gary looked at me a time then sneered. "Right, dick-head."

He hopped off the bench. "I'll ask Teddy and Ethel if they've seen anything and get back to you."

For the very first time I felt good, maybe even a little smug, about the way my conversation with the gnome had ended.

Fifteen

I knocked on Jessica's door promptly at seven. My lack of enthusiasm for a face-to-face meeting with Jessica's father was tempered by my reluctance to be late.

"Hi, Mickey. Come on in," she said.

I immediately sensed reserve and decorum in her bearing. Her father sat on the couch at the end of the living room, holding a beer. I wiped my feet on the mat and nodded in his direction. "Mr. Jones."

He nodded at me. "Please. Make it Devon."

"Okay . . ." I swallowed and finished, "Devon."

After the social signals I'd received at our first meeting, casually using his first name felt uncomfortable. But if nothing else, I'm adaptable.

"Can I get you a beer?" Jessica asked.

There was a six-pack on the kitchen bar. I'm not a big beer drinker, and Jessica doesn't drink beer at all. However, Devon had one in his hand. Evidently he had chosen the refreshments for tonight.

"Yes, please," I said. One beer, and I would sip it slowly. I needed my wits about me this evening.

I sat in the chair across from Devon, and Jessica handed me a can. She retreated to sit next to her father on the sofa. As she walked behind the couch, she pointed at her father's beer and held up two fingers. He was on his second? Good to know.

Devon and I exchanged a couple of comments about the weather.

Awkward social banter out of the way, Devon set his beer down and crossed his arms across his chest.

"My daughter says I should hear your side of the story."

I glanced at Jessica, but she was focused on her father. His bearing didn't have quite the feel of an inquisition. She'd said he was interested, but I saw skepticism in his manner.

I'd thought about what I was going to say tonight, and I tried to relate events in an order that made sense. As I went along, I addressed a number of statements to Jessica so she could back me up.

When I mentioned the Time To Go organization, he nodded. "Heard of it," but that was all he offered.

When I finished, he sighed and picked up his beer again. This time he took a long pull. Reminded of the beer in my own hand, I took a sip of bland.

"So . . ." He paused to look down and swirled his own swill. "I've asked around the department about you."

He frowned and speared me with his eyes. "Talked with detective Dickensen over in the Fourteenth Precinct. He called you a feckless wimp."

Dickensen? I thought back. "Yeah, that was a couple-three years ago. Henly Meyers, he was Bobby Parks' lawyer. Anyway, Meyers hired me to question some people who Bobby said could place him at . . ." I took a deep breath, but the memory wouldn't come. I shrugged. "Some bar Bobby claimed he'd been at the night he'd knocked over the liquor store on Bakersfield at Ninety-Sixth."

The more I talked, the better I remembered the incident.

"Bobby was a regular at the bar. I talked to a lot of the other regulars, but nobody could place him there on that particular night. I think Dickensen got his shorts in a bunch when he asked me what I'd gotten from the interviews, and I wouldn't tell him."

I smiled slightly. "He didn't have a warrant, so I said no. That meant he had to either get a warrant to serve me or go interview all the people I'd already talked to make sure the prosecutor would know what the defense had before they made a decision to take the case to trial."

"Yeah, DA's looking to keep his winning percentage up." After another sip of beer, he smiled slightly. "Dickensen also called you a smartass."

"Uh-oh," I said and held up my hands in surrender. "Guilty as charged on that one."

We both chuckled a little.

Devon got serious again. "From what I hear you say, Jessica is your best witness."

A moment later, I realized what he was saying. We weren't talking about Dickensen anymore. Bart had researched Stuyvesant for me, and Bart was dead. Jessica not only had been providing me with information on Stuyvesant, but also could confirm the timeline I'd laid out. Devon was saying his daughter's association with me put her in peril. That thought made my hands go cold.

I wanted to make sure I understood. "So you believe my story, and you think that puts Jessica in danger because of what she knows."

He nodded curtly and finished his beer. "It sounds like you've been set up to take a fall for Samantha Stuyvesant's murder. I also think you're right about the gun. When it shows up, I'll bet it's the same gun that killed your friend Bart."

He crunched his beer can. "I—" He flicked his eyes to Jessica. "I don't want anything like that to happen to her."

Neither did I. As angry as I had been about being framed, the fear that the murderer might strike at Jessica almost unmanned me. My thoughts were all a-tumble. I looked at her, but she was looking at her father.

I focused back on Devon and nodded to show I understood him.

There was one more idea I had to run past him—Kurse's theory about a feigned suicide for me. I hadn't shared this speculation with Jessica yet.

When I finished, she got up and came over behind my chair to put her hand on my shoulder without saying a word. As I started to reach up to take her hand, Devon's eyes flicked to his daughter's hand.

I canceled my idea to connect with Jessica and diverted the motion to become a thoughtful tap on my chin.

Devon looked me straight in the eye. "I don't think either of you are safe if it really is this Sherman guy."

He pursed his lips thoughtfully. "I'll ask around. See what the word is about him and his BlackOut company. Meanwhile—" He poked a finger in our direction. "You and her gotta stay outta sight."

After Jessica went back to the couch, Devon repeated a quick summary of what we'd talked about. I nodded agreement and thought we were done.

However, Jessica wasn't. "Mick, there's one other thing I found today that I haven't had a chance to tell you about. I ran across a notice that Stuyvesant filed a law suit yesterday against a land trust that's registered in Samantha's name."

She shrugged. "There weren't many details in the filing, but I printed a copy of it in case there might be something you want me to follow up."

I took the single page from her and glanced at the list of names and official legal identifying codes.

I'd started to nod my thanks when my eyes stopped cold. The name of the trust was Monoceros Land Holdings. Even with my modest foreign language schooling, I knew monoceros was Latin for unicorn, a clear signal that this might be the property Mel was worried about.

Moreover, the name implied that Samantha or at least whoever set up the trust knew about the land's significance. If that really was the case, it meant another human knew about unicorns, gnomes, and the rest of the faerie world—something I'd not encountered before.

I don't think well when I'm flabbergasted. At the moment I was still simmering with anger about the possible threat to Jessica. I couldn't think about this new idea while sitting across from her and her father.

I blinked, trying to un-pop my eyes. As casually as I could, I folded the paper and put it in my pocket.

I cleared my throat and said, "I'll check into this later."

Belatedly I added, "Thanks, Jessica."

From there our conversation segued to general topics where I saw a more genial side of Devon. It may have been the beer, but I liked the mellow Devon a lot better than the steely-eyed daddy I'd seen earlier.

It turned out he'd played professional baseball for a few years when he was younger.

"Yeah," he said with a smile. "Double A for the Indianapolis Indians."

He told a few anecdotes about his playing days.

I was struck by the thought that he was much happier talking baseball than talking about being a cop.

I returned to my apartment preoccupied with thoughts about unicorns and land trusts as well as a resurgent need to do . . . something. I'd just hung up my jacket when my phone rang.

I fished it out of my pocket. Jessica.

She didn't even say hello. "What was it? What'd you see?" she demanded. "I know you didn't want to say anything in front of Dad, but there was something on that paper I gave you, wasn't there?"

Busted.

Again.

The thing was, not only had Jessica gotten good at reading me and my reactions, I had trouble lying to her. I couldn't tell her that Monoceros was nothing because it might be important.

"The name Monoceros Land Holdings—it could mean something," I said truthfully. "I'm not sure, but I want to check."

Half an answer was better than none—maybe. But if I'd given her the full answer that included unicorns, she'd call the men in white coats to lock me up.

When she didn't say anything, I knew she thought I didn't trust her. "Look," I said. "It's something really . . ." I took a deep breath and tried to un-fumble my thoughts. "It's kinda far out—a long shot that would make me look really stupid if it's wrong."

Not to mention really demented.

"Okay, Mick," she sighed. "Be that way. One of these days I'll figure you out."

I snorted. "Yeah, and when you do—"

"I know. I'll be sure to include you in the brief."

I was about to try for a lighthearted farewell, but I realized I had to say more about another topic. "Look, JJ, I'm really worried about your father's idea that what you did for me could blow back on you like it did on Bart."

She sighed. "Yeah, after you left, he persuaded me to go home with him and use his spare bedroom for a while. That's where I am right now."

I hadn't counted on her next question. "What about you?"

I was about to reassure her that I could take care of myself, but I knew she would hear the message that I didn't think she could do the same. "Maybe we'd both better keep our heads down for a while."

She sighed. "Maybe we should run off to Hawaii."

Late evening.

Long day of worry and frustration.

"Tempting," I responded, trying not to let on how much the idea appealed to me. "Unfortunately as a condition of my release, I have to stay in the city."

But I had another bad thought. "Besides, we'd have to come up with completely new identities, or the BlackOut boys would track us down."

"So I guess we'd better solve this, huh?"

We indeed. Her implied participation comforted me, but it also reminded me of what the she of our "we" could do to help. "Listen, could you look for more details about that land trust that Stuyvesant is suing? If they hold the property I'm looking for, I don't need to know the physical appearance of the deed."

"Back to Monoceros and the property thing, huh?" I heard her yawn into the phone. "I'll see what I can do.

"Night, Mick."

124

After I went to bed, I lay there thinking thoughts instead of sleeping. I mulled over the information about Monoceros and what it might mean. I considered in what other ways the faerie folk might be involved. Then I worried about Jessica and the possibility the killer might go for her.

But another thought rankled and wouldn't go away. A feckless wimp? Dickensen had a better vocabulary than most detectives, but in the dark of my bedroom his casual characterization of me festered.

Hearing Devon offer the observation that I was useless in front of Jessica had made me feel embarrassed in a way that still bothered me. She was diligently pursuing the same law degree I'd given up on. I'd made light of that fact several times when the topic had come up, but tonight I again questioned my motives.

Had studying law really bored me as I'd remembered, or was I rationalizing my own avoidance of hard work?

Dare I even say its name—*laziness*?

I rolled to my other side and wriggled my legs around until I was comfortable again.

I conjured up memories of my last semester in law school and especially the courses in contract law and legal arguments. I'd always wondered. Was the goal to produce detail-oriented, logically reasoned justifications or was it nit-picky, redundant, and repetitive ass-covering?

I had to smile at the approach my mind took to frame the questions in the most self-serving way possible.

Yes, I had been bored, and boredom had amplified my lack of focus and effort that had made the work double-difficult. But did I lack the necessary intellectual skills and tenacity to succeed, or had it been that law school and the legal world were not suited to my character and temperament?

Know thyself?

Good old Socrates had it right. But did I actually know myself, or did I merely know how to fool myself?

I tried lying on my stomach, a position of last resort when all others failed to lull me to sleep.

None of my academic classes at school had ever really challenged me. In classrooms over the years I'd often let my imagination roam—even in law school.

I smiled at a memory from a session of the legal arguments class. One day, my stubbornness as well as my imagination had gotten me into a "But-what-if . . ." exchange with the professor about possible interpretations of ambiguous evidence. Even though I didn't expend much effort on the formal written work, I'd done all the readings. On that particular day I actually opened my mouth in the face of his smug self-assurance. I'd spent a delightful few minutes dancing him through a series of alternate scenarios until he finally closed the discussion by ordering me to leave the class. He'd trashed my required final essay as well, but I'd still accumulated enough points to pass the class—barely.

So, lazy until riled out of boredom by a challenge? I liked that thought.

I sighed. No, my mind was too restless for the rigid structural confines of the legal profession. In business for myself as a private investigator, I enjoyed a wide variety of questions and problems. Unfortunately even here most of my cases were pretty routine because most people are routinely stupid.

My current predicament was different. Stuyvesant and Sherman undoubtedly had more skills and resources at their disposal than I did. Worse yet, those skills and resources directly threatened me— and Jessica.

Therefore, I would have to outthink and outwork them.

Sixteen

The next day was Samantha's funeral.

I wasn't going to the service. The presence of her accused murderer probably would not be appropriate.

Yet, since Stuyvesant had arranged to point the finger of guilt at me, I needed to know what family relationships within the Stuyvesant's household might tell me. Graveside services were at Kingdom Fields, a small cemetery where I knew I could watch some of what went on while keeping my distance.

The gloomy drizzly morning matched my dreary mood. I used a broad-brimmed hat to keep the light rain at bay while also shadowing my face. I sheltered under the covered entrance to a movie theater across the street from the cemetery's small parking lot where I could see the family assemble.

They'd followed the pall bearers with the casket into the cemetery under a parade of umbrellas when Patricia Wentz arrived.

I blinked in surprise. Her connection to Samantha had been deeper than I realized. She parked on the street and hurried after the procession.

The memorial service was a short one, and the damp mourners hustled back to their cars.

Wentz was one of the first back to the parking lot. A young man trotted ahead of the rest and called out to her before she left the cemetery.

I'd seen him arrive with the family in the limousine, so I figured he was one of the Stuyvesants' sons, either Shane or Jeffrey. He gave Wentz a warm hug, and they talked for a few moments under her umbrella.

I was too far away to hear their conversation, but he'd called out "Aunt Pat" to get her attention.

She held his arm fondly as they talked before he left to rejoin the family.

I recalibrated my thinking. Obviously Patricia Wentz meant something to the young man and vice versa. If Wentz had a close connection to the family, she would have important information about Samantha.

Our previous conversation had been awkward and uneasy. At this moment, Wentz's emotions would be raw. She might not be so defensive this time—if she was willing to talk to me at all. On the other hand, if I approached Miss Martial Arts now, she might be even more strongly protective of her privacy and flatten me.

Wentz's car was not far from where I stood. I took a deep breath as she approached and went to intercept her. Fortune may favor the bold, but was I being bold—or stupid?

"Ms. Wentz. I'm sorry for the timing, but could I speak to you?"

I knew she remembered me when her eyes went cold. "Your maggoty little newspaper's interest in this sad story is beyond contempt."

I nodded agreement and put it out there. "It's worse than you think. I lied to you when I interviewed you. I'm not a reporter. I'm a private detective named Mickey Holmes."

She processed the information, and her glare of frigid contempt melted in rising fury. "You're the one—"

"Yes. Alexander Stuyvesant accused me of murdering Samantha," I said bluntly. "Do you believe him?"

Her angry scowl eased to a skeptical glower. "I've got to get out of here," she said. "If you've got a car, you can follow me."

I trailed along behind her as she headed north. After twenty minutes, we were in the neighborhood near her Time To Go office. We ended up in a cafe bar. It wasn't eleven o'clock yet. I ordered coffee, but Wentz asked for an expensive Scotch.

"Samantha's favorite," she said.

Before the server left, I said, "Give me a shot of that as well."

I looked back at Wentz. "If you'll let me, I'd like to join you in a toast to Samantha. From what I already know about her, I'd like to honor her as well."

A moment later, I added, "And let me pay for this. You're doing me a big favor just by speaking to me."

The first thing I did was to apologize again for deceiving her. I described how Stuyvesant had hired me to follow his wife then went on to tell her what I had seen the day I had shadowed the two of them.

"What I saw you two doing looked like a rescue. When I talked to you, I was trying to confirm it. Rather than tell you I was following her, I lied about being a reporter." I tried to look humble and sincere. Given the circumstances, it wasn't hard.

Since she hadn't punched me yet, I continued. "From what I've found out about your Time to Go organization since then, I plan to tell my friend, Sean Martin—who, by the way, really does run that paper—to do an article about you and what your group does."

The server brought our drinks. We held up the glasses and together said, "To Samantha."

After a ceremonial swallow, Wentz set her glass down and sighed. "Samantha was such a help to us. How will I ever replace her?"

Her eyes watered, and she turned away. I said nothing waiting for her to recover herself.

When she turned back, she took a deep breath and continued. "We were friends in college."

She stopped to take a sip. Her eyes stared off in the distance.

After a minute, she swirled her Scotch and took a larger swallow.

"We were more than friends." She looked directly at me, her eyes full of challenge. When I didn't react, she took another drink. "For her it was an experiment, an experiment that lasted until . . . he charmed her away."

"Stuyvesant?"

She nodded and smiled slightly. "I've moved on. My wife and I are perfectly happy, but you never forget your first."

Since I had my own bygones that were not completely gone, I toasted the thought and finished my own shot. Delicious stuff, but I had to stop if I wanted to keep using my higher-level brain cells.

Since we seemed to be putting our cards on the table, I tossed out another.

"I'm also thinking she was a major financial supporter of your group. Will you be able to go on?"

She sighed. "Yes. Samantha really helped get us established. It wasn't just her money; she knew people with money and convinced them to help us too."

She looked at me and gave me a small smile. "And she loved to get her hands dirty with the rescues too."

"Is she why you were touchy when I asked you about your group's support?"

She nodded. "Of course I was trying to keep her name out of it, but funding is a tender area. Samantha . . ."

She looked at me and smiled wryly. "Samantha allowed me to be lazy about fundraising. For the first few years, I hustled my butt just to keep us afloat. Once we had her help, I got to do what I loved doing."

She sighed wistfully. "Now I'll have to go back to work."

"Your recent track record should help."

"I will always treasure that as Samantha's legacy to us."

Neither of us said anything for a time.

Finally she said, "You said you were looking for evidence that she was having an affair?" She shook her head sadly. "Samantha and I were in regular contact, mainly about Time To Go. But from some of the comments she'd made over the years, I know she was unhappy."

She looked at me sharply and snorted. "But an affair? Hardly. In fact, from what she'd said recently, I think Alex was the one playing around."

"Do you know a guy named Louis Sherman?"

"Screwy Louie?" She snorted. "He came to my dojo once some years ago. He'd signed up for a class, but as soon as we started, he got all obnoxious about how I was doing it wrong."

She smiled tightly. "Since he already knew so much, I suggested he hike his ass right back to the street. I had no idea why he'd signed up unless it was to cause trouble. I gave him back his money, and that was the end of it. Since then I've only seen him in passing at social functions. Samantha's mentioned him a couple of times."

She studied what remained of her drink then said, "My impression of him is equal parts scary and creepy. Samantha told me that whenever he and Alex get together, they like to talk about the nasty things that they used to do in the service. Things that Louie's company still does."

"BlackOut, Inc.?"

Wentz nodded.

From the way she'd opened up, I decided to see what she thought about my idea for the murderer. "The police know that Alexander was in Brussels, Belgium the night Samantha was murdered."

I looked her in the eyes and raised my eyebrows questioningly.

Her eyes got bigger. "You think it was Louie," she breathed.

Her first thought matched my own conclusion, but I held up my hand as a caution. "I have zero evidence of that. The only thing I'm going on is an extension of the idea that he and Alexander were both special forces, and somebody is trying to frame me for her murder. At the moment, I have no idea where to look except at Sherman's company."

"Try the MMA scene."

"Mixed martial arts?"

She nodded and smiled slightly. "Entertainment for the testosterone-inflamed. He and Alexander are both fans, and Louie still likes to get into the ring—at least until he got kicked out of the local league."

"Do I want to know why?"

She smiled grimly. "He refused to follow the rules against head butting, eye gouging . . . that kind of thing."

"A fun kind of guy." While I recognized the theoretical need to kick someone in the head occasionally, I never thought much of it as a sport.

"He likes to hang out at a fight club called Only the Valiant over at Broad and Third."

"A fight club?"

"And training. Self-defense classes too. They do a little bit of everything." She snorted. "They have a couple of public fight nights a week. They sell drinks, take illegal bets, and indulge in other male dominance rituals." Then she shrugged. "I've heard Louie owns at least a piece of the place."

Wentz had little more information about Sherman, so I moved on to ask her about the land trust.

As soon as I mentioned the name Monoceros, she started nodding. "That was Samantha's treasure. It had been handed down to her through . . ." She waved her hand and shrugged. "I don't know how many generations. She said it was an important natural preserve that's been in her family forever." She smiled as she went on to recount Samantha's dedication to her family trust.

As soon as she finished, she frowned. "But it's in danger, right? Otherwise you wouldn't have brought it up."

"I think so. I think Alexander has some sort of development project in the works."

Her eyes widened. "That's the motive, right? That's why he had her killed."

I held up my hand. "Careful. You're jumping way ahead of me. I don't have enough to say that, but I'm looking into it."

I knew Jessica was doing research, and Gary had said he'd look into it as well. But how well could a gnome do research? For that matter, could a gnome even read? Still, Gary and the other gnomes could go where I couldn't.

The key here was that Wentz had just reinforced my opinion that the land deal was an important part of this.

Since I could think of nothing else to ask, I offered my sympathies again and stood up. "Thank you for your time, Ms. Wentz. If you think of anything else related to what we've talked about, please get in touch." I handed her a card.

She finished off the last of her Scotch and looked at me coolly. "You know, Holmes, I've revised my thinking about you. You're not a completely insufferable prick."

I smiled ironically. "Yes, I am. Ask anybody who knows me."

As I turned away, her sardonic half smile was the first trace of amusement I'd seen from her.

Seventeen

After my conversation with Wentz, Louis Sherman was on my mind when I walked into my apartment. That meant I was a little slow on the uptake.

Gary the gnome stood up on my couch and crossed his arms. "Now you've done it."

I blinked. "Done what?"

Just then, I noticed the tall, dark figure silhouetted in front of my balcony door. Involuntarily I took a step back.

The gnome jerked a thumb at the spectral form. "You asked me about our lawyers, and now a predactor wants to talk to you."

"What's a predactor?"

I'd addressed the question to Gary, but the creature stepped closer. "I am." it announced in a flat, toneless rasp of a voice. "I want to talk to you about a particular property involved in your investigation—specifically Monoceros Land Holdings."

The figure loomed over me, its words clipped and precise.

I was intimidated, so I gave it attitude. "Right. I was hoping to talk to someone about that." I plopped into a chair and motioned an invitation for the thing to sit.

The predactor remained standing. Evidently it wasn't a social creature—or maybe it couldn't sit.

From my new position the light was no longer behind it. Its triangular head and bulging eyes reminded me of a praying mantis, except it was blue—a dark, steely blue. A cloak of the same color closely wrapped its body and concealed any details of its gaunt form.

The creature tracked me with its head. Once I'd settled, it continued. "The property retained by that trust is one of twelve around the world that must remain inviolate. Undisturbed."

"Why?"

It seemed an obvious question, but the predator acted as if I'd trespassed into an indelicate topic. It took a step closer and raised its chin imperiously. "These sites root the tree of the world that is Faerie. Without that restraint, the chaos of the fey would throw your world into turmoil . . . as it has in the past."

"The past?"

The predator didn't sigh, but it stared at me—at least I think it was staring at me. Its large rounded eyes had no obvious center. Finally it answered. "When the trust was set up, it was intended to stop a threat to that root. Hunting had disrupted the natural system of the area. It had to be protected, but damage had been done. The results were catastrophic to your world and are yet present."

I thought about the western United States and the timing of the land trust. "Was it the Indians and the American bison? You know, the settlers hunting bison?"

"That was not hunting but unrestrained slaughter. The root of Faerie is anchored in the natural world. The settlers changed the fundamental structures that supported the root."

That sounded dramatic, but it explained nothing—at least to me. I rubbed my chin thoughtfully and looked at Gary. "Sounds bad, all right."

The gnome shrugged. "Yep. It was a few years before my time, but the way I hear it, the mess they made let several glacat leeches get loose. Caused what you anthros call your Civil War."

Caused the Civil War? The statement startled me. "How did — what kind of leeches did you say, glacats?—start the Civil War?"

"They feed off human passions and make 'em worse. Disagreements become unforgivable insults. Arguments get bloody. The glacat leeches got everybody stirred up back then. Took a while to get people back steady again." He sniffed. "Not that it's over."

Before I could pursue the topic, Gary jerked his thumb toward the blue creature. "But come on. The predactor's here to help. Like I said, they're what passes for lawyers in our world. So what's your question?"

Lawyer? Reminded of my more immediate concerns, the visit began to make sense. I had been trying to track down information about Monoceros, and the predactor could answer questions.

Or eat me. The huge insectoid still reminded me of an oversized mantis.

"I'm trying to make sense of Samantha Stuyvesant's murder," I told him, her, or it—I hadn't decided. "And Samantha's control of Monoceros Land Holdings, given its value in our world, could be the motive."

"The trust agreement declared that the land would be held henceforth, permanently inviolate and untouched."

"Right. Monoceros was probably set up as some kind of a conservation land trust. I've got someone looking into the details." I thought for a time. "Can you tell me when was it set up? How old is the trust?"

"It was the spring season when we agreed. In anthropoid reckoning, the year was 1835. We signed the original agreement with John Jacob Astor as representative of his heirs in perpetuity."

I raised my eyebrows. We? The predactor made it sound as if he'd been there to sign with old man Astor himself. Since I now had a date, I made a mental note to have Jessica check the date currently on the trust. In a couple of centuries, a lot of reincorporations, reestablishments, and other legalistic fiddling can take place. Was Monoceros the original trust or a reincarnation of it?

One part of the predactor's answer particularly intrigued me. "Astor must have been a sensitive. Most of us humans, you know, anthros aren't able to see your people."

The predactor nodded slowly. "Astor was one such as yourself. At the time, he was acquiring land in the area. We worked with him and provided resources to buy properties we valued on the condition he create a land reserve with them. For this he was paid a commission. A quid pro quo, as you call it."

Although the big blue bug had just quoted Latin to me, I refused to be distracted. Since a lot of real estate law had been changed and reinterpreted in that time, I asked, "Do you have contact with any current legal advisors?"

"No. I assume the original principals are all dead. We deal with anthropoids as little as possible. Since you know us, you will do."

"But I'm not a lawyer." Nor had I wanted to be.

"Hire one."

I was about to object that I wasn't sure I would be able to pay next month's rent when the predactor added, "Find the best. Alexander Stuyvesant has filed a suit disputing the trust's ownership, and we must fight it. We will provide you any needed resources, as well as a suitable commission."

Its long cape moved—or what I had thought was a cape. The creature had large wings wrapped around its body. Long, bony fingers jutted from one of the wing's articulating joints. The fingers extracted a leather pouch and dropped it into my hands.

Its weight surprised me, and I fumbled it. I knew immediately what "resources" must be inside, but I untied the wrap anyway.

Glints of gold gleamed back at me.

I looked at the predactor. "This is not exactly coin of the realm. I'll have to figure out how to turn this into money." I didn't know what a modern law firm's preferences might be, but for my commission, I needed something closer to legal tender.

The predactor made a dismissive flicking gesture with its fingers and wrapped its wings back around itself. "Astor found it convenient."

"I'm sure he did, but he wasn't dealing with the Federal Reserve system back then."

I hefted the pouch. More than a pound. Maybe two? Of gold? Okay, I had a new client. "I'll get started as soon as I can."

"Good. Please deal through Garhezeigenbusch."

The gnome smiled smugly at me from the couch. When I turned back to look at the predactor, he—or she, or it—had gone. I hefted the bag again and smiled. My old client was trying to frame me, but my new client was willing to pay me. Maybe I'd even have enough left to make bail if Client One's scheming got me arrested again.

Fortunately Eli Dushinsky was in his law office and could see me.

"Welcome, Mickey." He rose and reached across his battered wooden desk to shake my hand in greeting. "What's new?"

I dropped the bag of nuggets on his desktop with a weighty thud. Perhaps it was a little too dramatic, but it immediately focused his attention on my issue.

He plopped back down into his chair. After a brief stare, he pulled the bag closer. He extracted one of the nuggets and spent several minutes rolling it between his fingers. Once he'd inspected it with a magnifying glass, he poked it with the tip of a ballpoint pen.

Finally he looked up at me and narrowed his eyes. "I trust you came by this in a way that was moral, ethical, and most importantly legal?"

I shrugged. "An eccentric client." Could eccentric stretch to having sixteen-foot, bat-like wings? "He insisted in paying in gold. I told him I'd have to see about cashing it in."

Eli continued to look at me without saying anything. To fill the awkward pause I added, "Since I wanted to be sure I did it legally, I came to you."

"Do you have any idea what this is worth?"

I shrugged.

Hefting the bag again, he twisted up his mouth. Was he doing mental arithmetic? I had no idea of the numbers involved. Besides, I don't like to scare myself.

"I don't know the purity, but as soft and heavy as it is, it must be high." He dropped the nugget back in the bag and looked up at me. "I would guess this is in the neighborhood of fifty thousand dollars."

Some neighborhood. I'd figured the pouch was dangerously rich, but hearing a number spotlighted the issue of safety—both the gold's and mine. My apartment had already been burgled once, and I had no safe.

"Can you handle it for me?"

He continued to look at the bag doubtfully while he stroked his chin. "I will not sell this for cash. That opens too many questionable legal doorways. It will have to go into your account so a record exists of the transaction."

Immediately I snapped up halt signals with both hands. "Whoa! Not in my account. No way do I want a sudden big deposit to appear. Any district attorney would turn that into evidence against me."

I pointed at the bag. "Besides, this has to be used to protect Monoceros Land Holdings from the claim Stuyvesant's filed against it. I don't care how you set it up or how you do it, but that bag's not mine. It's my client's, and he"—*or she, or it*—"wants it to be used to defend against that claim."

Eli stared at me a time then looked down at the gold. "Eccentric doesn't do him—or you—justice."

I had an essential afterthought. "He's promised me a fee for my services. That's the only thing that should show up in my records."

Sill looking at the bag of gold, Eli nodded. "Given the mode and quantity of payment, I assume your . . . client wants the best possible representation?"

"That's what he said." But what did a predactor know about modern lawyers' consultation fees? "I'll want to confirm an estimate of the costs ahead of time."

Eli's eyebrows were still raised in rampant skepticism, but he nodded. "I should think so."

Jessica called that evening with more details about Monoceros Land Holdings, including the fact that it was the firm of Tyler & McKinley who had filed the possession suit against it.

Before I could ask, she added, "There wasn't any mention of Alexander Stuyvesant or any indication of who it was that had hired Tyler & McKinley."

I would pass on Jessica's information on to Eli for whomever he found to take the faerie world's case. Whoever those hotshot lawyers turned out to be, would they need to meet with a faerie world lawyer cum predactor? My lips started to curl upwards. What would the meeting be like? Who would eat whom?

"So what's next, Mick?"

Jessica's question brought me back to matters at hand.

"Where do you go from here?" she asked. "Are you going to investigate Stuyvesant?"

I took a deep breath. "Well, I'm not going to follow him, if that's what you mean. They'd put me back in jail and call it harassment at the very least. No, I think looking into the land transfer case will have to do for now."

I went on to tell her about my conversation with Patricia Wentz after the funeral.

"You're going to look at this Screwy Louie?"

"She said Sherman owns a fight club down by the river."

"You're not going in there yourself, are you? I've seen videos of those guys' matches. You're not a trained fighter. They'll knock your block off."

Her note of certainty rankled. "What do you mean I don't have training?"

"I heard about that night at Murray's when Leroy White put you down."

"It was a lucky punch," I protested.

"You took the first shot at him."

Okay, she really had heard about it.

I turned back to my main point. "Actually I was thinking of looking into his BlackOut company first. Your dad got me a list of BlackOut's clients. I'm going to ask some general questions to get a sense of what kind of business Louie runs."

"Mick, if this Sherman really is part of Stuyvesant's plot, he could be using his outfit to keep tabs on you. Ever consider that?"

"Oh, yes," I acknowledged. "I know that while I'm looking at him, he'll be looking right back at me."

I waited for her to protest that action as dangerous, but I was beginning to understand that Jessica didn't play conversational games like that. She'd just wait, and I'd hang myself by admitting my real plan.

I rolled my eyes and gave in. "You're right. I'm not going to look at him directly. I'll stick to companies that use their security service. I'll tell them I'm thinking of hiring Louie's company and see what they have to say."

Or don't say. Damning with faint praise can be quite eloquent.

After a pause, she said, "Sounds safe enough—I guess."

Before I could reassure her, she added, "And speaking of safe, where are you going to sleep tonight?"

Her tone was serious enough that my wisecrack about her dad letting us sleep together died on my lips. I started to offer up a platitude about being safe enough, but she cut me off.

"I don't think you should stay in your apartment tonight."

It was late.

I didn't have a place to go.

I was tired.

My excuses were legion, but I heard her concern. "I . . . I guess I didn't get around to thinking about that today."

"Mick? Think about it. Right now. Please?"

After we ended the call, I did think about it. I looked around my apartment. All my stuff was here, my life really—an eloquent testament to underachievement.

Rather than let my thoughts continue toward self pity, I focused on anger. My home had been invaded. Stuyvesant was trying to frame me.

I got up and checked the locks on the windows in my bedroom and my office. Back in the living room, I looked at the apartment's door. It had a standard knob lock plus a security chain. When I'd moved in, I'd paid extra to have the landlord put on a new deadbolt lock.

I stared at the door for a time. Having used that door a few thousand times, I had no confidence that it would survive a hearty kick.

After a little thought, I jammed a wooden wedge doorstop under the door and dragged my recliner over in front of it as an additional obstacle.

I looked at my precautions. They might give me a few seconds to get out to the fire escape—straight into the arms of the second member of the assassination team sent to do me in.

The late hour and my heavy eyes encouraged confidence in my protective measures.

I blinked at the door again and decided to spend the night fully dressed on my couch.

Eighteen

Leroy White was Black, a contradiction that always amused me.

Last night's conversation with Jessica about martial arts had reminded me of Leroy, an amateur fighter I knew. I'd learned he was a fighter the hard way one fateful night at a party when I'd had one drink too many that led to one smartass comment over the limit.

Leroy and I still greet each other cordially when we happen to run into each other at the Coffee Berry Ferry. He doesn't hold being a jerk against me, and I don't hold the black eye against him.

At least not much.

After an uneasy night's sleep, I went to the Pumpkin Pub the next morning. Leroy was the manager of the off-beat smoothie bar that specialized in vegetarian and fruitarian recipes. He was working the counter, and I ordered a lemon tofu smoothie. When he brought it, I asked him if he knew Louis Sherman or the Only the Valiant club.

"Never heard of Sherman, but, yeah, I know the club. They pay pretty good for a match, but you gotta *be* pretty good. Better than me, anyway."

He glanced around to be sure he wouldn't be overheard. "Never been in the club myself. Most brothers give it a pass unless they're fighting. Not the most welcoming establishment if you know what I mean."

"What? Macho attitude or racist?"

He smiled. "Yep. That pretty much covers it. Why? Think you'll fit in?"

I barked a laugh.

"I'm just looking for some information on Sherman. Thought I might drop around and see where he hangs out."

"If you want to see the fights, go Friday or Saturday nights. That's when they have the best fighters. They have some fights on Wednesday nights too, but those are kind of hit or miss. The guys who fight on Wednesday are trying to build a reputation. It can get pretty bloody if there's a bad mismatch."

Leroy White was right.

I'd spent that evening watching the entrance to Only the Valiant club from a cafe down the street. The club was in a seedy part of town not that far from my apartment. I made watching it a part of an evening stroll.

From what I saw of the clientele, it was obvious that I'd fit right in—like a Mahjong tile in a stack of poker chips. The men were big and burly. The women on their arms had lots of makeup and their jeans looked painted on. Many had shaved heads—the guys I mean.

The next Friday night, I walked into Only the Valiant, hoping Sherman would be there watching while the premier fighters were doing their thing.

If Sherman was the one behind my difficulties, I didn't want him to recognize me. Since I knew I wouldn't blend in at all, I'd opted for some camouflage. I bought a fatigue cap with a long, rounded bill to shadow my face. While I don't usually do elaborate disguises, this time I wore a long bushy, walrus-style mustache. While it didn't hide my face, it distracted the eyes and broke up the regular lines of my features. I hoped I looked enough like a different person to escape notice.

My goal tonight was to look around the club and get a feel for the place, a feel that might help me understand who Sherman was. If he was there, so much the better.

No maître d' appeared to show me to a seat, so I found a table in a shadowed corner of the big room that put a wall at my back. The menu card the waitress handed me was not pretentious. It featured mainly variations on burger and fries combinations. However, there were nine different meat selections for the burgers—deer, goat, 'gator . . .

I went through the list and didn't recognize any endangered species. Still I decided to play it safe and go with a standard cow-burger.

"So what'll you have?" The waitress was back and ready with her pad.

When I gave her my order, she said, "You new here?"

"Not to the city, but I've never been to this club."

"I figured that. You look like a guy who treats his body with respect." She chewed her gum, delivering the sentence in staccato bursts between chomps.

"I try."

I picked up the menu again. "So you're telling me I don't want the beef burger?"

"It's good, but pretty greasy. I figure you'd go for the buffalo burger—or maybe elk. They taste good and got less fat."

"What kind of buffalo are we talking about?"

She waved her hand uncertainly. "I don' know. Buffalo? Bison? Whatever the things are the Indians ate. Chuck buys 'em from Wally out at Wally's Wildlife Adventure. That's a ranch out west of the city where they got a herd."

"Oh? I haven't heard of that herd."

She stared at me blankly, so I focused back on the menu. "Okay, I'll try a buffalo burger.

She guided me through the selection of sauce and fries before I handed her back the menu. "Thanks for your help."

Her smile was well practiced. "And thank you, dude. I'll have it right out."

While a number of customers were eating, most of the crowd's attention focused on the raised, brightly lit fighting ring at the center of the main room. There were no tables or chairs surrounding the ring. Instead, spectators milled around the open area. When the next bout started, I saw why. The standing audience engaged with the action vicariously. They waved their arms and legs miming punches and kicks. Along with all their hooting, hollering, and jeering, they spilled a lot of beer.

The first fight was between two beefy guys with no necks. It lasted until one brute broke the other bully-boy's nose in a gush of blood.

The place erupted in cheers at the sight.

The second fight featured two men more my size, one White, one Black. The patrons reacted as they had before, but this time I heard racial epithets among the taunting.

My burger arrived, and in the distraction, I missed the takedown less than a minute later.

The crowd erupted in boos, and I looked up.

The White guy lay on his back, out cold.

Two husky guys in T-shirts with the Valiant logo on the front escorted the winner back to the locker rooms while a man in a white doctor's coat tended to the unconscious man.

The bison burger was good.

While I ate, I ignored the fighters. Instead, I surveyed the room, trying to match Sherman's face from the two ID pictures Jessica had sent me.

He wasn't hard to find. Ensconced in an easy chair, he sat on a raised platform beside a table where two men were taking bets. Not part of the wagering himself, Sherman looked like he was holding court with people coming and going from his presence. Dressed all in black, he had on a suit with a dress shirt but no tie. He looked darkly dramatic and much more stylish than his clientele.

Although Sherman didn't appear to be paying much attention to the betting, at one point he reached out and grabbed a burly man's arm just as the man handed his money to the cashier. Sherman casually reached with his other hand to pluck the money from the bettor's hand.

Once he'd tucked the money away, Sherman pulled the man closer. With his free hand, Sherman snatched the man's little finger and twisted. The man went to his knees and cradled his hand. I was too far away to be sure, but I was certain Sherman had just broken the man's finger.

While the man cowered before him, Sherman reached down and tipped the man's face up to look at him. Sherman's mouth moved, and the man, still carefully holding his damaged hand, did not look away. From time to time, the man nodded.

Finally Sherman released his hold and pushed the man away. Sherman held out his hand and waited. The man fumbled one-handed for his wallet. Pale and shaking, he said something to Sherman as he handed it over.

Sherman pulled out a sheaf of bills, then flipped the wallet back. He pointed at the door. The man scrambled to his feet, and hurried away toward the exit with his head down.

A gambling debt? Overdue bar tab? Whatever the cause, Sherman's small smile as he physically dominated the man showed me Sherman enjoyed inflicting pain on customers who screwed up. I didn't see him break any more fingers, but his customer's body language was eloquent. Sherman was in charge, and he made sure everyone knew it, an alpha male even amongst his macho customers.

I dawdled over my dinner while trying to understand what I could about the business Sherman was running within the active club. People came and went from his exalted presence. From across the room, their conversations were inaudible, but I saw a few envelopes exchanged hands. Loan sharking? Recreational drug dealing? One thing I was pretty sure of, there was more going on at the club than martial arts.

My potato fries were rough cut and tasty with a tang of saltiness. Dry-mouthed after the buffalo burger, I sipped at my beer while I finished the fries. As I neared the bottom of the basket, an attractive woman in skinny jeans slunk up to my table.

"Hey, guy. How they hangin' tonight?" She smiled broadly at me.

I nodded carefully. "Heard about this place and dropped in to see what's goin' on."

She was good-looking but the crinkles at the corners of her eyes told me she was no ingénue. Her tight crimson shirt called attention to her mammary assets, but it also highlighted the substantial love handles at her waist.

"L-u-u-u-v that mustache," she drawled. With a wink and a broad smile she added, "Looks like it would really tickle a girl's fancy."

While I'd used good spirit gum on the mustache, I doubted the resin adhesive would be up to the task. Fortunately the question quickly became moot.

"Hey, Clarice! Quit flirtin' and get your ass over here." A big bear of a man glared at us from three tables over. He was hunched over the table with two other guys with similar build.

My coquette whirled around. "Shut the fuck up, Leo," she shouted. "You want to thug-out with those guys, go ahead. I'm gonna have myself some fun . . ."

The shouting match continued. I didn't stick around for the end of the argument. As quickly and quietly as I could, I stood up, dropped a tip, grabbed my tab, and headed for the door. I was satisfied with what I'd found out about Sherman and how he did business.

Nineteen

"Feranald, Ennings, and Yost, LLC," Eli announced to me at one o'clock that afternoon in his office.

He'd called that morning and said he had news. Rather than take it over the phone, I told him I wanted to hear it in person. Whatever he had to say, I didn't want to give anyone from BlackOut, Inc. a chance to listen in.

"They're the local affiliate of an international law firm headquartered in Switzerland," he continued. He smiled thinly. "Your, ah, remittance provided them a substantial retainer. You said you wanted the best firm for real estate conservancy lawsuits anywhere, and that's what they are. One of their specialties is legacy protective guardianship agreements, both national and international. They are particularly interested in this agreement because the trust's main asset has potential to be recognized as a world heritage site by the UN if you choose to go in that direction."

I nodded. "Sounds good."

His smile broadened. "You said you wanted the best."

Yes, I had, but what was the predactor's budget? "So how much will they want by the time it's all tied up with a bow?"

He pursed his lips thoughtfully. "I asked them that question. They said another, uh, payment should cover all the research and preliminary court filings on an expedited basis. Subsequent court appearances, filings, and other activities will add to the bill." He waved a hand uncertainly. "They can't be sure. If it's highly contested and drags on for a couple of years, it could take up to five more payments."

The legal work was going to be heavy lifting in more ways than one.

"I'll see to it," I said with more confidence than I felt.

Ordinarily the thought of confronting an intimidating client face-to-face with bad news about the bill—and the predactor had intimidation in spades—would have given me pause. However, personal bitterness for what Stuyvesant was trying to do to me gave me a steely resolve that overrode my normal tendency to avoid conflict.

Besides, a predactor, as a lawyer in the faerie world, he (or she, or it) would surely accept a well-reasoned legal argument.

Or eat me.

I nodded decisively to Eli. "He said he'd do what has to be done, so let's do it. I'll get back to you if there are any problems."

I thanked Eli before I left.

By the time I got to my car, I had more thoughts about another part of the deal. In my role as a go-between for the faerie world, how would the predactor—or the unicorn for that matter—value my services? The big blue bug had implied a commission when he mentioned the *quid pro quo* agreement they had had with John Jacob Astor.

I was in business to support myself, so I was definitely very pro quid. But how much would they be willing to pay me? Astor's needs were different from mine. At the moment my current preoccupation with staying out of jail had severely limited all my other income possibilities.

I smiled, savoring my new resolve to bring up the topic with the intimidating creature handing out the gold. I have all kinds of courage when I'm pissed off.

I'd just gotten back to my apartment that afternoon when Jessica called to tell me her father had some information for me.

"He wants you to come over to his place after supper," she said. "And don't worry, I'll be there to protect you."

"Protect me?" I chuckled. "You're just afraid of what he'd say about you if you're not there to protect yourself."

I'd meant to be amusing or at least annoying, but she ignored my jibe. "Dad's heard some things about BlackOut."

And it was not likely to be good news. Her next comment reminded me of something I'd neglected to consider. "He said to make sure you're not followed tonight."

After the call, I thought more about the possibility I was being followed. While I was practiced at spotting tails—I'd been looking—I was playing with the big boys now. If Sherman wanted to track me, BlackOut, Inc. wouldn't have to rely on the human eyeball. They'd surely have tracking gizmos more sophisticated than my GPS unit.

I needed help. Therefore, I contacted Kurse and asked her if she knew anything about finding tracking devices.

"I don't do that," she said. "But I know somebody who does."

"Can I come over so they can check my car?"

"Hell, no. If somebody's tracking you, that's the last thing I want you to do. Think about it. It would point them right to me. It'd be smarter to let my guy come to you."

And that's how I came to meet Hank, an expert on tracking devices. I met him in the parking garage by my car. Hank turned out to be tall, lanky, and young—young at least by my eye. His hair was long and unkempt. A scraggly beard that was incomplete in scope appeared to be a recent development.

"S'whatchagot?"

From the inflection on the end, I gathered it was a question, but Hank's diction needed work. "Excuse me?" I said politely.

Hank sighed condescendingly. "Isedwhatchagot!"

I thought I heard enough familiar sounds to answer. "There might be a tracking device on my car. Kurse said you could find it for me."

"Yup."

He fished a gizmo out of his pocket that was about the size and shape of a deck of cards. He extended a collapsible antenna and fiddled with a couple of controls on the face of the unit. He pointed the antenna at the front right fender, then walked it along the side of the car. At the right rear fender opening, he stopped fussed with a control. A moment later he ducked down and reached into the wheel well.

He came out holding a small button I recognized. I nodded sagely. "GPS tracker, right?"

He started to reply but stopped and sighed heavily. With careful enunciation he said, "Sup-posed t'find this one. Prob-a-bly more."

While his words weren't encouraging, at least I understood them. "More?"

"This's an active unit," his said casually tossing and catching the unit. "Puts out a regular signal all on its own."

I pointed at his gizmo with the antenna. "And your detector found it."

"Yup."

And that led me to another thought. "So if that's an active unit, you're saying there could be a passive unit? What's that?"

"Only transmits when it's pinged."

He held up his signal detector. "This's useless for that. If you don't know the frequency of the transmitter and the code, you have to look for the hardware."

Hank's exaggerated articulation felt patronizing, but at least I could understand him. "How long will that take?"

His shrug was an eloquent enough answer, but he added, "Donno."

Opening the driver's door, he reached in and popped the hood. "Use'ly 'bout three—four places t'look."

He leaned into the engine compartment and used a small flashlight behind the grill.

Shortly, he pulled back and muttered, "Nah."

He went around to the passenger side and tipped himself in over the fender, leaning into the engine bay to the point his feet were off the ground.

A moment later, his highly inflected "Ahhh!" told me he'd found something interesting.

Pushing back, Hank got his feet back on the ground and turned to face me. "Really slick set up. If you want, it'll take about two seconds to pull out."

I frowned. "Why wouldn't I want you to take it out?"

Hank rolled his eyes, but he didn't sigh this time. "Take it out, and they'll know. Come lookin'."

Ah! I had the power to mislead.

If I found another ride to go see Devon and Jessica, Sherman and his company would never know I was gone . . . probably. If Hank disabled this device, BlackOut would know. The next time they would be double careful.

If they didn't kill me first.

"Hey, yougottabug."

"What?"

Hank had his scanner out again. Instead of answering my question, he walked over and waved his antenna up, down, and around me.

He pointed at my belt buckle. "Gimme."

I took off my belt and handed it to him.

He fiddled with the leather strap that held the buckle and pulled out a flat little piece of something with a tiny wire attached. He held it out for me to see. "GPS."

He nipped off the little wire with his teeth then ran the detector around me again. "N'dead."

He looked me up and down. "But thr'could be more in your other clothes."

In that moment, I felt as if I'd had a towel whisked away from my nude body while on stage in front of an audience. How long had the locators been in place? Ever since they'd been in my apartment? I shuddered. What did they know about my movements? My habits? My friends?

I looked at the tiny tracker, then looked at Hank. "So how do I get rid of these if they put them in my other clothes?"

"Clothes dryer'd probably kill 'em." He shrugged. "Prob'ly."

A faint smile traced across his lips. "Put 'em in a microwave. Itidkillem, but careful d'sparks don't set stuff a'fire."

That evening, I went to see Devon.

I let my own car sit and borrowed Murray Linster's. Murray is my cross-the-hall neighbor who owes me several favors. I took a circuitous route and checked for a tail all the way.

To make sure I wasn't followed or overheard, I took Hank's advice about running all my clothes including my shoes through the dryer. I even gave them a short burst in the microwave, but I didn't see any sparks fly.

Devon lived in a small house in an older suburb near the downtown area. Jessica let me in.

As I stepped into the living room, Devon hit me with both barrels. "Stuyvesant's really pressing the department to put you back in jail."

He sat on his couch with a beer in one hand. With his other he waved an invitation toward his refrigerator.

"Let me get it," Jessica said, allowing me to stay focused on what her father was saying.

Devon pointed at a chair across from him for me to sit. "He's filed a petition in court that you be charged with his wife's murder. At the minimum, he's demanding specific justification for the decision not to arrest you that includes an inventory of all evidence found in your apartment."

I frowned and asked the obvious question, "Why?"

He shrugged. "Don't really know. The DA's against it." He smiled. "In fact he's hoppin' mad about it. He says other than your disputed surveillance activity, there's no reason to charge you. Other than Stuyvesant's accusation, there's no other directly incriminating evidence."

"Stuyvesant wants to see the list of what they found in my apartment? I'm not following. If there's no evidence, what's to see?"

"Okay, the department's list would not be just evidence specific to the crime. When we do a search, we list any *pertinent* items we discover. We're supposed to record all items observed that could possibly relate to the criminal investigation. Things like ammunition—"

"For my gun that was stolen."

"Right, right." He nodded. "Basically they'd list receipts, pictures, other documents—everything they looked at which might conceivably be relevant. They're looking for paper with the victim's name, tools that could be used for breaking and entering . . ."

He paused and looked at me. "And you know, things like those sex toys they said they found under your bed."

I was thinking and only half listening. My head snapped up at his last comment. "What!"

Devon cackled with laughter. "You're blushin', man. Don't tell me you actually had a stash?"

I smiled gamely. I was beginning to understand where Jessica got her sense of humor. She hooted with laughter at his remark and smirked at me. I felt my cheeks color at her amusement.

However, I was still trying to understand the situation. I took a deep breath and returned to the subject at hand. "Okay, but why would the police release that information? I understand that the defense can request the details of everything the police have when they do discovery before a case goes to trial, but why would Stuyvesant want it now?"

He looked at me expectantly and watched me think.

I took several sips of beer as I mulled my understanding of the situation. I thought out loud. "He's trying to frame me for his wife's murder. There's the missing contract, my missing gun, plus evidence that I've been following her."

After I took another sip, I continued. "But what about my gun? As long as the murder weapon hasn't been found—"

I flicked my eyes up to look at him. "It hasn't been found yet, has it?"

He shook his head, no.

"Okay, they didn't arrest me because there's no direct evidence I killed her."

No direct evidence? That finally triggered a chilling thought. "They were supposed to find something else in my apartment, weren't they? Something that would have made the case against me. Now he's worried because the people who searched my apartment didn't find it."

Devon smiled smugly. "That's pretty much the way I figured it, and that's why I wanted you to know."

Twenty

I had no more than arrived back at my apartment when my phone buzzed. It was Jessica. "Is it true, Mick?" she asked eagerly. "Do you really have a stash of sex toys?"

I'd had a feeling she would want to tease, and I was ready. "Yeah, they found my Suzy the sex doll under my bed, but they missed the leather straps, whip, and other bondage stuff I keep hidden in a secret compartment behind my book case."

There was a satisfying silence on the other end.

But my smugness dissolved in a moment as a memory surfaced. Under the bed? The fancy shoes? I'd dismissed them when I'd found them, but now in this new context a suspicion blossomed. "Hey JJ, do you know anything about Fendi shoes?"

"Fendi?" She sounded puzzled at the sudden change in subject. "Sure, Fendi shoes." She snorted a little laugh. "Yeah, buy me a pair of those, and I'll be your sex doll."

"They're that good, huh?"

"I don't think I'd want to go hiking in them, but if you want to drop a quick thou, that would do the trick."

A thousand dollars for a pair of shoes? That was right up there with paying eighty-six bucks for a fried fish lunch.

"I found a pair of Fendi shoes under my bed the other day when I was cleaning my apartment. I tossed them, but now I'm thinking—in fact I'll bet you anything that they belonged to Samantha Stuyvesant. Whoever took my gun and my contract with Stuyvesant must have planted those shoes. That's what the police were supposed to find when they searched my apartment."

"And now Stuyvesant's worried."

I didn't answer right away. Stuyvesant's original plan hadn't worked, so of course he was worried. Would he try something else?

"He's feeling pressure," I said. "His set-up to frame me didn't work, and he doesn't know why."

There was an additional factor Jessica didn't know about—my work through Eli to fight the transfer of ownership of Monoceros Land Holdings. The push-back on his suit for control of the land would add to the pressure he was feeling.

"It's getting worse isn't it, Mick?"

Jessica's comment brought me back to the situation at hand. I hadn't said anything to her or her dad about the trackers Hank had found on my car and on me. Jessica had once accused me of keeping too much to myself, and I'd been doing it again. I'd gotten her involved in this, and she deserved to know.

I took a deep breath and filled her in about what Hank had found.

Although I hadn't taken time today to make plans for a new place to stay tonight, my priorities shifted. I'd been thinking of this a bit cavalierly as an adventure. Talking with Jessica forced me to look at reality. Barricaded door or not, I was sure I wouldn't sleep if I tried to spend another night in my apartment.

Since I knew Jessica would ask, I brought it up myself. "I'm going to check into a hotel for a couple days and make myself hard to find."

I tried to communicate how seriously I was taking this. "I know you've been staying, uh, away. Your dad's right. We're both in danger. Somebody's tracking my movements. So I . . . I can't help but think of you and what happened to Bart."

Reminded that the same thing could happen to her that had happened to Bart, I couldn't go on. I paused and took a deep breath to steady myself. "We both need to stay out of sight."

She tittered nervously. "What? You want me to run away with you?"

"I don't want to kid about this. Don't go out. Stay . . . where you are."

The fact that I'd again avoided mentioning her dad gave her pause.

"We really are in trouble, aren't we?"

"They've got surveillance capabilities I don't even want to think about. Bart's funeral was hard enough. Please, Jessica." My chest was so tight I could scarcely finish.

To add to my concerns, I remembered what Kurse had said about my phone. "And why don't you turn off your phone and wrap it in aluminum foil? Get someone to pick up a contract phone for you, and use it until this blows over. Give the number to you-know-who to get to me."

She didn't say anything for a long time, and when she did, her tone was subdued. "Okay, Mick, I was worried before, but now you've scared me. I'll be careful, but I want you to be careful too."

"I always am," I said trying to sound more confident than I felt. "You take care."

Once I finished talking to Jessica, I thought I was done for the night—except for that part about finding a place to sleep. I was on my feet headed out when my phone buzzed.

I figured Jessica had something else to tell me, but the caller ID said, "Unknown."

I answered, expecting a sales pitch about my car's extended warranty, but it was Kurse.

"Got some stuff," she said. "Come to my apartment, but don't drive your car."

"Can't you just tell me what it is?"

"Not on the phone. And how long has it been since your apartment was swept for listening devices? If I meet you somewhere outside, can you guarantee someone doesn't have a parabolic mic trained on us? And remember. No car. No phone."

Fortunately I still had Murray's car keys. "Right," I agreed. "I can be there in fifteen."

"Stuyvesant's hurting." Kurse announced.

Her words left me a step behind. It took me a moment to catch up. "Hurting? You mean for money?"

She nodded. "Two brokerage houses have sent him a low funds notice. Prescott, Trumble, and Donner suspended his license to trade their insurance equities pending repayment of an advance on a commission."

I felt a flush of satisfaction. The good book says that love of money is the root of all evil. If Stuyvesant's finances were under stress, his plot to kill his wife and pin it on me made even more sense. I was more convinced than ever that I was on the right track.

I smiled. "If he needs money, he's after either insurance or her estate."

"It's the estate. He's got a big oil deal cooking out west to develop the property you're checking out. Since the investigation into his wife's death is still open, the court put a hold put on the settlement of her estate."

Kurse hadn't mentioned the actions taken by Feranald, Ennings, and Yost to protect the safety of the Monoceros trust and the unicorn breeding grounds. When that hit the court, the sparks would really fly.

I had a more immediate concern. "What about Louis Sherman?"

"A tough nut to crack."

"Yeah, he's into martial arts."

She waved away my wisecrack. "I mean his digital accounts are highly protected."

It seemed obvious, but I wanted to make sure I had the whole picture. "His firm's services must include digital security."

She nodded and smiled. "And yet, I managed to track the source of your sexy phone file to his company."

I smiled in return at that news, but what she'd said left me wondering. "But you said you can't get into his accounts. How do you know?"

Her smile broadened. "I didn't say I *can't* get in. It's just that his system lets him see everything I do *while* I'm in."

"Ah. So you must be disguising yourself?"

"You bet. I have multiple shell accounts, all with fake IP addresses. So far he's tracked me as far as Outer Mongolia."

Not quite on the opposite side of the world, but close enough. "So what's he up to?"

"Mainly surveillance from what I can tell. Plus, he's moving money around in accounts that are associated with Stuyvesant. It's obvious they're working together, but I can't tell exactly what the purpose is."

I nodded. "I wouldn't be surprised if he's laundering money of various sizes, shapes, and colors. Take a forensic accountant to figure out, but he must be trying to find money. Maybe to help Stuyvesant cover his shortages."

She nodded, then pointed at me. "He's also monitoring you."

I snorted. "Of course he is."

"Relating to you and Samantha, he's also looking at your friend Jessica Jones and two lawyers, Patricia Wentz and Tony Meyers."

I told Kurse that Wentz was Samantha's friend who maybe did some legal work for her as well. Although Wentz had known about the Monoceros trust, from the way she'd talked, she wasn't involved in work for the trust itself.

But who was Tony Meyers? I had plenty of loose ends that weren't going anywhere, so I welcomed a new name. I didn't know Meyers, but if Sherman was looking at him, he could be Samantha's lawyer for the trust—or not.

A lawyer would never give me information if I asked about a client, so I asked Kurse. "Do you have any idea who Tony Meyers is?"

"There's a family connection."

She pulled out a tablet. After a few taps and swipes, she studied the screen. "One of the emails Sherman intercepted is from Tony Meyers to a 'Jeff' in reference to Samantha's estate, and a little later makes reference to 'your mom.'"

She looked at me. "That tell you anything?"

I nodded. Meyers had emailed Samantha's younger son, Jeffrey. The fact that he'd addressed him as "Jeff" made their relationship sound familiar.

"Jeff is Samantha's son," I replied. "Is there any reference to Monoceros trust?"

She nodded. "Yep. I'll send you a copy of the email, but basically Meyers is briefing Jeff on the status of the suit that was filed against his appointment to the Monoceros board."

It sounded as if Meyers was working with the son, but was he working *for* the son? The fact that Sherman was monitoring Meyers's email gave me the idea that Meyers could be Jeffrey's lawyer. Patricia Wentz might know.

Before I left, I had one other question for Kurse.

"Can you tell me if Sherman or anyone in the company is doing physical surveillance, you know, tailing any of us?"

She shook her head. "If they don't digitize their records, I don't see it."

When I got back to my apartment, it was even later. Yes, I had told Jessica I was going to disappear.

But I was tired. The familiar surroundings urged me to just settle in for one more night.

Then I remembered Bart.

I remembered his wooden casket.

I sighed and dug out my overnight bag. I left by the building's back entrance. It was dark. Few people were out and about.

My eyes were sandy, but I kept them peeled on the two-block walk to the neighborhood rent-a-flop. Their rates were posted by the hour, but I rented a room for the whole night. All I wanted to do was sleep—sleep somewhere the BlackOut boys wouldn't find me.

Twenty-One

The next morning, my first priority was the same as it had been last night—to find a new place to sleep. Unfortunately the room next to mine had been in use during the night.

Twice.

I hadn't bothered to check the times. The bed next door's distinctive "thump, thump, thump" sounded clearly through the thin wall and told me more than I needed to know about what was going on. I pulled the pillows around my head and hoped for the successful—and swift—completion of their mission.

Problem was, my finances were limited. Last night's temporary shelter was quick and available—but expensive. At the moment, I had zero income. My current client had accused me of murder, so he probably wouldn't be paying me. I had a little money laid aside for a rainy day, but this current rainy day had turned into a deluge.

I sighed with self-pity and refused to think about the yet-unproven benefits of being an agent to a unicorn.

Fortunately Jessica called me first thing that morning with a better offer. "Mick, do you need a place to stay?"

Even short on sleep I couldn't resist a dig. "What? Did your dad say we could use his spare room?"

"I don't know."

I blinked in confusion. Her answer sort of made sense in the context of her question, but she had ignored my wise crack.

My brain's transmission finally clunked into gear. "He's right there where he can hear you, isn't he?"

"You bet."

I had to laugh. "This feels like high school. Hey, babe. Want to go to the prom?"

I heard a little snort of amusement on the other end, but she kept her focus. "Dad's friend Sandi Smith, is going out of town for a few weeks, and he suggested you call her. He says you could bunk at her apartment for a while. If you promise to collect her mail and look after the place, she won't charge you."

"Sounds better than what I managed last night." That was a gross understatement. I sighed into the phone. "In fact it's immensely, hugely, amazingly better than last night."

"I'll give you her number, so you can call. Try not to use so many adverbs when you talk to her."

Another worry assailed me. "Are you going in to work?"

"I called Clarence at the Berry Ferry. He said he can give me a week off, but if I'm not back after that, he'll look for someone else."

"What a peach. How about school?"

"I've got two more class meetings on campus. I'm going to ask the instructor how much I can do online maybe with a trip or two to the main library."

"Sounds like you're covered."

After Jessica gave me the contact information for her dad's friend, I thanked her, saying, "You're a real life saver."

After I ended the call, the aptness of the phrase I'd just tossed off gave me a sudden chill.

While I felt safer in Sandi Smith's apartment, my sense of safety came with a side dish of awkwardness.

First of all, Sandi was Devon's relatively new girlfriend. While that made no difference to me, it made Jessica uncomfortable any time I mentioned Sandi or her apartment. Whenever my conversations with Jessica veered in that direction, I got self-conscious.

The apartment itself made me uneasy in a different way.

I'm a simple guy, and I like basic and simple guy stuff. Sandi's tastes leaned heavily to the ornate and elaborate. There were frills, tucks, and ruffles everywhere I looked.

She also liked knickknacks, bric-á-bracs, give-a-dog-a-bone type doodads. A large collection of small stuffed animals of various species decorated all the rooms. Some of the figures were recognizable creatures, but others were extravagant adventures in cryptozoology.

The rooms had different themes. Her own bedroom had mainly cats and dogs. I put my bag in her guest bedroom where, irony of ironies, there was a herd—a pack? a flock? a gaggle?—of plush, stuffed unicorns. Most were white in color and smiled with serene bliss. Except for their single horns, none of them bore the slightest resemblance to Mel.

Atop the end table by the living room couch, a stack of furry teddy bears reached up the wall a good three feet. I took time to study the structure of the pile. The arrangement appeared random, but I've known people who are quite systematic in their haphazardness—me for instance.

Since the stack appeared somewhat precarious, I took a quick photo so that if I should inadvertently topple her teddy tower, I might be able to recreate it.

Aside from the busy clutter of her decor, Sandi's apartment made a good hideout. I felt lucky. In return for a few small chores, I had a refuge. Therefore, I aimed to keep my footprint on the space as small as possible.

With one less worry, I had more time to investigate Stuyvesant and Sherman.

I strongly suspected—so far without evidence—that Louis Sherman had been the one who murdered Samantha. Obviously a dangerous man, I intended to stay well out of his reach. Still I needed information both about him and his organization. Devon had given me a list of the BlackOut security company's current clients who had registered their security status with the police. However, since I'd originally asked for it, I'd had second thoughts. If I started interviewing people still doing business with Sherman's company, someone might mention the fact to him. Even if I used an assumed name, I didn't want Sherman to know anyone was checking.

After a little thought, I asked Devon for a second list, this one of BlackOut's clients from two years ago. Cross checking the lists would show me any customers who had terminated their security contracts with BlackOut. Perhaps their reasons for discontinuing service would tell me something.

Devon saw my point and had agreed to do it, but he bitched about having to get the extra information. Blackout's current customers were in the department's active files. Access was easy. Records from two years ago were in the archives and hadn't yet been digitized. Since BlackOut wasn't associated with any of his assigned cases, Devon couldn't ask the clerical department for help. He would have to do the extra work of searching through the files on his own time.

However, when I picked up the second list from him, I was surprised to see him all smiles when he handed it over. As a veteran of the force, he'd finagled a rookie into doing the work for him—as a training exercise.

Once I had the list, I assembled a file of five former BlackOut customers and started calling. Pretending I was thinking about hiring the firm, I told the companies I wanted to check the quality of their service. Feigning ignorance that they were no longer customers of BlackOut, I asked about their experience with the company. On the second call I struck pay dirt.

"Did you know we cancelled our account with them a year ago?" asked Milo Shuck, owner of Master Gems, a jewelry store downtown.

"Oh, really? Did you have a problem?"

"No, no. Nothing like that." He chuckled. "We'd been with them four or five years, but they raised their prices. Orenthal Guardians offered me a better deal."

"Ah," I said, pretending eager interest. "How much did you save?"

"It was around two hundred a month, but then again, we got robbed six months after we started with Orenthal."

"Really? Was it Orenthal's fault?"

"The police didn't think so," he said. "They said the theft was a pretty slick operation. Somehow the thieves had disabled the alarm system and made off with a lot of our best stuff."

"Did Orenthal use the old alarm system, or did they put in a new one?"

"It was a brand new one with net-linked motion sensors and the works. The company said it was state of the art."

"Was it?"

"Well, the cops agreed with them. They said it was good even though we were robbed."

I thought for a minute. "Did the new alarm have an uninterruptible power source?"

"Sure. BlackOut put one in when they set the system up originally."

"Did Orenthal use that one, or did they replace it with one of their own?"

After a long pause, he said, "You're thinking the thieves turned off the power, and the backup failed? I'm not sure the police checked that."

Yes, the backup might have accidentally failed, but since I was already suspicious, I immediately saw another possibility. BlackOut might have installed their "uninterruptible" power source with a secret off switch.

There was one more jewelry store on the list of BlackOut's former customers. Following my suspicions, I called Timeless Treasures, a store in a sprawling suburban shopping mall north of the city. Their story was the same except they had been robbed three weeks after they'd changed to a new security firm—just days before their new security system was due to be installed.

I knew I was onto something when Advanced Electronics said they'd suffered a ransomware attack three months after switching their service. They'd done a comprehensive forensic study and found the computer virus that had infected their system and held it hostage. However, they were unable to determine when the virus had entered their system or where it had come from. They'd hired a specialist in order to trace the ransom payment itself, but the money had disappeared into a squirrel's nest of cryptocurrency transactions.

By the time I'd finished the fifth call, I'd found that three of the five companies had been hit with a major crime after they'd discontinued their contract with BlackOut. The methods were different, but three of the firms I checked had been robbed in some way after discontinuing BlackOut's service. I'm no expert on security systems, but that looked like a pattern.

I called Devon and shared what I'd found.

"I think you might be right," he agreed. "That sounds fishy to me too. Detectives Eckersall and Hatchett are handing Samantha's case. I'll pass on what you've found about BlackOut. As far as the theft cases themselves, I don't know who's assigned to them right off hand, but they'll need to hear this too. Are you willing to talk to them?"

I remembered talking to Eckersall and Hatchett. Hopefully this would change the topic away from my guilt. "Sure. No problem."

And since I'd just shown Devon that I could do a favor for the police, I was ready to ask Devon to help me find a car to use.

Before I could bring it up, he said, "Jessica told me you found a locator beacon in your car."

I related what Hank had told me about the devices he'd found. I finished up saying, "He warned me that if he took out the one in my car, they'd know."

"Right. And if you don't drive the car, they'll figure it out in a day or two anyway. But in the meantime, they won't look too hard. You want something else to drive?"

"Like what?"

"I've got an old pickup. I don't use it much except to haul my bass boat up north to go fishing. If that'll do, you can drive it." He chuckled. "At least until the next time I want to go fishing."

Happy to have a problem solved so easily, I was speechless for a moment—but just a moment. "Gee, that would be great."

"Can you get a ride out here sometime after six to pick up the keys?"

"Certainly, and thanks so much!"

"Just don't you take my daughter out parking in it or nothin'." He growled as he said it, then hooted with laughter.

I still wasn't impressed with his humor, but I gave it a half-hearted chuckle. "Oh, she's got nothing to worry about. And thanks again for the help."

I'd been more than a little embarrassed by Devon's wise crack, but I didn't spend time wondering about my reaction. I got busy finding a ride out to pick up his pickup.

Kurse's information that Sherman was watching Jeffrey Stuyvesant's lawyer raised two obvious questions. Why would Jeffrey need a lawyer like Tony Meyers, and why would Louis Sherman care? I suspected the common element had to be Monoceros Land Holdings.

Lawyers are defensive about their clients, so before I went fishing for information in that pond, I decided to see if my faerie friends knew anything.

Since I didn't have Gary the gnome's contact information, I went looking for him. Once I had Devon's pickup, I swung through a Speedy-Mart for a cup of coffee and drove back to the park where I'd met with Mel and Gary before.

It was a temperate Tuesday evening in the middle of summer. The children's play area near the entrance was loaded with noisy kids. I wandered farther back along the walking paths to the quieter areas, headed for the bench where I'd met Gary before. The sun was warm, but the bench was shaded by a grove of trees. I settled in with my coffee to do some work—and wait.

Kurse had helped me set up a blind account to check my email so BlackOut wouldn't be able to backtrack and identify my new phone. That gave me confidence to work my way through a backlog of unread mail.

I was almost at the end of the list and wondering what I would do next when I heard, "Yeah? What's up?"

Gary stood, hands on hips, looking at me.

I put my phone in my pocket. "Lately, quite a bit. Do you know who Jeffrey Stuyvesant is?"

"Sure. Samantha's kid. The younger one."

I nodded. "How about Tony Meyers?"

"Nope. Never heard of him."

I explained who the lawyer was and my suspicion that, because Louis Sherman was looking at both of them, there might be a connection with Monoceros Land Holdings. "I think this is relevant because Feranald, Ennings, and Yost, our lawyers for the trust, should know if there's a common interest with Jeffrey."

"You anthros really like to make things complicated, don't you?"

Unfortunately he was all too right.

Before I could reply, I caught motion out of the corner of my eye. A mother with two youngsters in tow was coming along the path, headed toward the play area. She'd seen me sitting there earnestly engaged in a conversation with . . . nothing.

I smiled at her and nodded sheepishly. "Practicing asking my boss for a raise," I said.

She smiled in return, but didn't break stride while hustling her children along.

Once they were past, I turned my attention back to Gary. "So will you check with Mel before I give the trust's lawyers Jeffrey's name?"

He smiled. "Sure, I can do that, but wouldn't you rather talk directly to the predactor?"

"Not unless it's absolutely necessary."

"You'd probably be safe. I've never know one of those big blue bugs to eat anything much bigger than a cat."

He was trying to intimidate me. I was sure of it.

Pretty sure, anyway.

"Look, just let Mel know, would you? Unless he's dead against it for some reason, tomorrow I'll contact the lawyers for the trust through my lawyer."

"Will do." He gave me a half mocking salute. "What else you got?"

"You remember Jessica, right?"

"Saw her yesterday. I tell ya, she's a good lookin' babe. Just your type. You should do her."

My first impulse was to snap at him about his obvious goading. However, by this time I'd learned that if I took the bait, it only encouraged the gnome to more aggravation. "Look, I'm worried that by helping me, she's in danger too."

"You should stay with her." He wiggled his eyebrows suggestively.

And ignoring his jibes encouraged him as well.

"Come on, I'm working to help you and the rest of your world. I'd be reassured if I knew you were keeping an eye on her."

"No problem. You want a picture of her in the shower?"

The hassling continued, but finally I heard him agree to my request. I made him repeat it just to make sure. That reassurance that they'd keep an eye on Jessica was all the business I had for the faerie world.

"Thank you," I said. "And let me know if you hear more about the trust or what Stuyvesant is doing."

"Sure. And that UN heritage site thing? Mel told me he actually thought it was a good idea."

"That almost sounds like a compliment."

He grinned. "Yeah, and old Mel has high standards. You could go far."

After the gnome departed, I sat for a moment and contemplated what I had accomplished by pleasing a mythical beast. What kind of world was I living in? The real world or some fantasy world? Even if I was off my nut in a big way, the gold had been real enough. Eli had seen it.

And did it really matter if it was real? If the rest of the world never noticed the faerie world, what difference could those creatures make?

Then again, just because no human except me and maybe Samantha and an Astor ancestor of hers were aware of them, did it mean they couldn't cause problems in our world? Gary had claimed some kind of an emotional leeches had caused the Civil War. I found that unlikely, but he'd also mentioned that a troll was Mel's enforcer. But what would he enforce? And the predactor had said other creatures rooted deeper in the faerie world were dangerous. If this was all my own private fantasy, I certainly had an impressive imagination.

Another inconsequential—but amusing—thought popped into my head. What could a troll do in an MMA round or two at Sherman's Only the Valiant club? That gave me a momentary smile, but I took out my phone again. I had a few more people to contact in the real world.

Twenty-Two

"What's new?" Patricia Wentz asked, leaning forward on the table at the coffee shop.

I took the first big swig of my tall coffee and treasured the bitter bite of an additional shot of caffeine for my brain. I'd felt safer spending night at Sandi Smith's place, but a first night's sleep in a new bed was never restful.

"Glad you had time to see me," I said. "I wanted to get your reaction to a couple of things."

I told her about Stuyvesant's financial problems, but I really got her attention when I warned her about the monitoring that BlackOut was doing.

"Screwy Louie is bugging me?"

"Your name was on the list, but I think they probably wanted information about Samantha rather than you directly."

She crossed her arms over her chest and leaned back. "Maybe, but there might be something personal in it too. I didn't tell you that Louie came on to me a couple of times before I finally made it clear I wanted no part of him."

She had smiled slightly as she said that last part. I had to ask. "You punched him?"

"Knee to the go-dads." Her smile broadened. "Action speaks louder than words—especially with a creep like that."

I had yet to actually meet the man face-to-face, but picturing her in action gave me a momentary smile—but only a moment.

"He's also watching Jeffrey Stuyvesant."

"Jeff? What about his brother Shane?"

I shook my head. "He's not on the list. I was hoping you'd be able to tell me why."

She paused a moment. "You were watching at the cemetery the day they buried Samantha?"

She looked at me, and I nodded.

"That was Jeffrey who came to say goodbye to me. I was much closer to him than I was to his brother, Shane."

With a sigh she went on. "Jeffrey reminds me of Samantha. He's a sensitive kid who relates well to other people. On the other hand, his older bother is more like Alex."

She made a sour face. "He and his dad both have narcissistic tendencies. They're much more concerned about winning in their own world of dollar signs and status symbols than they are in others. He . . ."

She looked down as if embarrassed. "Samantha was worried about Jeffery because he didn't seem to think much of either his father or his brother."

"So why would BlackOut be watching Jeffrey?"

"Probably the trust."

"Monoceros? How so?"

"Samantha had named Jeffrey as her successor on the board of directors if anything ever happened to her. She told me once that Alex was upset she hadn't named Shane, since he's oldest."

"Did she tell you why she did it? Named Jeffrey as her successor, I mean."

"Samantha thought Jeffrey was more sympathetic to the trust's mission of preservation. If Shane ever got on the board, he'd see the land as an asset to be developed."

"Help me understand how this works. How does Samantha get to designate someone to the board like that?"

She shrugged. "I don't know the details, but the whole setup came down through the Astor family. The trust has a provision that a family member must sit on the board and have veto power over certain board actions. I don't know how or why, but Samantha had the right—no the duty, she told me once—to name her successor."

She cocked her head to one side. "How did you get into this successor thing?"

Although Wentz obviously thought I was asking because of Samantha's family, I had an additional interest in unicorn families—a topic I did not care to get into with her. I opted for a bit of deflection. "I'm in contact with a group that's opposing her husband's case for control. I thought it might be relevant."

She actually smiled at me. "The ones who are fighting it? The environmentalists? You do get around, Mr. Holmes."

I snorted. "Make that floundering around, and you'll be closer. But if it's okay, I think I'll let them know what you told me about Jeffrey. They seem to have a common interest."

"You're right, Mickey. Alex and his allies are trying to keep Jeff off the board. He'll appreciate any help you can give him."

I nodded. "And thank you for clarifying the reasons behind it." I wasn't about to get into the additional details of unicorns and predactors, but things made more sense after talking with her.

In addition, I noticed Wentz had called Jeffrey Stuyvesant a *sensitive* kid. By now I had a hunch Samantha herself had been sensitive to the faerie world. Naming her younger son as her successor to the board suggested to me that Jeffrey might be aware of the faerie world as well. Maybe when this was all over, I'd have a chance to find out. How much would it be worth to me personally to find out I wasn't completely crazy?

I thanked her and started to go, but she reached across the table and touched my arm.

"You're not thinking of confronting Louie face to face, are you? Have you had any martial arts training?"

My first instinct was to be flip, but her eyes were concerned. "Not like you mean. I've been through some physical training sessions where they showed us basic police take-downs, things like that."

"That might work on punks, but none of these BlackOut guys will be easy to handle by yourself. They'll attack like a macho ninja, and they've got a power thing. If they take you down, they'll hurt you."

I'd seen that, and I bobbed my head gratefully. "I'll keep that in mind. My sense of virility doesn't include personal bloodshed."

I looked into the distance. Wentz was warning me that there was serious danger. "Look, I'm just gathering information. I know I'm not in a position to do anything myself. I'm going to turn over what I find to the police."

Now I felt I could add a little levity and smiled at her. "I'm not as dumb as I look."

She snorted. "So far there's evidence to the contrary."

But then she smiled back. "Take care of yourself, Mick."

"Mr. Holmes? This is Detective Mort Eckersall."

My phone had warned me of who was calling before I answered. This was a call I wanted to take. "Yes, Mr. Eckersall, what can I do for you?" My last conversation with the detective had been in the interrogation room at the police center—under duress. Today, I actually wanted to talk to him.

"Devon Jones gave me your number and suggested I get in touch." Eckersall's more solicitous attitude today was immediately apparent in his tone. "He said you had information about Louis Sherman and his BlackOut company my partner and I should hear because it relates to what you've told us about the Samantha Stuyvesant case. We'd like to set up a meeting with you. We could come to your office if you like."

"I'm avoiding my office because I think it's under surveillance. What if we meet at Armando's Beanery? Do you know it?"

"Love their Pancho Villa burritos. You free in an hour?"

Not only would I be free, talking to the detectives could help me remain free.

"Certainly."

The beanery was a hole-in-the-wall place—actually two holes since Armando had expanded last year. It was still too early for lunch, so we had coffee and shared guacamole and chips. Eckersall even popped for the guac.

"So how you been, Mick?" he asked after he sat down on the opposite side of the booth beside his partner, Lionel Hachett.

"A lot better than the last time we talked."

I was struck by the difference a few days had made in our conversation. Today Eckersall spoke as if we were good buddies. Just over a week or so ago, I'd faced these same two cops on their home turf, a sterile, harshly lit interrogation room. Their grim faces that day contrasted markedly with their friendly demeanor now. Of course at the moment, rather than demanding information from a suspected murder, they wanted to solicit information that I had found that might help them solve the case.

Context is everything.

We chatted about the beanery and the weather until the food arrived. At that point Eckersall got down to it. "So what did you find out about Sherman and his BlackOut company?"

The man was in his mid-forties and had been a detective for years. He might be in a more genial mood today, but he still had a job to do. Hachett was younger, an apprentice to the veteran. Although Eckersall led the questioning, Hachett had his own sharp questions and was quick to follow up on any inconsistencies.

I told them what I knew about the connection between Sherman and Stuyvesant, the incriminating evidence that had been planted on my phone and in my apartment, and the surveillance that Kurse had traced back to Sherman.

As soon as I mentioned Kurse, they immediately asked for more information.

I held up my hands. "You can have it, but that part of it will take a warrant."

They looked at each other and frowned.

Before they could growl and threaten me, I opened my arms expansively. "Come on, guys. I'm telling you what Kurse told me. Sure, that means it's hearsay—inadmissible. If comes down to it, I'll give you the contact information. At the moment, I want to stay on Kurse's good side, so if I need help in the future, I can get it."

I'd even kept any gender-revealing pronouns out of the conversation without a stumble.

I shrugged and tried to emphasize my earnestness by leaning forward. "Okay, maybe Sherman's looking, but that's not a crime—or maybe it is, but it's not what you're after. To me, it's suspicious as hell, but it won't convict him of murder."

I knew I hadn't satisfied them. Cops are seldom content until they'd squeezed out every last drop of detail. Therefore, I tried to get them interested in something else. "Besides, that's not the good stuff."

I laid out what I'd learned about the thefts from BlackOut's former customers. By the time I finished, they were smiling again.

Summing up my sales job, I said, "If this is what it looks like, you won't have to have Kurse to go after BlackOut for more information."

As we got up to go, Eckersall said, "Thanks, Holmes, but I'd appreciate it if at this point you stopped looking at BlackOut. If you continue, you'll be in our way. It's police business now and not related to your problems."

He tapped his finger on his note pad. "We're homicide, so we'll pass the theft stuff off to another team. But we do appreciate you bringing it to the department's attention."

"Only too pleased to help."

Only too pleased to keep my butt out of jail by doing favors for the police.

And it was a cheap favor. I didn't have the resources—or the courage—to investigate BlackOut any more on my own. As a bonus, if BlackOut got wind that the police were looking at them, it might take some of their attention off me . . . and Jessica.

I called attorney Tony Meyers after lunch. I wanted to see if he would give me any information about his connection to Jeffrey

Stuyvesant and the Monoceros trust. He was defensive at first, but as soon as I mentioned Feranald, Ennings, and Yost, the firm helping defend Jeffery's interests in the trust, he warmed up considerably. So much so he invited me over to his office.

"Mr. Holmes." He greeted me at the door and shook my hand. "Won't you come in and have a seat. Can I get you a coffee?"

He didn't actually get me the coffee. His administrative assistant did. Still we were off on the right foot.

He frowned when I got to the part about how I'd been arrested for the murder of Samantha Stuyvesant, but he listened.

Once I'd explained my suspicions about Stuyvesant and Sherman, he nodded slowly. "I won't say I support what you're implying, but your idea about the husband's motive lines up with what we're seeing in the lawsuit Tyler & McKinley filed opposing Jeffrey's right to his mother's seat on the board."

"I've been in contact with the party who hired Feranald, Ennings, and Yost to oppose the suit." I waved my hand vaguely, hoping to convey that the identity of the party didn't matter—especially since the party in question was a unicorn. "When I found out about the suit opposing Jeffrey's seat on the board, I urged Feranald, Ennings, and Yost to contact you."

Meyers smiled broadly. "Their resources are certainly going to make difference. They've already shared relevant information. They're pursuing this suit on the federal level, and they've brought international implications into the case that I was totally unaware of."

He glanced at his watch. "As a matter of fact, they are going to call me in another hour to update me on their filing in Geneva at the World Resource Council. We are boxing in Tyler & McKinley at every turn."

And blocking Stuyvesant's plan. Couldn't happen to a nicer person.

Out loud, I said, "I'm glad I could be helpful."

We talked for another ten minutes. I probed for information about Jeffrey, and he asked about the police's investigation of me. Neither of us satisfied the other.

Before I left, he raised one more issue.

Setting aside his note pad, he leaned forward. "You know, Mr. Holmes, if this turns out the way you think it will, you would have grounds to sue your former client for defamation of character."

I sat back in my chair.

I hadn't thought of that aspect, but a moment later, reality intruded. With no definite commitment for any payment from Mel, I was a destitute private detective.

I shook my head and chuckled. "Well, maybe I could, but I certainly don't have the money to do it."

He smiled with suddenly crafty eyes. "What if I offered to take your case on a contingency fee basis? It wouldn't cost you a thing unless it's settled in your favor. At that point, I'd take a cut."

"Definitely an interesting idea," I answered immediately.

Although Stuyvesant was currently hurting for funds, depending on how all this turned out, Meyers might be able to extract at least some payback for the problems Stuyvesant had caused me.

I stood up and shook the hand of Tony Meyer, modern-day bounty hunter. "I will think about it, counselor, and let you know." I made sure to take his business card.

On the way back to Sandi's, I smiled. While I'd not resolved the police's suspicions about me that Stuyvesant's accusations had triggered, I felt like I'd at least made progress on the part of the case Mel the unicorn was interested in—progress in blocking Stuyvesant's efforts to develop the land.

Twenty-Three

I was in bed that evening reviewing my notes when Devon called.

"Jessica with you?"

As soon as he said it, my heart sank into my gut. "No. When did you last see her?" Even as I asked, I threw back the covers and got out of bed.

He sighed heavily. "She went out late this afternoon. Said she had to see Clarence at the Berry Ferry. When she didn't come home for supper, I figured she was out with you."

He paused. When he resumed, his voice was strained. "I'd . . . hoped she was with you."

I'd started to dress without any clear idea what I was going to do. "Did you check with the Berry Ferry?"

"I called them, but they hadn't seen her."

"What about Clarence?"

"He was at home. He was supposed to meet her at 4:30, but she never showed."

"So she disappeared between, what? Four and four-thirty?"

"Yeah, it's been about six hours."

I thought furiously about where to start. "What's Clarence's last name?"

"Applegate, but I doubt it will do any good to talk to him."

Although I agreed with him, I didn't tell Devon. "What about earlier? Did she go anywhere or see anybody?"

"I was on my shift from five this morning until two o'clock, so I can't say for sure. When I got home, she was bitching about being bored, so I assumed she'd been home all day."

"Do you want me to come over?"

"I won't be here. I'll be out looking for her."

"Hey, wait," I called, fearing he was about to hang up. "Are you calling on your cell? I'm going to go looking too, and I want to be able to get you if I find anything."

After the call, I sat back on the bed and stared dumbly into space. *Jessica.*

I shivered and quickly finished dressing while I churned through the places I knew she frequented. By the time I stood up, I realized she wouldn't be at any of her usual haunts. Stuyvesant and Sherman had kidnapped her.

They'll tie her up, take her some place, strip her clothes off, and—

I gasped, nearly panicked by the direction my imagination wanted to take me.

I headed for the kitchen to grab a quick cup of coffee. I had to focus on something productive. Jessica's disappearance was not a random act. Stuyvesant wanted the Monoceros property, and my investigation of his attempt to frame me for Samantha's murder was a problem for him. If he had gotten wind of the fact that I was involved in the court action against his takeover of the trust, the problem I'd created became a direct threat.

Because Jessica had been helping me . . .

Because Jessica was special to me . . .

Sum it up, Holmes.

I took a deep breath. They had taken Jessica to get at me. The kidnappers wanted to use her as leverage. They would contact me about a price.

Me. I would be their price.

The coffee was ready. I'd been unwinding before turning in for the night, but now I had to get wound back up again. Hot and bitter, the taste of the brew tasted like the guilt I felt.

But my self-reproach wasn't helping. I had to do something, but I had to do the right thing. Stuyvesant would be out of the country climbing a mountain, or some other place equally inaccessible, to be sure his hands were clean. Sherman would be the actor. He and his crew had kidnapped Jessica.

Where would they take her?

Someplace not too far away.

Somewhere he controlled.

Somewhere he was comfortable.

The best fit would be someplace Sherman owned. That meant I had relevant information. When Jessica had researched Sherman's operations, she had given me a list of all his assets and business ownerships.

I fired up my laptop and found the file. Early on I'd scanned the list more out of curiosity about the man's background than anything. This time, I was looking for Jessica.

Where would Sherman hold her? If they had her at someone's personal residence or some location not on the list, I was screwed. However, most residences had neighbors—not what he'd want for an operation like this.

As I went through the file, the entry for the Valencia Bar and Grill caught my eye because it had a familiar address. Sherman had owned the property for eight years. Under the "doing business as" entry, I saw the name "Only the Valiant," the fight club I had visited. I frowned. The club was too busy to be a good place to hold a hostage. Sherman would have her somewhere much farther off the beaten track.

Jessica had categorized her list according to types of businesses. Under "Other" I spotted the name BNG Enterprises. Unlike the rest of Sherman's companies, BNG's entry had no business operations on file. I looked at the entry thoughtfully a moment, then checked a separate record to see the list of company assets. BNG had only one asset cataloged—ownership of the ABC Storage Company.

Sherman owned a company that owned a storage company?

Undercover storage?

Half a hunch was better than none. I checked the address of ABC Storage. It was out in Chatham, a suburb west of the city. I called up a map and tried to orient myself to the surroundings. I'd never worked in the area, but I'd driven its main streets.

The storage company was in a sprawling industrial complex developers had creatively named the Chatham Enterprise Center. The district surrounded the intersection of the city's outer belt with a major east-west interstate highway as well as a rail line. The enterprise center catered to light manufacturing as well as warehouses and shipping companies.

I rubbed my chin thoughtfully. With no housing nearby, the neighborhood would be quiet. A private place. Perfect for—

"Hey, big guy. Your girl's been snatched."

Gary the gnome's voice made me jump. I'd been totally focused on my search for Jessica.

I took a deep breath and turned to see him standing on my couch. "I'd already heard. Do you know who did it? Where they took her?"

"Nope. It happened so quick, the pixies got left behind."

I closed my eyes and sighed. There was nothing to do but to go back to work.

I tried to focus again, but Gary's interruption had broken my concentration. Darting little thoughts about Jessica and what her kidnappers might be doing to her chased around my brain. The idea that she was in the hands of Sherman and his henchmen knotted my guts with anxiety. Wentz had said they liked to hurt people. My chest kept getting tighter. I panted with short, tight gasps. My head felt light.

I turned away from the screen and took a deep breath. I stared out the window. My hands were cold, but hot prickles danced along on my skin.

Fear?

The darkened cityscape outside showed a thousand points of light and told me nothing.

I looked back at my computer. No, I wasn't afraid. I was angry. I was exasperated by my powerlessness to do anything more concrete to rescue Jessica. But my fury centered on Stuyvesant and Sherman—and whoever else was involved in this.

I took another deep breath and let it out slowly. I had to recover my composure. Anger was not a good emotion for me. In the past, my anger had triggered rash responses I later regretted. I tried several of the calming mental tricks I've used before to reign in my impulsive recklessness.

Going for a run would calm me but waste precious time. I closed my eyes. Taking my hands off the keyboard, I scrubbed them over the day's stubble on my chin. After I'd stretched my arms high over my head, I looked back at the monitor. I had control of my thoughts again.

A grim and relentless determination had replaced my anger, and with it came an idea. I turned to look at the gnome. "I'm on Mel's good side, right? Do you suppose he would do me a favor?"

Gary chuckled. "Mel ain't got a good side as far as anthros are concerned, but, yeah, he owes you big-time."

He smiled, and his eyes sparkled with excitement. "Why? You got an idea? What you got in mind?"

"Is there any way he can track down where they took Jessica?"

He thought for a moment and nodded. "Yeah. Mel could round up a couple of chupakus and go looking, but it could take a while."

"Chupakus?"

"Dark dogs. They only come out at night, but they can track a scent across a lake. They'd find her."

Trackers would be good, but there was a critical question. "How long do you think it would take to find her?"

Gary shrugged. "Depends on where they took her. Got any ideas?"

"Right now I'm looking to see if I can figure that out."

"Yeah, that'd sure help." He shrugged. "If you're right."

I was desperate for progress of any type. "Can you get to Mel and ask him for help?"

"Sure. Anything's better than sitting around while you type and swear at the screen. Do your stuff, hot shot. I'll be back in a bit."

He turned to Sandi's teddy tower. "And Mel says thanks for your help, Ullya."

One of the teddy bears in the third row up flashed Gary a thumbs up. At least I think it did. The movement was quick and unexpected.

I watched until the gnome was out the door, but saw no other sign that the teddy was anything other than another of Sandi's souvenirs. Then again, knowing the faeries were watching me was certainly better than discovering one of Sherman's bugs.

With the gnome gone, I focused back on analyzing Sherman's operations. By the time I'd reached the end of the file, I knew he had a finger in a number of businesses all over the city. And Blackout wasn't just a local company. Sherman himself had a condo in the Washington DC metro area. BlackOut, Inc. had operation centers in DC as well as in South Miami.

However, I was the target of this operation. The other cities were irrelevant. They'd hold Jessica nearby to use as bait. That put ABC Storage at the top of my list: non-residential area, anonymous ownership, no on-site business enterprise—and not too far away.

The gnome had not yet returned. Rather than let my apprehensions and self-recriminations get out of control again, I walked to the window and gazed at the scattered dots of the nighttime cityscape. I'd connected isolated speckles of information into a picture of what I hoped was the solution to the kidnapping, but what happened next?

Sherman had lots of resources and was no dummy. I had to be realistic. Even if I was correct about where they were holding Jessica, how could I possibly rescue her? Although I could summon up some pretend swagger and support it with a lot of baloney from my mouth, I was no superhero.

The police were good and had lots of resources, but Sherman would have considered police action in his planning. Even if the police were able to trap him and his men at the warehouse, that didn't mean they'd be able to save Jessica. Besides, if Sherman saw them coming—

I blinked. My worried musing had triggered an idea. I was certain that if Sherman saw the police—or anyone else—coming to save Jessica, he and his men would take off and kill her as they left.

I smiled grimly.

But what if Sherman couldn't see who was coming?

I was doing a double check of Jessica's information when I heard the ghostly quiet chunk of the door latch. Without looking up I said, "Gary, I think I've found her."

"You're getting better, Sherlock."

He hopped up next to me on a chair. "What you got?"

"I think they're holding Jessica in a warehouse on the west side of the city."

The geography reference bumped my thinking into a new track. "Where's Mel anyway? Are he and the—whatevers—out looking?"

"They started following her trail from her dad's place."

"That's too far to the north."

I started to read the address of the warehouse to him, but Gary immediately started shaking his head. "Anthro addresses don't mean squat to me, and that'll be a double diddly-squat with a half twist for the unicorn, let alone a chupaku. 'Course them dogs ain't got much—"

"Can you read a map?"

"Sure. Five years ago, me and three other gnomes were down in Georgia. We had a map to where a band of Confederate soldiers hid some gold. We were trying to help out the whangams who wanted it."

At another time, the story of the whangams and the gold might have been fascinating, but I had another problem that was considerably more urgent.

"Here." I flipped to the map I'd been using on my pad. "Take a look at this." I zoomed in on the location of the warehouse, then expanded the view enough to include where Jessica's father lived.

After a couple of questions, he nodded. "Yeah, I've been out in that area. I'll get word to Mel, and they'll head that way."

I took a deep breath and felt the cruel edges of the smile that crawled across my cheeks. "So how much is Mel willing to help?"

The gnome saw my smile. His eyes lit up with eagerness. "Hot boppit! You've got an idea, right?"

I nodded. "You once told me that Mel had a troll to do his dirty work?"

"Yeah, a troll!" He hooted with excitement. "That's exactly what you need."

He laughed and jumped down off the chair. "Time to call out the troops!" he crowed as he started for the door.

Before he got there, I called out, "Hey! What can I do to get this started?"

"Nothing, hot-shot. Sit tight. Mel's gonna love this. I'll get back to you when it's set up."

He smiled and jerked a thumb at Sandi's table-top teddy tower. "Why don't you cuddle one of them bears 'til I come get you?"

I didn't find his suggestion the least bit amusing especially since at least one of the fuzzies was probably a faerie critter of some type. "I'm not going to wait. I've got to do . . ."

My mouth curled up in a snarl. My anger was back. "I don't know, but I'm going to do something."

The gnome shrugged. "No problem. We can find you when it's set up."

Once the gnome had gone, I was alone again. Breathless in my urgency to take action, I swallowed hard. I had to get a handle on my emotions so I could think. A couple more deep breaths didn't help.

I was tight as a twisted spring. Stomping around the house, tearing my hair, and ranting would be worse than useless. I would waste time and energy. I had set things in motion, but Jessica was in danger right now.

I closed my eyes.

Jessica, I'm going to find you.

And with that thought, I had another idea. I had a suspicion about where they were holding Jessica, but Kurse had the tools to confirm it. With her digital connections and methods, she was a bit of a "dark dog" herself. More importantly, Kurse hunted in the same electronic territory where the BlackOut boys worked.

I tucked away my pad and headed for the door.

Twenty-Four

"What?" As usual, Kurse confronted me in the hall outside her apartment door.

Having run up the stairs, I had to stop to catch my breath. "Jessica's been kidnapped."

"Your girl, right?"

Jessica wasn't my girl, but I didn't take time to correct her. "Is there any way you can help me find her?"

She scowled. "Shit. Why can't you get into something interesting like embezzling bitcoins?"

She paused. "Wait, Jessica? Bart's friend? The one who's helping you investigate Sherman and those guys?"

I nodded, still breathing heavily.

She opened her door and waved me inside. "Get out of the hall."

Once I was inside she said, "You're getting to be a pain in the ass for just showing up like this."

"Then give me a way to contact you."

"Go fuck yourself." I didn't think it was possible, but her scowl deepened.

She stared hard at me before she looked away. "Shit," she snapped and pounded her fist on the wall.

She took a deep breath and looked back at me. "All right, I'll help, but don't get your hopes up. If they're taking precautions, they could be hard to find."

Precautions? The BlackOut company portrayed their security operation in paramilitary terms, but that told me nothing about their standard operating procedures. They might communicate only with combat hand signals for all I knew. At least by having Kurse help, I felt that I was doing something.

By now Devon would have the police department searching. Unfortunately the police solved most crimes after the fact when there was a dead body to examine—an outcome I didn't want to think about.

Kurse's apartment had little furniture. Her one couch was ratty and vaguely blue. A rusty-brown overstuffed chair at right angles to the couch was in better condition. Tables full of electronic equipment and monitors lined two walls of her living room. Cords snaked here and there, and two large fans circulated the air.

Kurse slid into a padded leather and chrome office chair, the one high-end piece of furniture in the apartment. She sat at the focus of multiple display screens.

"This is for Bart," she reminded me. "If I didn't want to stick it up the asses of the guys who killed him, I'd never do this. I stay away from those militant, macho dick heads."

She pulled the center of three keyboards to her and started typing. A moment later, she looked back over her shoulder to where I stood. "And don't touch anything!"

I had no intention of interfering in any way. "I'll sit in your chair if that's all right."

She waved absently and kept working.

She ping-ponged her attention between three screens. A fourth display held five rows of static icons, while a fifth sat in blissful dark serenity.

My eyes roamed over her workstation's elaborate and precisely ordered setup. I recognized I was looking at an impressive mustering of high-end equipment. How much had all of it cost? I had no idea. One car's worth? Two? Were those cars Fords? Bentleys?

In her kitchenette a clutter of plates and pans crowded one side of the sink. Two more dark screens sat on the short counter by the stove. Did Kurse use those screens for business or entertainment? Maybe both?

A half-opened door revealed a darkened bedroom with the foot of an unmade bed dimly visible inside. Her name might be Karen Hernandez, but she was Kurse. Nothing showed that more truly than this apartment's contrasts between the big ticket resources she put into in her online digital world compared to the humble way she lived the rest of her life.

So what had been the source of her connection with Bart? Other than a physical relationship, had they shared anything else? They were both deeply involved in computers, but had they found common ground in any other aspects of their worlds? I felt a twinge of envy for whatever parts of each other's lives they had held in common.

"Sherman's west of the city," she announced, bringing my attention back to the matter at hand. "He's out in the warehouse district. I can't find Stuyvesant."

"How—"

"Cell phone."

Impatiently she flicked through several screens.

"Given the tower spacing out there, the location's probably accurate to about half a kilometer."

"Pretty big area." But I had an ace up my sleeve. I recited the address of ABC Storage Company. "Is that anywhere close?"

She went back to her screens. A moment later she turned—and smiled. "Bingo. Right near the center."

She went back to work. "I'll tighten the location by accessing a history of cell tower pings and average the midpoints."

Additional accuracy would only confirm what my gut already told me. "It's going to be ABC Storage."

Now that I was more confident of my information, it was time to let Devon know.

"Mind if I go out into the hall to make a call?"

Her eyes shifted to the door. "I'd rather not have anyone see you here. Use the bedroom."

I flipped on the light. The overhead bulb was dim. The shadows it cast, dark. Kurse's bed was unmade, but neat rows of technical manuals lined shelves that covered the opposite wall. A book case near the head of the bed held ranks of paperbacks lined up within easy reach. The titles looked to be all fantasy and science fiction. Kurse, for all her electronic legerdemain, liked to read actual paper books.

Devon answered on the first ring. "Did you find her?"

"Not for sure, but I'm making progress."

I gave him a quick synopsis of how I'd reviewed Jessica's information and Kurse's phone location confirmation, but I didn't give him the name or actual address.

"So where is she?" he demanded with a little heat.

"They're holding her out west in the Enterprise Center—"

"I repeat—*where?*" he snarled, putting heavy emphasis on the last word.

Okay, he shouted it.

Rather than answer, I asked, "What's the standard police response if you get a tip on the location of a kidnapping victim? Is it still to lock down the area?"

There was dead silence for a time.

"You're not going to tell me, are you? You son of a bitch. When I get my hands on you I'll strangle your flat ass."

His growled threat didn't make sense, but the message was clear. I also needed to calm him down. "Look, these guys are special forces, not some whacked out druggies. If you show up in force, they'll disappear."

It was time to be straight with him.

"I know they took Jessica to get to me. I'm the one they want. If the police show up before I do, she's disposable."

Heavy breathing on the other end of the connection told me he was listening, but I had more selling to do.

"These guys are smart," I continued. "They planned all along to pin these murders on me. They still think they can. They're going to shoot me with my own gun and sell the idea it was suicide."

193

"They'll kill Jessica anyway."

The thought made me sigh. "I know that," I admitted. "But they'll keep her alive until they have me. When they're ready, they'll call me to come to them. They're pros. If they see a hint of the police, they'll vanish."

I swallowed heavily. "And they'll kill Jessica along the way."

"I still haven't heard anything from you that says she'll be alive at the end of this."

"I want to see if I can work out some sort of a trade. You know, persuade them to let her go if I promise to go with them."

I'd been arguing to convince Devon, but once I'd said it, I knew it was true. I'd trade my life for hers.

"When they contact me," I said, "I'll tell you where they want me to go. I'll meet with them but delay things by dickering. That way you and the police can get there in time to save her and take 'em down. "

We went back and forth. Devon called me several other graphic epithets, but over the phone all he could do was threaten.

Colorfully.

I ended the call and went back into the living room.

Kurse looked back over her shoulder. "What?"

"I called Jessica's father. He's a policeman."

"They'll fuck it up."

"I didn't give him the address. Not yet, anyway."

"Ballsy."

"Stupid's more like it."

Now that I knew where they were, I thought about my next completely idiotic step. "I'm going to head out and see if there's any way that I can help Jessica. Would you please give me a phone number so I can contact you if I need help with anything?"

Her eyes were as sharp as laser beams. She called me one of the same expletives that Devon had used—but then she reeled off a phone number.

Still frowning, she added, "Don't get dead."

Twenty-Five

I fired up Devon's pickup and headed west toward Chatham. All kinds of crazy ideas swirled in my head. The most heroic were the least likely to work. Fortunately for my distracted driving, it was after midnight and traffic was light.

The first thing I wanted to do was scout ABC Storage, so I headed for Enterprise Center. Certain that BlackOut hadn't seen me in Devon's truck, I drove leisurely by the front of the warehouse, trying to see everything at once. The ABC warehouse was a nondescript building, one of a long, utilitarian string of bland boxes. There were no signs of life outside, but that didn't surprise me. Any action would be behind the blank beige walls.

I didn't want to stay in the neighborhood and wait for Gary to find me. No, with the capabilities of the BlackOut guys, they might spot me if I stuck around. Instead, I drove out the approximate route Mel and Gary would follow from Devon's house. Gary had said he'd find me, so I hoped that meant the faerie world was tracking me somehow.

Pixies?

Or maybe some sort of Gnome Positioning System?

Mel's white coat stood out under a street light in a residential section. I pulled to the curb and hopped out. I'd taken two steps heading across the street when I spotted a huge dark figure shambling along behind the unicorn. The streetlight glared in my eyes, making it hard to see details. All I could make out was a misshapen lump of a thing that stood a good seven or eight feet tall.

"Hey, it's Mick the dick." Gary the gnome's voice came from the lump's direction.

I shaded my eyes and looked more carefully. The creature carried Gary cradled in its hand as it lumbered along after the unicorn.

Was this a troll?

"Hot tiffles," Gary crowed from his elevated perch. "You brought a truck!"

I stood in the middle of the street, still trying to make sense of what I saw.

"Hey, Bud. Close your mouth or say something."

The gnome hopped down a long way to the ground and trotted over to me. He jerked a thumb back toward the looming figure. "Introduce yourself to Finical the troll."

My eyes scanned up the troll's long, furry body as he strolled into the street toward me. His squat head rested on broad shoulders with no noticeable neck. A bulbous nose sat between two large eyes, eyes that were fixed on me at the moment.

Ugly would have been a compliment. Long hair framed the troll's wide face and flowed into a braided beard that hung most of the way down his hairy chest. He might have been wearing a loincloth down there, but his heavy pelt made it hard to tell.

I had asked for help from a troll, so this must be one in the flesh.

At this point, my plan was ill-formed to say the least. I finally blurted out, "He's here to help? So what can he do?"

Gary smiled, then shrugged. "Finical? Well, trolls can do just about anything. General butchery, slaughter, extermination . . ." He shrugged again. "They're pretty good at all kinds of carnage and stuff."

"I don't want Jessica hurt."

"Look, trolls are big and ugly, but they're not stupid."

He looked up at the monster, who had strolled closer. "Are they?"

The troll had been looking at Gary. Now he looked at me again. More precisely, he looked down at me. Up close the troll loomed at least a foot over the top of my head with at least twice my bulk.

He grinned a wide smile that showed many sharp white teeth stretching across his broad face. "Good evening, sir," the troll said in carefully modulated tones. "As Garhezeigenibusch said, my name is Finical. I understand there is a spot of trouble to resolve?"

I blinked in surprise and stood in stupid silence.

The troll's knuckles rested on the ground.

He was butt-ugly.

And yet, the words he spoke were refined, and every one of them was pronounced with perfect diction.

Having zero experience socializing with trolls, I gave him a respectful nod of a bow and answered with similar formality. "And I am Mickey Holmes. I'm very pleased to meet you, Finical."

After he returned my nod, I continued, "And you are right. A girl is being held hostage, and we would like to free her."

"Yes, Melocartazenilis told me of the fair Miss Jessica, and how she has been abducted. I am here to slaughter the miscreants."

I blinked.

Slaughter?

"Uh, I'd really rather you didn't kill anybody. The police will be coming, and it would be really difficult for me to explain dead bodies to them. I could end up in trouble myself."

The troll frowned—a truly unpleasant sight. "I dare say, that is unfortunate. I was hoping for a massacre."

"Hey," Gary called up to the troll. "The idiots took her, so let's not count them out. They may give us a good reason for a bloodbath before this is all over."

The gnome turned to me. "Keep him interested," he whispered. "We need him."

The gnome was right. I needed allies, especially big allies. I had gotten over my surprise, and my anger had me ready to consider anything.

I looked back at the troll. "Gary is correct. There may well be need for your particular talents before this is finished."

Like if they harmed any one of the short little hairs on Jessica's head.

197

My eyes were caught by a dark shadow across the street. It slithered along, coming back from the direction the others had been heading. As it got closer, I saw two red eyes glowing from a dark, dog-shaped shadow—a very large dog. The eyes flicked in my direction for a moment. The thing stopped about fifty feet from us and sat down.

"Chupaku." Gary's unexpected announcement made me jump.

In a moment, I remembered—dark dogs. "They've been tracking Jessica?" I asked. "What have they found?"

The gnome looked up at me. "They lost her trace back where they must have snatched her. Now they're following . . ." He shrugged. "I don't know, something like her ambiance? After you called and got us headed in this direction, they could tell it was the right way."

A moment later he added, "Good work on that, by the way."

A second dark shape, similar to the first, emerged from the darkness and took its place beside the first. Two pairs of smoldering crimson chupaku eyes, each about as far above ground as my own, stared in our direction.

At that moment, my phone buzzed for attention.

My first thought was Kurse, but an instant later the speaker burbled Jessica's ringtone.

A chill went down my back.

Jessica?

Or her captors?

I held up my hand to silence Gary. "This could be it."

It may not have been my regular phone, but I'd set it up with an app that Bart had given me to record phone calls. I activated it and answered.

"Jessica? Where are you?"

"Wouldn't you like to know, shithead." The male voice taunted me with a cruel laugh. "So sorry to get you up in the middle of the night, but we took your girlfriend."

The kidnappers had made a faulty assumption if they thought they'd awakened me. I pretended confusion. "What? Where are you? What do you want?"

"Mick?" It was Jessica's voice. "They took me to—"

There was a fumble of sound, then the man was back.

"So you see we've really got her." He chuckled. "And if you want to see her again, you've got an hour to get your weak-ass carcass over to this address." He recited the address of ABC Storage.

I smiled. My research had paid off. Since I was in the neighborhood, an hour would be plenty of time. I could have strolled there in an hour stopping for coffee on the way.

"And be sure you come alone, jerk-face," he said. "We've got a drone up. We see any sign of the cops, and you're pickin' up her body parts."

"How much money do you want?"

"Now this is your lucky day. We don't want nothin' except to talk to you about all the nosin' around you been doing."

He broke the call before I could reply.

I stared at the phone for a minute while I thought. They didn't want to talk ransom. No, I'd gotten too close. They planned to kill me—if I gave them the chance.

I looked at the others. My phone had been on speaker, and they'd all listened.

I focused on the gnome. "Is your troll as hard to see as the rest of your people?"

"He's not my troll. Finical is a friend of Mel's. But, yeah, the anthros will never see him comin'."

I'd been counting on that, but I had no plan of action—yet. Up until now, my thoughts had been consumed by trying to locate the kidnappers. That and worrying about Jessica.

Now I knew Jessica was still alive.

I'd met the troll.

And I finally had the beginnings of a plan of how to rescue her.

I put my phone away. "They're holding Jessica at the warehouse I told you about. It's not far, but they've got eyes in the sky watching for me."

Watching? As soon as I'd said it, a nifty new idea popped into my head.

I smiled at them. "Hang on. I need to make a call."

I called Kurse, but I didn't call on the phone I'd used to talk to the kidnappers. Since they had used Jessica's phone, I knew for sure they now had that phone's number. Sherman probably would use that phone to track me even if he couldn't listen in. It was a chance I couldn't take. As soon as they ended the call, I'd killed that phone. I'd brought another contract phone to use and given Kurse the number so she'd know who was calling.

"It's ABC Storage for sure," Kurse said when she answered. "I was going to call you."

"Right, and we're in the area. The kidnappers just called me. They said they've got a drone up watching. Is there anything you can do about that?"

"Depends on what they're using. If it's a commercial unit, I should be able to find the IP address they're using to link with the drone's wireless signal. If that's the case, it shouldn't be too hard to block it. I'll let you know when I neutralize it."

"Tell you what. I'd rather not have you do anything to the drone until I'm in position. I'll call you back when I'm ready."

"Gotcha. I won't do anything until you tell me. Text me when you're ready."

She paused. I was about to thank her and end the call when she added, "You're gonna insist on being a dumbass and go in there, aren't you?"

"Yep, but it's not completely hopeless."

"I . . . Take care, Mickey."

She sounded worried. That was the first time I'd heard that from Kurse. Maybe she was human after all.

"Thank you. I will," I replied and ended the call.

"So what's goin' on?" Gary asked. "The bad guys got their own pixies watchin'?"

"Something like that."

I thought about the logistics of our expedition. I could drive to the warehouse in an easy ten minutes, but this party was on foot. "How long will it take you to get to the warehouse?"

Gary folded his arms and frowned. "What? You gonna make us walk when you've got a truck?"

"There's not all that much room in back."

"Sure there is. Finical will fit in there easy."

"But what about Mel?"

The gnome sneered. "You think a unicorn would ride in a pickup?"

I turned to Mel. "Can you get to where they're holding her in time?" Did he even want to get there? The unicorn had stood stoic and apart from us the whole time we'd been talking.

Stoic?

I reevaluated that assessment. He was looking down his nose at me. The sneer gave it away.

Gary answered for him. "Don't worry. Mel don't need a lift. Unicorns come and go when and where they please. He was just helpin' the two of us find our way."

With one more glance at the unicorn, I went to the back of Devon's pickup. It was time to load, but Devon had never showed me how to unlatch the tailgate. I pulled the latch right in the middle upwards, but nothing happened. I started to fumble with it, but Gary hopped up and nudged me aside.

"Right here," he said and touched a keyhole. "Put the key in, turn it, and it's open."

Gary didn't use a key, but when he pulled up the latch, I heard the chunk as the tailgate unlatched.

Finical climbed gingerly aboard. I hadn't asked the troll how much he weighed, but given the way the pickup swayed and the back end sagged, the troll's mass was real enough, even if the rest of the world couldn't see him.

"Would you move forward, please?" I asked. "The truck needs to be level."

He shuffled up a step and leaned on the top of the cab. Once satisfied the truck was on an even keel, I checked the springs. They had maybe an inch or two of travel. I slammed the tailgate up.

"I'll take it easy until I see how it handles." I told them. If the motor could move it at all.

I handed Gary up into the back with Finical. The little guy weighed more than I expected, but the bulk of the troll made the gnome look small.

"Let, 'er rip, big guy," Gary called. "Lay some rubber."

With a heavy load in the bed, I took it easy getting the pickup in motion. If the street's pavement was in decent repair, the suspension on Devon's truck might still be intact by the time I reached the warehouse. The truck's sluggish response confirmed I had a substantial load in the back. I pressed on as fast as I dared. Concentrating on avoiding potholes kept me from thinking about Jessica.

Twenty-Six

At ABC Storage I parked on a parallel street a couple of blocks from the warehouse. Mindful of the drone, I dared go no closer until I heard from Kurse.

Meanwhile, I had another interested party to bring up to date.

Devon answered instantly. "You find her?"

"I got a call from the kidnappers. They're holding her and want me to come talk to them. They said no cops, and they've got a drone up to watch."

He snorted. "And you believe they just want to talk? You're dumber than you look."

"No, they want to kill me. They'll probably get rid of Jessica too."

After I said it, I had to take a deep breath and swallow before I could go on. "But they need me to come to them first. Look, I think I can handle this—"

"Famous last words—and the dumbest. Give me the address, or so help me God, I'll piss on your casket. You're going to get my little girl killed, dammit."

Not if I could help it, but I didn't think he'd be reassured if I mentioned the troll.

"How about this? When I'm ready, I'll give you the address, but only when I'm ready to go in. I'll stall the kidnappers. While they deal with me, the police should get there in time to rescue Jessica."

I hoped.

That kernel of hope didn't mask the hollow feeling in my gut. Even as I talked to Devon, the thought that Jessica might already be dead made my knees tremble.

Unfortunately I hadn't sold the idea to Devon. He'd seen too many bad situations in his career. He swore some more and demanded information.

Finally I said, "Look. I've got help. I'm not doing it alone."

I didn't mention my helpers were two and eight feet tall and that a third had four legs.

Devon remained skeptical.

He was still spitting jagged blue curse words when I ended the call.

Mel came around the corner from the direction of the warehouse. Gary hadn't been kidding when he'd said the unicorn could get around quickly. Another gnome trotted along behind him. As Mel approached the truck, Finical stepped down from the pickup. The sudden absence of the troll's weight made the truck bounce and tossed me in my seat. I took that as an encouraging sign that the pickup's suspension still functioned.

I climbed out to meet the unicorn.

"Mel wants to talk to you" Gary said. "Teddy's been checking out the situation."

I bowed respectfully to the unicorn. "Mel, can you tell me what the situation is? Do you know how many are inside?"

Mel bobbed his horn toward me. I took it to mean he wanted to touch me, so I stood stock still. With his horn on my shoulder, Mel's words formed in my mind.

There are five anthropoids inside the building. Jessica, the one you seek, is locked in a small room at the back with no windows. Another is imprisoned with her. The three others are in the main room.

Two hostages? "Who's the other captive?" I asked. "Are they guarded?"

I had other questions, but those seemed good starters.

Mel turned to the second gnome—Teddy?—and dipped his horn to touch him. While they were in contact, Teddy looked up at me and made a thumbs up gesture.

While I wanted to take his signal as encouraging, I knew his gesture didn't mean the same thing in all cultures. Was he indicating, *We got this*, or *Up your bum*?

The gnome scurried off, and I impatiently checked the time. My deadline to appear at the warehouse was approaching.

Thankfully the gnome came back quickly. "The other anthro is Jeffrey Stuyvesant," Teddy announced.

I was surprised, but I didn't have time to think about it. With Jessica, Jeffrey—and me—the kidnappers could tie up all the loose ends, but was Stuyvesant heartless enough to sacrifice his son? At the moment, the only loose end I cared about was Jessica, and I was already worried enough about what might happen to her.

In my distraction, I'd failed to notice the unicorn had approached to offer a thought. I bumped his horn. Mel pulled back and scowled at me.

"Sorry," I said, "but I know who Jeffrey is. He's involved in the Monoceros trust."

I thought rapidly about what to tell the unicorn. "I'm pretty sure Alexander Stuyvesant and Louis Sherman are in this together. They want the development rights to the property held by Monoceros, but with Jeffrey on the trust's board, they won't get it. They must have some sort of plan to eliminate Jeffrey and blame it on me."

I took a deep breath and admitted, "They took Jessica to get me to come here tonight."

Mel nodded and touched me with his horn. *We know Alexander Stuyvesant, and he is not here. Teddenhauperwelt says one of the men in the main room is Louis Sherman.*

Finical stepped forward and folded his long arms in front of his chest. When he did, his elbows jutted out to either side of his body. He wore a most impressive frown. "If I am to help resolve this situation, I must have at least one person as a reward for aiding your cause."

The troll, bent on mayhem and slaughter, still talked like a British butler.

Jessica was nearby. Sherman and the other thugs who had kidnapped her had put her in danger. That made my decision easy. I smiled at Finical. "In a minute, I'm going to go to the warehouse's main door. Louis Sherman will undoubtedly be the one who answers the door." My smile stretched to a grim grin. "You may have him."

I turned to the other gnome standing with Mel. "Teddy, I know there are loading docks around back of the warehouse. Is there a regular door as well?"

"Yep. Two of 'em," he reported. "The one in the middle between the two loading bay doors goes into the main room. The other's an office door."

"How closely are the two prisoners guarded?"

The gnome smirked at me. "Garhezeigenibusch says the woman is your girl friend. You afraid they're having fun with her now that they've holding her prisoner? I've heard anthros do that."

Evidently Gary wasn't the only gnome who enjoyed raising difficult topics. It was my worst nightmare, but I tried to control my annoyance. "Where are the guards? You're sure there's no guard in the room with them?"

"Don't worry. It's like Mel said. They're locked in by themselves. Sherman's all over the place in the main room talking on his phone a lot. Another guy's sitting at a table in a coffee lounge near the room where your girlfriend's locked up. He's playing on a computer. The third guard's got a long gun and is hiding behind some barrels near the guy at the table."

"Thank you," I muttered automatically. I was already lost in thought.

Based on the gnome's report I figured Sherman was running the op and probably communicating with Stuyvesant. The guy on the computer was flying the drone. The third man was there to back them up and make sure nothing got out of hand. While they might have had another member of their team watching on the outside, I thought it was more likely they would be depending on the drone to prevent surprises. Guys enamored of their technology can develop blind spots.

Although I had a plan for a rescue, the mention of guns gave me a new worry. How would a faerie creature like a troll deal with real world weapons?

"Finical, they've got guns," I said to the troll. "Is that a problem for you?"

"Ah, those noisy rascals do sting, something like a hornet might do to you I've heard." He flicked his hand dismissively. "I have been pricked several times in the past. However, I vanquish my foes quickly enough that it is not a problem."

He smiled that wicked-wide smile again showing a carnivore's set of teeth. "Do not forget. They cannot see me."

Yes, there were certain advantages to being a monster of the faerie kind.

"How long will it take for you to handle Sherman and the two other guards?"

The troll sniffed contemptuously. "Humans give me little trouble, sir, but a moment please."

He conferred with Gary then turned back to me. "Had to establish a common frame of reference, you know. To complete the action, I believe it will take between three and five, ah, minutes."

He pronounced the last word carefully, as if he'd never used it before. Then again, maybe he hadn't.

There was one more part of my plan, and it was crucial that the troll understood.

"Finical, I know you can handle these guys, but you've got to make it look as if humans were the only ones involved."

"Hoo, ha!" Gary interrupted. "Gonna grab all the glory, huh, big guy?"

"Shut it, gnome." I glared at him. "When the police start asking you questions . . ." The gnome laughed at me, and I finally got it. "Okay, they won't ask *you* the questions, but how am I supposed to explain how I took down three ex-special forces troopers?"

I made my voice a mocking sing-song. "Gee, officer, it was a troll what tore off their arms."

Both gnomes thought my improvisation was hysterical, but Finical looked thoughtful—at least that's how I interpreted his frown.

Since I needed the troll to understand, I focused on him. "Finical, it would help me explain what happened if you made it look as if the men were fighting each other. The police would think they'd had a falling out—a disagreement."

The troll was inexperienced in the art of misdirection. His brute force gave him little need for subtlety. Describing how humans fought each other, I gave him a quick anatomy lesson. While Finical had disassembled humans before, he was unfamiliar with the idea of maiming without completely dismembering or stomping a wiggling body flat.

I also encouraged him to leave at least one man alive to tell a confused and garbled tale to the police. The key factor I emphasized was that the police should see evidence of a brawl between the men from BlackOut—a human-type fight.

Finical was quite experienced at mayhem. Once I'd laid out the choreography I wanted the police to infer from the fight scene, he was confident he could produce an authentic-looking final tableau.

He did ask for clarification on one point. "But you say I must handle them in such a way that their limbs remain affixed?"

"Humans have trouble tearing arms and legs off each other without substantial help. It would be hard for me to explain afterwards."

"Heads too, I presume?" When I nodded, he sighed and rubbed his chin thoughtfully. "But I do get Sherman, correct?"

I bowed at the waist and made a polite gesture of acceptance. "Yes, please take Sherman. I want the police to think the three got into a fight, and Sherman ran off. That makes him yours to do with what you will."

Cultivated as my response to the troll had been, inside I was darkly satisfied at sending Sherman to his fate. After what he and his helpers had put Jessica through, he deserved it.

The troll nodded. "So when shall we begin?"

Gary chimed in. "Yeah, enough talking. Let's go get your girlfriend."

I took out my phone. "Real soon, but I have to make a couple of calls first."

Kurse answered by saying, "Found it. I can cut their link to the drone anytime you say."

I sighed with relief at that news. The kidnappers expected to see me alone, and they would. They'd never see the troll coming. But I had to time it right. The kidnappers might kill their hostages and take off if they lost their eye in the sky before I showed up.

"That's great news, but hold off for now. I want those guys to feel safe right up until things start to happen."

"Like when the cops show up? You are going to call them, right?"

"Definitely." And hope they didn't show up until the main event was over. "Like I said, I'll send you a text when it's time to take down the drone."

With that business concluded, I called Devon. I wasn't about to leave Jessica's father hanging. Besides, Devon would bring the police. I wanted them to show up soon after the carnage, so they wouldn't have to think too deeply in order to reach the wrong conclusion.

I punched in his number.

Devon didn't say hello. "Where is she, shithead?" he barked.

He held his tongue while I gave him the address and a quick summary of the situation.

When I'd finished, he growled, "We're rollin' on this right now. You'd better hope she stays alive."

Even if he hadn't hung up, I couldn't have said anything after that reminder. I just looked at my phone and took a deep breath.

Did I have it right?

The troops were on the way. Now I had to start my end of the rescue—the distraction.

I handed the troll my wristwatch. "All right, Finical. I've explained how the timing works. You know what to do from there."

The watch fit nicely on the troll's thumb.

He smiled showing many, many teeth. "Certainly, my good man."

Twenty-Seven

The metal door on the street side of the warehouse had ABC stenciled on it in large block letters. The lettering's black paint had peeled in spots, and the door itself was scuffed and dented.

Once under the shadow of the canopy at the entrance, I tapped my phone to send the text that would signal Kurse to disable the drone.

I delayed a minute, then gathered my courage before I pounded on the door three times.

Faint, hollow echoes reverberated inside.

I waited, but not patiently. After a slow count to thirty, I hammered on the door again.

This time, it opened promptly.

Inside, the warehouse was bright with light. The glare silhouetted a large, broad-shouldered man in the doorway. It was Sherman, dressed for action in camo.

Fatigue hat pulled low over his eyes, he eyed me up and down scowling impatiently. "About damn time, Holmes."

He pulled the door open and waved me inside. "She's waitin'."

He'd answered the door empty-handed. I'd worried he might greet me with a drawn gun and finish it right there. I'd counted on his confidence in his martial arts skills to discount any threat from me.

I took a step across the threshold of no return.

Sherman grabbed me by the arm and slammed the door behind me. "If you're wearing a wire, your dead right now," he muttered as he waved an object in his other hand over my body.

When he'd finished, I smiled at him blandly. "And good evening to you, Mr. Sherman," I said. The troll had disarmed me with his elaborate politeness, and I thought it might do the same with Sherman. "Has Alexander paid you yet for murdering his wife and my friend Bart?"

He blinked in surprise, and a slow smile spread across his face. "As a matter of fact, he has." By now he was grinning broadly. "And besides that, I've got a little settling up to do with you myself. Seems you've given the cops the idea that my business should be investigated."

He huffed an unfunny laugh. "Alex was exactly right. You're not stupid, but your nosiness is a righteous pain in the ass."

"Ass-pain is a specialty of mine." Still deferential, I inclined my head modestly. "Thank you." Considering the source, his epithets were high compliments.

The man had just admitted to two murders and had as much as told me that he planned to kill me too. Still controlled and deliberate even as my heart hammered in my chest, I asked, "So where's Jessica?"

His eyes flicked toward the room holding the two prisoners. I wasn't supposed to know that, so I pretended not to notice. "We'll get to that in a bit," he said.

He thumped his right index finger firmly against my sternum. "But first I've got some questions about what you know and who you've been talking to."

Questions he was obviously going to enjoy asking, especially if I gave him an excuse to beat the answers out of me.

The questions he asked made it obvious the he and BlackOut had been tracking me. I held nothing back as I answered, giving him full, honest—and elaborate answers.

We got through his first three questions.

A crash from the back of the warehouse echoed through the cavernous space. Finical was right on schedule.

Sherman turned to look, and I snapped a sucker punch at his head.

The man was unbelievably quick. My fist had covered maybe half its planned distance when he batted it away. His return stroke slapped the side of my face, walloping my ear.

My head rang.

My eyes wouldn't focus.

As I stumbled for balance, he whipped up his leg and kicked the outside of my right thigh. I tumbled to the floor.

Once down, Sherman booted the side of my head for good measure. "Stay," he commanded and bolted for the pandemonium at the back of the building.

My brain buzzed.

My eyes didn't work.

But I had to get to Jessica.

Desperately I struggled to get up. The leg Sherman had kicked was numb. It wouldn't support me, and I collapsed back to the floor.

The racket at the back of the warehouse was punctured by a ground shaking thump that reverberated through the warehouse. A moment's calm was punctured by two gunshots.

That fight was elsewhere. I concentrated on getting to Jessica.

Impatient for my scattered wits to catch up, I crawled toward her prison. My injured leg tingled with returning feeling while its muscles spasmed randomly. The prickly numbness eased as I dragged it along the floor.

Once I'd mastered crawling, I struggled to my feet again. The first step on my bad leg sent me sprawling. I crawled a little farther and tried again. This time I kept my feet, but my right leg still didn't work right.

I staggered toward the door like a drunk—a drunk on a mission.

The din continued in the warehouse. Although cluttered with boxes, shelving, and pallets, the building had a lot of open space. Thoughts of a stray bullet worried me, but I focused on staying upright. I aimed for the door and kept moving.

A bellowing roar rattled the roof trusses.

I held onto a shelf and looked to the back of the warehouse.

Finical had a camouflage-clad man in each hand. The troll shook them until they had both dropped their weapons. Once disarmed, he tossed them aside. The men lay motionless where they had landed.

The troll turned and stood silently staring at the floor. A large lump of camo lay there beside a section of overturned shelving. It was Sherman. As I watched, the ex-Ranger pushed himself up and staggered to his feet. He crouched low and drew a pistol from a holster at his back. Head swiveling to find a threat, he backed cautiously toward a tumbled pile of large boxes.

I smiled. Finical stood silent as a post not more than twelve feet away from him.

Sherman's obvious desperation to find a threat delighted me. I didn't know what Finical had planned for him, but the man was doomed—doomed and didn't know it.

Sherman, still in a tactical crouch, rotated slowly, studying the warehouse for the peril only I could see. Lest he spot me, I edged behind the shelves and watched over the tops of the boxes.

When he turned away from the troll, Finical bent down and tossed a wooden pallet against the metal wall of the warehouse twenty feet from where Sherman stood.

The man snapped into a perfect shooter's stance and put two quick shots through the blank wall.

Before the echoes died, Finical pounced and batted away Sherman's gun.

Sherman stared blankly at his empty hand for a moment, then looked around frantically.

The troll smiled his over-wide smile and reached for Sherman. Once in Finical's grasp, the man fought back with a frenzy of kicks and punches to whatever part of the invisible beast's body he could find.

Finical took a good two-handed grip on the man and flipped him roughly up over his shaggy back. Sherman's gut hit Finical's boney shoulder, and his breath whooshed out audibly. I have no idea whether or not trolls have a humerus bone at their shoulder, but I thought the expression on Sherman's face was hilarious.

I remembered my goal. I stumbled on to the locked door that imprisoned Jessica.

A large padlock secured the steel-clad door.

I hammered the door with my fist. "Jessica! We're here to get you out."

Could they hear me inside?

A rumbling crash from the back of the warehouse boomed through the space and interrupted my concentration.

I waited for the echoes to die away before I beat on the door again. I listened, but there was still no reply.

"Mr. Holmes, sir?"

Finical stood smiling down at me. Sherman was draped limply over his shoulder. "The other two miscreants are disabled, perhaps dead. I did not stop to check. I have placed them in the back near where I entered. As you requested, all their limbs are still attached."

He patted Sherman's rump almost affectionately. "And am I correct that this is the anthropoid you promised me?"

What did the troll have planned? Sherman had admitted murdering Bart and Samantha Stuyvesant. He had stolen Jessica away and locked her behind this door. Had he hurt her? Assaulted her?

And why had Jeffrey Stuyvesant been kidnapped? No matter how venal Alexander Stuyvesant might be, I couldn't believe that he was actually planning to do away with his own son to insure his control of the Monoceros property. Was Sherman freelancing? Had he decided to take Jeffrey as a bargaining chip to make sure Stuyvesant ponied up Sherman's share of the loot?

At the moment, those questions didn't matter. While I don't like to think of myself as particularly vengeful or vindictive, at this point I had no sympathy for Sherman. I smiled up at the troll. "Yes, Finical. You have completed all that you agreed to do. I am profoundly grateful for your help." Echoing the troll's formal manner of speech made me feel righteous.

Finical smiled. "You are more than welcome, old boy. I enjoy a good romp now and again." He gave me a slight bow. "If you should perchance have something sporting for me in the future, please let me know."

215

He mimed tipping an imaginary hat atop his hairy head. "So for now, I will take my leave. Good evening, sir."

"And a good evening to you," I responded.

Watching him leave the building through the hole he had made to come in, I realized I was grinning.

Twenty-Eight

Bam! Bam! Bam!

My eyes had lingered on the troll's exit, and I jumped at the unexpected sound from the locked door. Somebody behind the heavy barrier wanted out.

I pounded on the door in return, then examined the lock. Shiny new, it was as big as my fist.

I rolled my eyes in frustration. I needed a key to open the lock—the very key that was undoubtedly in Sherman's pocket. And Sherman had just left with the troll—a troll who probably could have torn down the whole wall was his free hand.

Stupid and double stupid, Holmes!

I had started to wonder what a gnome could do with the padlock when the cavalry arrived.

"Police! Hands up! Nobody move!"

Carefully I raised my arms into the air and turned slowly toward the front of the warehouse. Two officers, guns drawn, had taken flanking positions inside on either side of the entrance.

"Over here," I shouted. My damaged head throbbed. I winced in pain, but I kept my hands high.

One of the officers crept cautiously in my direction, checking over, under, and behind the scatter of boxes and stacks of pallets.

As he approached, I called out to him. "The kidnappers had a fight at the back. I think at least one of them got away."

Once the officer got closer, I continued in more normal tones. "My name's Mickey Holmes." I pointed an elevated thumb toward the steel door behind me. "Sounds like somebody's locked in there."

The officer was professional and smart enough to search me to make sure I wasn't an immediate threat. It felt good to put my hands down when he'd finished.

"Two men down in the back," his partner called from the back of the warehouse.

Just then, someone pounded on the other side of the locked door again.

"See?" I nodded in the direction of the door. "Somebody's in there."

The policeman went to the metal door and struck it twice.

An immediate answer boomed back.

The officer holstered his gun and hefted the padlock. "Big sucker." He held it in his hand and studied it. "Not sure our bolt cutters will be enough for this bad boy."

Outside, sirens wailed. More police stormed through the door. They fanned out to search the entire warehouse. I stayed with the first cop at the locked door while he put in a call for a heavy duty bolt cutter.

While we waited, a heavy-duty police officer came through the warehouse door—Devon.

"Holmes, you son-of-a-bitch! Where are you?"

As soon as he saw me, he charged to confront me. "Where's my daughter?"

Before I had a chance say a word, he slugged me. "You prick. You got her into—"

The other officers grabbed his arms and pulled him off me. He struggled briefly, but stopped when the pounding on the inside of the door began again.

"She in there?" he snapped.

Once the other officers saw he was back in control of himself, they let him go. Devon shrugged his uniform shirt back in place. He looked down at me on the floor and pointed. "That her?"

I looked up at Devon. His eyes burned into mine. A bit woozy from his punch, I sat up slowly. "Yeah." I started a nod, but I winced as my head bloomed with pain. I gingerly felt the spot where he'd hit me. It was on the same side where Sherman had smacked me.

I cleared my throat and started over. "Yeah, I think so. They're trying to find a bolt cutter to take the lock off."

Devon, now fully into his professional officer mode, offered me a hand to help me to my feet. "Tell me again how you found this place."

I was still a little dazed from his punch but not so much that I gave him a straight answer. "I had Jessica's list of properties these guys owned. This one seemed most likely, so I had some guys check it out."

I felt a little proud of myself for not telling even one lie—at least not if you used a fairly broad interpretation of the word "guy."

He looked at me skeptically. "Huh," was all he said.

It's tough to lie to a cop. They hear so many falsehoods every day, big, small, and all around the mall, that they develop an almost sixth sense about when there's more to a story. Fortunately, the bolt cutters arrived before Devon could ask any follow-up questions.

All attention turned to the lock. The cop with the bolt cutter was a big, beefy guy, larger even than Sherman, but he struggled with the cutters on the lock.

After straining ineffectually a couple of times to cut through the shackle, he backed off and wiped his sweaty brow. "Must be special hardened steel."

"Gimme the cutters, Jerry." Devon held out his hand.

The large man smiled skeptically but handed over the big bolt cutters.

Resolve flared in Devon's eyes. The lock was between him and his daughter. Even though he was smaller than Jerry, I wasn't going to bet against Jessica's father.

Devon took time to set himself and get the cutter into the gash it had already carved into the metal of the lock's shackle. He stared hotly at the offending bar for a moment before he bore down on the handles of the cutter.

He pressed harder. His hands shook from the effort. Devon had big hands. The cutter bit deeper into the shackle, and the gap between the cutter's handles narrowed. Red faced, he reached a finger across to bridge the gap between the grips. In a moment, he had both his hands wrapped around the handles as he forced them closer together. Teeth clenched, he growled as he squeezed.

Veins stood out on his neck.

The lock vibrated with the force of his effort.

Snap!

The metal shaft parted. Pressure gone, Devon stumbled, and Jerry caught him. A third policeman pulled the broken lock out of the staple and swung back the hasp. The door burst open pushed from inside.

Jessica and a young man tumbled out.

"Daddy!" Jessica called as Devon wrapped her with a big hug.

She wriggled away and held up her wrists bound with a zip tie. Devon used his knife to free her arms.

As soon as she was free, she threw her arms around him.

I felt a twinge of envy. However, Devon, bless his big blue heart, was more than willing to share her thanks. He pointed her in my direction. "Mickey here was the one who found you."

Jessica turned and enthusiastically embraced me "I knew you'd come." She laughed happily with tears in her eyes. "It just had to be you."

I put my arms around her. We hugged. Slowly it dawned on me how good it felt to hold her like this.

I smiled and snuggled her closer, but she tugged away. "Oh, geez. I must stink. It was hot and sweaty in there, and it's been hours—"

She shut up when I dragged her back into my arms and kissed her. It wasn't a long kiss, nor a passionate one, but it was emphatic. I don't think I'd ever enjoyed a kiss more.

"Thank goodness you're safe," I said and hugged her close again.

I would have held on to her a much longer time, but the police wanted to talk to her.

So did her father.

The young man who'd been in the room with her was right there as well. Once the police had freed his arms, I introduced myself. "Jeffrey Stuyvesant? I'm Mickey Holmes." I offered my hand and we shook. "I'm glad to meet you. Patricia Wentz has told me something about you."

Jeffrey perked up at Wentz's name. I didn't go into the details of how I'd come to make her acquaintance, but it gave us a connection. We shared a few words about his association with Wentz, but this wasn't the place to ask if her description of him as sensitive included his being sensitive to the faerie world.

The detectives on the scene wanted to interview Jessica and Jeffrey first, and I wanted to let them. At the moment, I had a different priority. Before the crime scene got completely locked down, I wanted to take a quick tour of the warehouse. I would be high on the police's interview list, and I needed details for my story. I didn't want to go on the record describing what I had seen and done until I'd had a chance to decide what exactly I had—sort of—done.

Finical had wreaked havoc on the boys from BlackOut. That was obvious. In case the subject came up when the police questioned me, I wanted to offer plausible cues to help them misinterpret what had happened to the men. I was rooting for them to create an explanation that did not include the word troll.

I had coached Finical to make his entry not by battering down the warehouse door but by wrenching it outwards to make it look as if someone inside had left in a hurry. I wandered toward the back and was delighted to see that the troll had not only followed my instructions, but also improvised. The doorway gaped open to the night air. A forklift sat outside the opening with one of its forks impaled in the steel sheathing of the door. Slewed off to the side, it appeared to have ripped the door from the frame as if someone was trying to flee. As long as the investigators didn't check the outside of the door for troll fingerprints, the setting clearly said "escape."

But then again, did trolls even have fingerprints?

Whatever the case, Sherman himself was gone. The police would think he'd gotten away, and I wouldn't disabuse them of that notion.

Sherman's two henchmen were laid out at the back of the warehouse near the smashed door. From my casual survey I didn't see any damage the troll had inflicted on them that a human couldn't have. One thug's arms were twisted up funny, but no heads, legs, or other body parts were scattered about.

Three officers attended the two, and I didn't linger. They had cuffs on one of the men, so there was apparently at least one survivor. That BlackOut operative would tell a confused story of an invisible attacker.

The police, hopefully, would nod knowingly as they listened to his tale. They were experienced with people claiming hallucinations along with other creative, drug-induced fabrications.

From the front of the warehouse my view of the action had been limited. I wanted to make sure I didn't say anything that contradicted what the police found. I'd already cooked up a hypothesis I'd offer if asked: Sherman had confronted me at the door, but while that had been going on, I'd heard his partners arguing. After Sherman had knocked me helpless on the floor, he went to see to his men.

If asked, I planned say I had no idea what had happened to Sherman after that. While that might not have been the complete truth, it wasn't entirely a lie. And if I ever did find out what fate the troll had in mind for Sherman, I was confident I'd approve.

Once I'd taken the lay of the land, I wandered aimlessly about the warehouse, trying to stay awake. It was very late. Now that the action was over, I was exhausted.

"Mr. Holmes? We're ready for you now."

I'd been staring vacantly at a stack of pallets, admiring repeating angular symmetries in the rough-cut wood. Yawning and blinking, I walked to where two detectives waited to interview me. They took me through my story once, then asked a few more questions bouncing around in a different sequence. They were doing this to test my veracity, so I kept things as simple as I could.

The place where Sherman had slapped the side of my face still glowed with heat—probably nicely red by now. Devon's punch had broken the skin nearby. I'd carefully not wiped the little trickle of blood I'd felt on my cheek, and I kept that side of my face turned so they could see it. My obvious head injuries and still gimpy leg helped my credibility. Of course I would tell the story with some muddled confusion.

While I talked with the detectives, Jessica came over to me and took my hand. She stood and listened while I spun my tale for the detectives. Unfortunately I had to tell a few lies along the way. While I had no compunction about making up a cock-and-bull story to protect my own hide, lying in front of Jessica proved harder than I'd expected.

Necessary, but harder.

When the detectives said I could go, I was weak with relief.

I also felt monstrously guilty about the worship I saw in Jessica's eyes. Okay, I had found where the kidnappers had been holding her, but I'd had a lot of help. First of all, I'd located her by using the information she herself had gathered. And the rescue? It's not like I'd swaggered into the warehouse with guns blazing. I'd been a distraction while the troll did the heavy lifting.

Given the potential for disaster, I was deeply relieved at the way things had worked out. Jessica's admiration made me uncomfortable, but there was nothing I could do about it. I wanted her to continue to think of me as a normal anthro, uh, human. Therefore, I would not be able to ever tell her the truth about the help I'd had.

"Mick?" Lost in my thoughts, I took a moment to respond to her. "Mick, would you . . . I mean, do you still have Dad's truck? Could you take me home?"

She looked flustered. "I told Dad I wanted to talk to you and that you'd give me a ride."

Head tipped down, she looked up at me with mesmerizing eyes. "So would you? Take me back to Dad's, I mean?"

Twenty-Nine

Jessica held onto my arm as we walked to where I'd parked Devon's truck. By now the hour was so late it was almost early. There was no traffic, so we walked in the street. Jessica was exhausted from her ordeal, and I wasn't far behind.

When we rounded the corner, I spotted the truck—and a new problem. Mel and Gary stood waiting.

To thank me or berate me?

I had no idea. I had no energy for speculating. Jessica was with me, so I fumbled for the keys and pretended to be oblivious to their presence.

Beside me Jessica looked up. "Hey, guys," she muttered.

Thunderstruck, I stopped dead in my tracks. "What?"

Sleepily she responded, "Huh?"

Abruptly she gasped and straightened. "Nothing. Oh, nothing, Mick. Don't pay any attention. I'm just confused. Forget it."

Had I dreamed what she'd said? Maybe, but I had to ask. I turned her to face me and waited until she reluctantly met my eyes.

"Jessica, tell me true. Do you see . . . them?" I fought against a life-time of secrecy to force out the next words. "Uh, you know, Mel . . . and Gary?"

Her eyes widened. "Mel?" Her eyes flicked in the direction of the unicorn. You . . . you know Mel? I . . ."

I crushed her to me and held on for dear life. Usually overflowing with the gift of gab, I had no words.

Jessica finally broke the silence between us. She pushed back far enough to look at me. Her eyes sparkled with tears in the dim light of a streetlamp. "You see them too, Mick? My mom told me when I was little to never say anything. Never let on."

She choked a sob and cleared her throat. "From some of the things Jeffrey said while we were locked in together, I kind of wondered if he might, you know, see them. But I never asked."

I had to blink away tears in my own eyes. "I've always worried it was my over-active imagination."

"Oh, Mick. This is wonderful—"

She couldn't finish because my lips got in her way.

We had been lost in the kiss for some time when I felt a tug on my pant leg.

"Hey, if you two are gonna be at this a while, we'll check in with you tomorrow."

I looked down at the gnome and smiled. "Thanks," I said. "We'd appreciate that."

Once Gary and Mel had departed, I sighed. As much as I wanted to continue kissing Jessica, Devon was expecting us. With what I'd discovered about his daughter, I absolutely had to stay on his good side.

I looked at her and smiled ruefully. "We really should be going."

She nodded. "Before we go, I want to say something. I know you said you were gun shy about women, but—"

"I love you, Jessica." I put my hands on her shoulders and relished her smile and the sparkle of affection in her eyes. "I guess I've been in love with you for a long time, but the kidnapping was the slap in the face I needed to wake me up."

I looked away and debated with myself the chance I was about to take. "Look, would you . . ." I took a deep breath. "I want to have you in my life. Would you consider moving in with me? Maybe in a couple of weeks when things settle down a little, and maybe after we have a few, you know, uh, dates, we could . . . "

I stopped as my train of thought chugged to a halt. Jessica was shaking her head.

I sighed and looked away. "Sorry. I guess I got too pushy and—"

This time it was her kiss that interrupted me.

When she let me go, she smiled broadly, but she shook her head again. "Mick, except for your office, your place is a dump. Besides, it's too small. We need to find a new place. I have to have my own office space to do class work."

I didn't go back to Sandi's that night. Jessica convinced me I was too tired. Once we were at Devon's, I slept on the couch in his living room.

In the morning, Jessica and I told Devon that we were going to live together. Actually Jessica told him while I sat beside her, nodding humbly and trying to remember to smile. Since my cheek remained tender where he'd punched me, Devon still intimidated me.

Ever since the morning we'd told him, Jessica's father had been more than helpful to us. He even used his contacts to help find us a place to live. He'd been nothing but pleasant to me. However, I'll never forget that moment when we broke the news to him. The look he gave me was a clear warning. Papa bear would continue to be very protective of his little girl.

Six weeks later, Jessica and I finally moved into our new apartment together. It was not far from her father's, and he helped us with the move. After a day of loading, lugging, and toting, Devon took us out to eat.

I'd had a day of hard labor. With a freshly filled belly, I was less than attentive to the after-dinner conversation. That is until Devon announced he had fresh news from the police investigation into the Stuyvesant/Sherman case.

I sat up on full alert.

"They're suspending the investigation," he said. "They say it's Sherman plain and simple."

Devon poked me. "You remember I told you they found your gun in the office at the warehouse?"

He'd told us a couple of weeks ago. I nodded.

"Well, the tests are all back. Sherman's prints were all over it. Since he hadn't bothered to wipe it, he must have been planning to use it again." He looked at me and raised his eyebrows meaningfully before he went on. "Yesterday we got the report from ballistics. They confirmed he'd used the gun to kill both Bart and Samantha."

That was all well and good, but there was something missing. A big something

"What about a motive?" I asked. "Why would Sherman kill his friend's wife? And why Bart? Why'd they take your daughter for crying out loud?"

I shook my head and slapped the table emphatically. "No, it only makes sense to me if it's wheeler-dealer Stuyvesant playing the lead to protect his fortune and reputation. Then he's got Sherman working as a partner to do the dirty work."

Devon turned up his hands helplessly. "Hey, I don't disagree. But that's the way the detectives called it. Sherman's disappeared. Nothing new has turned up in almost three weeks. The case has gone cold."

He shrugged and held up his hands helplessly. "By saying Sherman did it, they can issue a warrant for his arrest and put their investigation on hold. Besides, they've got other cases piling up."

I'd shared with Jessica but not Devon the fact that Sherman's disappearance was permanent. Although she was as pleased as I was, it now meant that if no new evidence surfaced, the case would never be solved. Stuyvesant would get off scot free.

Well, maybe not completely free. His financial empire was shaky. Devon had also told us that although Stuyvesant had not been charged, investigators had talked to at least two of the directors on the board at Sterling Fund Investments. Directors just hate that kind of attention especially when it concerns one of their top people.

Still, if Stuyvesant was as crooked as I suspected, he could have off-the-books assets to rely on. Maybe he could mortgage a third-world country or something to salvage his situation.

The good news was that whatever he did to save his financial reputation, it wouldn't include developing the land held by the Monoceros trust. While control of the trust had not yet been settled in court, Feranald, Ennings, and Yost, LLC had tied Alexander Stuyvesant's suit for control into a legal knot—a double bowline with a half hitch at that.

At least the unicorn happy hunting ground was safe.

It wasn't late when Jessica and I got back to the apartment for our first night our new place. After our day's labor, we were both tired and immediately set out to get ready for bed.

However, that usually normal routine took longer than expected.

First of all, coordinating our movements in an unfamiliar shared space was awkward. No, this was not our first night together, but always before, one or the other of us were on our home turf. Tonight we shared *terra incognita,* and that generated a mutual lack of finesse.

It had taken us the whole day, but we'd moved all of our stuff in and unpacked. Everything had been put away, but we were far from settled. During the relocation, we'd both made decisions on the fly about where to stash things—her stuff, my stuff, and some newly purchased joint possessions. We'd not always taken time to make those decisions together. Now we were at sea in an unfamiliar array of closets, cupboards, and drawers trying to remember our improvised organizational logic of just hours ago.

But we were here, and we were together in the privacy of our new home.

Once ready for bed, we had planned to share a quiet moment and a glass of wine in our new living room—and perhaps afterwards, an even more private moment or two in our new bedroom.

I was in my pajamas carrying two glasses of wine when I rounded the corner of the couch and saw Gary sitting right in the middle.

The gnome hopped to his feet and whisked off his pointed hat.

"Mr. Holmes, sir. If you could spare some time, Melocartazenilis would like to speak with you about a problem."

I blinked in surprise. First of all, his visit was unexpected. But maybe just as astonishing, I'd never before heard the gnome phrase anything so politely.

Before I could reply, Jessica joined me wearing the filmy little nothing I so enjoyed. "Not tonight, Gary," she said firmly. She smiled at me and took one of the glasses of wine from my hand.

Pointing at the door she said, "Tell Mel we'll talk tomorrow. Mick and I have business to attend to this evening."

Have I mentioned how much I love Jessica?

* * *

www.ingramcontent.com/pod-product-compliance
Lightning Source LLC
Chambersburg PA
CBHW060211180626
46813CB00007B/2779